SEA LIGHT

JANE MULLEN

BLACKSTAFF
PRESS

BELFAST

First published in 2006 by
Blackstaff Press
4c Heron Wharf, Sydenham Business Park
Belfast BT3 9LE
with the assistance of
the Arts Council of Northern Ireland

Jane Mullen has asserted her right under
the Copyright, Designs and Patents Act 1988
to be identified as the author of this work.

Typeset by Red Barn Publishing, Skeagh, Skibbereen
Printed in Great Britain by Cox & Wyman
A CIP catalogue record for this book is available from the British Library
ISBN 0-85640-781-X

www.blackstaffpress.com

For my daughters
Margaret and Elizabeth

The name *Hope-Ross*, scrawled in pencil across the top of the newspaper, gave Eve a start. She had come into the shop for an *Irish Times*, but it was late in the day and there was none left. Just this one copy, reserved for the Hope-Rosses. She had slept all morning, had slept most of the two days since her arrival and had stayed awake most of two nights, using all her energy trying to wake up or to go to sleep or to get warm.

There were other newsagents as well as other newspapers, but seven years ago she and Martin had settled on this shop, the smallest. No young girls behind the counter, bored and impersonal, contemptuous of Americans. Only florid-faced Mr Keneally, always pleased to see them. *Hello, my good people.* His shop was the size of a closet, crammed floor to ceiling with cigars, cigarettes, newspapers, magazines, paperbacks, guidebooks, sweets, school supplies, three-pound boxes of chocolates wrapped in dusty yellow and pink cellophane.

A man needed a refill for his pen, located only after a five-minute search. Another man bought twenty instant-winner lottery tickets, a present for his wife, and wanted them wrapped. A noisy cluster of schoolchildren, their uniforms giving off a cloudy smell of wet wool, held fistfuls of unwrapped peppermints and marshmallows, gummy snakes in lurid colours and sticky brown toffees scooped from a collection of open boxes ranged along the floor. Kindly Mr Keneally, a sibilant murmur of multiplication and addition escaping his lips, often lost count responding to their shrill chatter and had to begin again, totting up the figures in pencil on the back of a brown paper bag.

Then there was only one woman left. She turned and waved Eve ahead of her. 'Go on. Go on.' It was more a command than anything, but Eve misunderstood. She did not mind waiting. And that scrawled *Hope-Ross*. If she hung round long enough, she might run into Peter or Adele, come to pick up their paper. It would make everything so much easier just to run into them. She had looked up their telephone number that morning and started to dial it, then put the phone down, unable to think what to say, how to begin. Dropping in on them was not possible. How could you say you were just passing by when you had to drive three miles out of town to get to the gates and then another half-mile of winding avenue to the house? Derrymore was the kind of place where dropping by meant nothing less than trespassing.

The woman, small and sharp-faced, a wet floral scarf tied under her chin, glared at Eve, judging her dark hair, cut like a man's, her black clothes, black sweater, black jeans. Eve felt herself – her height, her slimness, her whole country – despised. The woman turned a scornful back and leaned over the counter, whispering. She had an instant-winner lottery ticket, a hundred euro. The shopkeeper embarked on congratulations, but the woman shushed him with a swipe of her hand. No one was to know; she didn't want word getting round to her husband. Mr Keneally was not to tell a soul, nor was he to post a sign in his window declaring he had sold a winning ticket.

'But there's no names used,' he said. 'It's a help to the business to have a sign. Lynch's has ten signs in the window. Everybody and his uncle buys his ticket there.'

'Did you not hear?' The woman leaned closer, as if she would take a bite out of his face. 'There's to be no sign for my ticket.'

'No one would know.' He spread plump red hands. 'There's no names used.' But the woman shook her head, adamant. He took her ticket, tucked it away beneath the money tray, and counted out her hundred euro.

'Bless you, bless you.' The bills rolled and stashed in an inside pocket of her black handbag, big as a suitcase, she rushed out into the mist. Eve stepped up to the counter. Mr Kenealiy's eyes, bluer than she had remembered, looked so sad she wanted to say something.

'Couldn't you put the sign up anyway?' A mistake. A curtain fell, his expression changed, he pretended not to have heard.

'Fine day,' he said.

'It's raining.' Eve's cheeks burned.

She asked if he would hold a paper for her the next day, and every day; she'd be staying for a while. He wrote down her name. *Alliver*. She had to spell it for him. *Oliver*. It had been the same seven years ago. They'd always had to repeat and spell it, hearing their own accents in the phonetic spelling. But clearly the name meant nothing to him; nor did he recognise her face. He must have seen a thousand Americans since then. And then, even someone who had known her one year ago would have had trouble recognising her now: eyes dark hollows, all colour gone from her face, all beauty vanished, snatched from her like a mask the night the two policemen had come to her door to tell her about Evan's death.

'Last time I was here. You kept a paper for – for us. We were here six months.' She hesitated, her fragile confidence now in shreds. 'It was seven years ago.'

'I thought so!' He smiled, beamed, a shut door flung wide open and all the lights turned on. 'I thought so! I thought I knew you. And how is your husband keeping himself? I remember him well. A tall, fine-looking fellow. How is he now?'

'I don't know.' She could think of nothing else. 'I don't know,' she said again, and fled.

A lorry, squeezing past a bus travelling in the opposite direction, swerved four of its wheels up onto the pavement in front of the newsagent's. Neither vehicle stopped or even slowed down and she leapt out of the way just in time, settling any doubts she might have had about her desire to go on living.

She walked quickly, hands in her pockets, eyes on the wet pavement. Why had she done that? Why had she said that? Why did she have to remind him? He would never have remembered her. She could have started all over again with him, been just another vaguely familiar face.

One of the things that had drawn her to Clonmere, aside from the fact that she knew it, was that it was small enough to walk from one end to the other in twenty minutes but large enough for anonymity. The population was less than three thousand, but half of them were right here, crowded into these three narrow streets, an elongated Y, with a few abbreviated appendages. On market days there were even more: farmers with cattle to auction or buy, carrots, turnips and potatoes to sell. And every day people poured in from the countryside and the smaller nearby villages to shop. In terms of negotiating your way down a crowded sidewalk, Clonmere was like a couple of blocks of midtown Manhattan dropped on the west coast of Ireland. It was a busy, bustling town: nineteen pubs, two small hotels, five tea or coffee shops, six hardware shops, dozens of tiny shops that sold clothes and shoes and bedding. Newsagents and food shops, butchers and chemists. Three concrete schools, out of which poured hundreds of children every day at one and again at four. And two churches, whose bells she had noticed, still chimed slightly out of sync.

An enormous, new Catholic church, at one end of town and reached by an imposing flight of wide steps, sat boldly astride a hill. At the other end of Clonmere the Church of Ireland, much older and much smaller, retreated unobtrusively to the far end of a tree-shaded drive, well behind the tall, black, wrought-iron gates that were kept locked six days a week. Eve, having walked from one end of the town to the other, stood outside these gates now, looking through the bars at the dripping lime trees and the nettles growing among the time-blackened tombstones.

She had been inside the church only once, on St Patrick's Day. The Hope-Rosses had invited them to a party at Derrymore, a buffet they were giving after the morning's special service, and the Olivers, having accepted the invitation to lunch, had felt obliged to attend the church service. Eve had been amazed by the numbers of brass plaques and stained-glass memorial windows commemorating the death or life of one Hope-Ross or another. She could almost see them all assembled there on Sunday mornings: brothers, uncles, cousins, grand-parents, aunts, guests, friends, visitors, filling the pews with rustling garments, their hymns swelling to the rafters. Then they evaporated; the congregation shrunk to Peter and Adele alone in the first pew, and a handful of others, their thinning voices brave.

In their hotel room later that afternoon Eve and Martin had talked about how only an outsider could move back and forth between the two worlds they had found in Ireland. The one almost invisible, existing in isolated houses, like small islands, at the ends of winding avenues, completely obscured by trees. The other highly visible, right out there for all to see, although in its own way just as inaccessible. Staring through the locked gates of the church, Eve saw instead the hotel room, where, sluggish from sherry and wine, she and Martin had lounged on the bed, talking, watching the lights come on outside their window. She saw them sleep, make love, sleep again.

'Excuse me. Aren't you Martin Oliver's wife?' The woman was short and dark, plump, middle-aged, American. Startled, Eve just stared at her.

'Sorry. I thought you were somebody else.' The woman started to turn away, but Eve stopped her.

'I *was* married to Martin Oliver,' she said.

'I knew you were.' The woman put out her hand.

'Dolores Depriest. I saw you at a party at the Hope-Rosses' once, some years ago. I asked your husband to point you out to me, but you got away before I could work my way over to you. I saw you a couple of times after that, down the street, crossing the road. You're so tall, you're easy to spot. I asked you to lunch. You didn't come.'

Eve remembered now. Martin had told her about meeting another American, another academic. She talked too much, he'd said; he'd had a hard time getting away from her. When he mentioned the invitation to lunch, he had already refused it.

'What are you doing here?' Dolores Depriest pushed at the bridge of her glasses with a forefinger. 'Do you mind my asking?'

'In Ireland?'

'In Ireland in January, yes.' This was accompanied by an exaggerated shrug. 'But I meant, what are you doing standing out here in the rain without a hat? Are you all right?'

Eve took in the older woman's masculine tweed hat, but said nothing.

'I was next door in O'Gorman's and saw you go by. When you stopped and stood here for such a long time, I got curious. Then I realised I knew who you were.'

Eve wondered how long she had been standing there. She looked at her watch, but except for the time it gave her no information. She hadn't even noticed when the mist had developed into a serious rain. The other woman took her by the elbow.

'Come in here with me. Come in out of the rain. I'm almost finished. Then I'll give you a lift. It doesn't do to get too wet. It's so damn hard to get anything dried in this country.' Eve was being steadily moved along the pavement.

'I don't need a ride. I have a car.'

'A lift, not a ride. You say *ride* here, it means something else entirely. Never ask a guy if he wants a ride. Where's your car?'

'At Ballard's.'

'Ballard's? The hotel? That's at the other end of town. That's miles away.' By this time they were at the door of what Eve saw was not a pub but an estate agent's. She had imagined Dolores Depriest sitting in the window of a pub having lunch or a lonely drink, hungry for someone to talk to, anyone, then rushing out to grab Eve by the elbow.

'Come in here. I'll be through in a minute. Come meet the O'Gormans. Wonderful people, wonderful.'

'No.' Eve pushed her now quite wet hair out of her eyes. 'No. I can't. I'm sorry. I can't.' Once again she turned and fled.

The next few days were much the same, more sleeping than waking, more rain, more aimless walking. Every morning, she picked up the telephone, then put it down again. Twice she drove the three miles out to the gates, only to turn and drive back into Clonmere. At home, looking at a photograph she'd taken in the woods at Derrymore, a vast carpet of bluebells under a high ceiling of pale spring green leaves, it had seemed possible to just step into it. She had seen herself back there again, walking through the woods and meadows and along the cliffs, painting the sea and the sky, and if not recovering the peace and joy of that other time, at least, perhaps, recovering.

Now she saw that crossing the Atlantic had been the easy part. Now that she was actually here, she could no longer envision herself entering the gates of Derrymore. And the longer she put off the attempt, the more improbable her success began to seem. *Easier for a camel to pass through the eye of a needle.*

But why? What had they done?

She had sent the Hope-Rosses a copy of Martin's book as soon as it was published. Then, as the weeks passed with no word, she thought they must have decided to read it first. But she never heard from them again. Nor did Martin.

Eve had never even heard of Evelyn Hope-Ross before Martin decided to do the book, but it seemed to her that it was, if anything, extremely sensitive. And it wasn't as if the Hope-Rosses hadn't wanted it done. Peter had answered Martin's enquiry practically by return mail, offering him every possible assistance, offering him access to everything: the original manuscripts of the novels, essays, stories, the paintings and sketchbooks, diaries and letters, the books and magazines Evelyn Hope-Ross had read growing up, her account books for the management of the house and farm and stables.

He said he was pleased there was finally going to be some critical attention given to his great-aunt – a great woman, he believed, who had been neglected, allowed to fall between the cracks. And he seemed pleased the book would be written by an American, an outsider, someone who was innocent ('ignorant, he means,' Martin had said) of class prejudices, who would be objective, who would see Evelyn Hope-Ross not as a privileged daughter of the landed gentry, but simply as an extraordinary woman, a daughter of the Victorians who had managed to break free and make her own way in a man's world.

The Hope-Rosses had offered not only assistance but hospitality, often inviting the younger couple for drinks or dinner or tea, lunch. They had even, after the Olivers had been in Clonmere for some weeks, offered them a room in the house, an offer that Martin declined. He wanted his autonomy and preferred to stay in the hotel. But he went to Derrymore every day to work in the library and Eve had been invited to come whenever she wanted, to paint, to wander in the gardens and woods and the sheep meadow ranged along the top of the cliffs. The Hope-Rosses had always been more than just helpful, and they had all parted on good terms. Eve was sure they had.

And the book had done as well as you could expect an academic book to do. There had been a couple of good reviews and it had even been taken up by a feminist press, which kept a few paperback copies in print. Yet not a word from the Hope-Rosses. When a Christmas card went unacknowledged, Eve was surprised, disappointed; but Martin was not. 'They don't want to be friends with us, Eve. We did each other a favour, that's all. They wanted this book done. I wanted to do it. Now it's done. Finito.'

But they *had* been friends, Eve knew they had. How could you be mistaken about such a thing? They had not only parted on good terms, the Hope-Rosses had even bought two of Eve's watercolours and had hung them on the same walls with Evelyn Hope-Ross's early oils and watercolours. Eve had not been able to judge if they really admired her work or were just being kind. But if the paintings were still hanging there, she would know. If she ever got inside the house again.

One morning she awoke to sun so bright she had to shield her eyes. Blazing into the town, it lit up, as if from within, the rows of bright-painted shops and houses – blue, pink, yellow, green – that had been blotted out by the rain. She felt brighter too after getting some sleep. Today she would phone.

She picked up her newspaper at Keneally's and bought postcards to send Lily and Rose. For the present, frequent cards were safer. Too much leaked between the lines of a letter; she wanted them to stop worrying about her. She went into Logan's for breakfast and wrote out the cards, then walked to the post office and on to the bank to change some money.

When she took her place in the queue waiting along the length of velvet rope, there were at least ten people ahead of her. She only gradually became aware that the man now second in line was Peter Hope-Ross. His grey tweed overcoat, its collar a little twisted, silver hair curling over it, giving him a genteelly dishevelled look, he was unmistakable even from behind. He moved to the front of the queue and then to the counter, conducting his business inaudibly, putting things into his pockets before turning away.

Eve's heart quickened. Now that he was here, standing not ten feet away from her, she was afraid to speak to him, afraid of his reception. She realised, actually seeing him, that he was almost a stranger to her now, and she to him.

She nearly let him walk past, and then almost clutched at his sleeve, but caught herself in time. 'Mr Hope-Ross,' she said, unable to manage the now too-familiar 'Peter'. He stopped and turned, looked at her.

'I'm Eve Oliver,' she said at last.

'Of course you are.' His lips twitched, the barest hint of a smile. 'Of course you are. On holiday?'

She nodded, unable to say why she had come.

'Lovely,' he said. 'And lovely to see you. Enjoy your holidays.' He smiled briefly, nodded, almost a bow, then walked the length of the bank and out the door. So much the gentleman, his voice so kind. No one witnessing the encounter would have guessed she'd been cut to the bone.

Monday, 19 January – *Sunny at first and then cold, cold, cold.*

She wrote in the still largely blank book Lily had given her, extracting from her, before going back for the second semester, the promise to write something in it every day, if only a sentence. Rose had extracted a promise too, one that had shocked her mother into action.

'I want you to promise me you'll speak to at least two different people every day. And not just hello or goodbye or thank you. I want you to exchange a couple of sentences.'

What must she look like to them, what must they think of her, that they should feel entitled to patronise her in this way?

She and Evan had done the same. They had worried about their father, about his loneliness, his health, his state of mind. They had gone often to visit him, much more often than was convenient. They had tried taking turns, but he preferred them as he had always had them, together. They would sleep in their old rooms, they would eat the same easy meals they had settled on after their mother died, and they would sit in their same places at the table. Their father seemed to wish for nothing more from life. He would look from one to the other of his children. He would smile. 'Now, isn't this nice?' The twenty- and then thirty- and then forty-year-old twins would glance at each other with identical expressions: What will we do with him?

She would not do that to her children, and she would not let them do that to her. She would not let them turn her into a greedy, needy old woman hungering for their visits. At the end of their Christmas holidays, which they had spent helping her get the house ready to put on the market, when they told her they weren't sure they'd be able to get home before their spring break in March – approaching her tentatively, Rose half-hiding behind Lily – she had made up her mind. She told them they might have to stay with their father over spring break, if they didn't have any other plans. She was going back to Ireland.

'Back? What do you mean, *back*?' Lily's eyebrows had shot up; she'd exchanged a glance with her sister.

They had no way of knowing. They had almost forgotten that

their parents had ever been to Ireland. Twelve years old at the time, they'd been offered a choice and had chosen, because of soccer and tennis and clubs and friends, to have Martin's mother, recently widowed and eager for company, move in and take care of them. They had no idea how reluctant their mother had been to come home, how often she returned in her head and in her dreams.

She may have gone to Ireland because of Martin, but it was she who had responded to the place and she, though she missed her children, who had wept when their time there had come to an end. At home again, she kept having the same dream, a dream within a dream. She would wake up in Clonmere from a dream of being back home; she would get out of bed and push the windows wide open, put out her head and inhale the sweet, intoxicating air. Then she would wake up for real, in her own bed, her windows shut, locked, and barred.

Then, packing up the house and coming across that photograph, she had been so possessed by the need to walk there once more, she knew that her life could not be over.

Saw Peter Hope-Ross in the bank today. He made it clear he wants nothing to do with me. But tomorrow I'm going out there. There is some serious misunderstanding somewhere. I mean to find out what it is, if they will tell me. I can't just let it go. Not this too.

The high iron gates stood open to the avenue. Inside, on the right, a vacant gate lodge with intricate mullioned windows was obscured by the unpruned branches of rhododendrons pushing up against it. These towering shrubs, flanking the entire length of twisting gravel drive, had been in bloom when she last saw them, great stars and bowls of colour: crimson, mauve, white. Now their dark leathery leaves created two walls of solid green that she drove between almost at a crawl.

The narrow, curving drive, according to Peter, had seen generations of head-on collisions. Rounding one of the curves, Eve surprised into flutter a grey wood pigeon that spread wide wings and glided ahead of her at eye level, as if leading the way. Round the last curve, the pigeon streaked away into the clearing in which stood the house, a two-storeyed slate-roofed Georgian that had seen better days, its granite face softened by the reddish leaves of the creeper whose vines were doing their best to burrow beneath the frames of the long windows that were Derrymore's best feature. Before the house, on a wide gravel sweep designed for turning a landau and four horses, was parked an incongruously small blue Morris Minor. Eve parked next to it.

Then, glancing back from the low steps that ran across the front of the house, she noticed the car's British number plate and instantly lost her nerve. She had not counted on their having visitors; the thought had never occurred to her. It would be difficult enough to have a heart-to-heart with the Hope-Rosses alone. How could she possibly talk to them in front of other people? She walked quickly back to her car, hoping she hadn't been seen. But just then the door of the house was flung open and a man she had never seen before came down a step, hand raised, calling to her.

'Hello! Hello! Don't go away. I must not have heard.'

Eve went back to the house and stood a step below the man, who loomed over her, unnecessarily tall and thin, with a long bony nose, high dark eye sockets, and a wide mouth. Black hair, threaded with grey, hung nearly to his shoulders. He wore brown whipcords, cuffed in a way Eve hadn't seen in years, and a thick-knitted white cardigan with bulging pockets. He presented a cold hand that was all fingers, and a smile crowded with long teeth no longer white.

'Henry Cole,' he said. 'Making a bit of a racket. Didn't hear you.'

'I came – I was looking for Peter and Adele Hope-Ross.'

'Come in. I can show you round.' He held the door open for her, but Eve remained where she was.

'You *do* want to see the place?'

'Well.' She hesitated. 'I did, but – '

'Right. I can show you everything. The Hope-Rosses are in Cambridge.'

'They're in England?' Eve didn't believe him. 'But I saw – I saw him yesterday.'

'They left yesterday.' The man examined his watch. 'At this very hour.'

'I'd better go. I don't want to put you to any trouble.'

'Happy to do it, really. I take a keen interest in these old Irish houses. This one is a veritable museum. They've never thrown a thing out, bless them.' He was growing impatient at having to hold the door open. 'I say, would you mind terribly stepping inside?'

Inside was as cold as outside. Eve remembered this now, and everything else was also exactly as it had been. The same long and heavy-legged tables and ancient grandfather clock and huge brass tub of umbrellas and walking sticks occupied the same spaces in the lofty, two-storeyed hall. At the far end, directly opposite the hall door, a double staircase of polished oak curved up from the right and left to meet at a landing beneath a long Venetian window on the sea side of the house. On the upper storey, arched passages, east and west, led to two bedroom wings; a central gallery circled the hall, its balustrade draped with the mouldering skins of a wide variety of Victorian animals and its walls hung with an equally wide variety of art works. Eve's eyes were immediately drawn up to the space, selected by the Hope-Rosses with much care and consultation, where her own two pieces had been hung and where, her heart jumped to see, they remained.

'Yes,' her guide followed her eyes, 'if ever a staircase were built for swagger, this one was.' He tossed his hair, then lunged toward the door of the drawing room. 'Come to the fire.'

He went straight to the great sculpted marble fireplace that was the centrepiece of the drawing room and added another log to the fire. Eve walked to the far end of the room to the French windows, whose distant view held the entire length of the glittering harbour right down to its mouth and out to the open sea. Beyond the windows was a levelled and still carefully mown area where lawn tennis and croquet had once been played. At the edge of the lawns a tangle of crabapple trees provided a screen from westerly winds, the orchard sloping to a meadow where black-faced sheep grazed. The meadow, Eve knew, shelved steeply to the sea.

'If nothing else, they knew where to build a house.' Henry Cole came and stood next to her, releasing the bolts at the top and the bottom of the French windows. 'Evelyn Hope-Ross put in these doors. I came across the glazier's bill for them just this morning. It used to be a long window, set rather near the floor. But there was a tax levied on houses according to their number of windows and she had the ingenious idea of turning as many windows as she could afford into doors. Extraordinary woman, really, the way she kept this place going.'

He excused himself to tend the fire in the library. He was

actually working in there, he said, but had taken a break to do some piano exercises and so had been in the drawing room when Eve arrived. She paused by the grand piano and looked at the Schubert score standing open there. Then her eye was caught by a reflection in the glass front of a cabinet against the wall next to the piano: the front end of her hired Nissan. He must have seen her sneaking away.

'You see, that is how we work in my line of history.' He burst back into the room. 'Glaziers' bills, cleaners' bills, masons, carpenters, physicians, schools, tax bills, cookery books and receipts. We reassemble the past from odd scraps of paper. Now how about some tea? India or China?'

The offer was made so enthusiastically Eve was surprised by his obvious relief when she refused it. She'd just had lunch, she said. Could she simply walk for a while, outdoors? But he insisted on coming with her. The Hope-Rosses would never forgive him if he didn't. And, really, he assured her, it was no bother at all. He excused himself again. Eve was not at all looking forward to being rushed round and then shoved off, but she did not want to hurt his feelings, which she guessed would be at the sensitive end of the scale. And he was so accommodating, or meant to be, he might be perfectly willing to let her come and paint during the weeks he would be in charge of Derrymore.

They went out through the French windows and walked briskly across the lawn. Henry Cole swung a walking stick toward a huge oak standing guard at the extreme curve of the gravel sweep. 'Derry is from the Irish for *oak*, you know. *Mór* means big, large, great. Hence Derrymore.'

Just before the crabapple trees, they struck off to the left and followed a path of laurels that led to the walled garden. On the other side of the orchard a similar laurel path led to the woods Eve remembered carpeted with spring bluebells. These paths used to be open, she heard now, wide walks designed for three and four people abreast. The laurels were planted when Evelyn Hope-Ross was a child and they had gradually crowded the walks to narrow, single-file paths. 'The Victorians had a passion for laurels, planted them absolutely everywhere.' Henry Cole tapped a brittle, yellow-spotted leaf with the tip of his stick. 'Could never see them myself.'

He walked swiftly alongside one of the high stone walls of the garden. Eve could hardly keep up with him. At the end of the wall he stopped suddenly and swung his stick again at a clump of shrubs. 'Laburnum,' he said lightly. 'Want to get rid of your husband? Slip a few seeds into his cake. Foolproof, absolutely undetectable. Or used to be. Probably not now. Modern forensics. Takes all the fun out of murder.'

He led the way down a narrow path to a fence with a wide cattle gate, the latch fastened with a twisted wire. He looked from the gate to Eve, and back to the gate. 'I *could* open it.'

'That's all right,' Eve said, 'don't bother.' She'd had enough. This forced march wasn't at all what she'd had in mind.

'Right,' he said, and to her surprise he climbed the gate and set off across the sheep meadow that ran along the edge of the steep shelf above the sea. She got herself over the gate but lagged behind, lengthening the distance between them. He never looked over his shoulder; when he got to the edge of the meadow, he veered left again and soon dropped from sight.

There was a path, Eve saw when she reached the edge, that sloped gently down to a narrow strand and a small, abandoned cottage whose slate roof she remembered looking down on when the cottage itself was unapproachable, buried up to its ears in a clotted tangle of brambles and shrubs. Now it stood in a small clearing, its low walls gleaming with fresh white paint. Her guide flourished his stick in the direction of the cottage, pointing it out to her, before leading her the rest of the way down the path and taking a long key from the pocket of his coat. As he opened the door, he touched the wall beside it. 'Two feet thick, all the way round. Will stand its ground in the worst of gales.' He stepped aside for Eve to enter.

Inside, one long room with a fireplace at each end had been made to seem like two rooms. A single bed and chest of drawers, a wardrobe, formed a bedroom. At the other end, two armchairs, a footstool, a bookcase and desk, and small rug made a sitting room, with a window on each side of the fireplace.

'The windows were Adele's idea. The Irish, you know, never used to look at the sea. Always turned their backs to it. That's why this place sits sideways on the strand. The sea got only a cold shoulder until Adele had those windows cut in. And do note the floors.'

Eve crossed the polished pine floor to one of the windows. The thickness of the walls formed a natural window seat. Outside, the silent sea was a Mediterranean turquoise, although she knew it could also be black and churning. White sea birds swooped and circled.

Henry Cole, who had not left the threshold, crossed the room now to a low doorway, where again the walls were two feet thick. It led to a narrow kitchen and small bathroom. These, he told Eve, had been rather cleverly added on to the cottage by the conversion of a small shed and an outhouse. He tapped at the green wainscot in the bathroom. 'No shower, as you see. Immersion heater takes one hour, but you'll get a full bath then. Firewood is not really available. You'll want to burn turf. Place called O'Driscoll's delivers.' He turned and caught her look of astonishment, and misunderstood.

'There *is* firewood for the house, as you must have ah, ah —' He swung his stick again, tapped a grey metal box with two dials on its face. 'Electricity runs by feeding two-euro pieces into the hungry maw of this meter. Again, you'll want to be careful.'

'I take it this place is for rent.' Eve found her voice. 'Did you think I came here to look at it?'

'Didn't you?' Now he was astonished. 'Aren't you the American O'Gorman telephoned about this morning? Oh, Lord,' he said, as Eve shook her head. 'Dreadfully sorry, really.'

More annoyed than sorry, he ushered her out the door, which he slammed behind them, and climbed the path at a bound. Nothing was said all the way back to the house, an uphill walk that took, even at that pace, a quarter of an hour. He crossed the level lawn and skirted past the French windows, leading the way round to the front of the house. On the gravel sweep a third car, a Porsche, had joined the Morris and the Nissan. A stocky middle-aged couple in bright blue padded parkas and white running shoes lounged on the steps. Eve was filled with dislike and at the same time seized by a violent proprietary jealousy. She caught hold of Henry Cole's surprised arm.

'I want it,' she said. 'I'll take it.

Wednesday

Went to O'Gorman's this morning to pay the deposit and first week's rent. Ran into Dolores Depriest again. She had just invited the O'Gormans to lunch tomorrow and asked me to come too, and would not take no for an answer. She told the O'Gormans to bring me. I'm to go to their office at half-twelve and drive out there with them, somewhere near Kilcreene Bay. I wanted to drive myself but they said it was too complicated to give directions to her place, they always drive people there the first time. They manage it for her when she's not using it herself, letting it to tourists. But she's on sabbatical now. Not sure how I feel about that.

Eve moved away from the fire and stood at the window, although at six o'clock it was so dark all she could see was her own reflection, then Dolores behind her, coming in from the kitchen with glasses of whiskey and a jug of water on a wooden tray.

The O'Gormans had gone back to town immediately after lunch, during which Dolores and Máire O'Gorman had talked mostly to each other. Jerry O'Gorman, a small, dark-haired man with bright, bird-like eyes, devoted himself to Eve, telling her how, when they were first married, his wife, who was just eighteen, could not cook, could not so much as roast a joint or boil a potato, and how he and the wife's brother had to cook the first Sunday lunch between them. He set himself to learn how to cook, he said, just so he could teach the wife, and they both came to enjoy it so much they not only became excellent cooks themselves but produced a daughter who now ran a fine restaurant in Dublin. The daughter was always wanting her parents to come for a meal, expecting them to show up at least two or three times a month.

'But how many times can you eat a salmon?' He leaned towards Eve confidentially. 'How many times can you eat a lobster? They never have a joint. They never have a stew. A month ago I had a piece of lamb that tasted like rope. I complained in the kitchen and your man says he doesn't know what's wrong with it, it was just walking around yesterday. I said, "That's *exactly* what's wrong with it."' His hand slapped the table. 'I said, "That lamb should still be hanging in the cold room three weeks from this day." But it just goes to show,' he shook his head. 'You never know how things will turn out. You never know a thing.'

Eve found his conversation soothing and undemanding. He asked no questions. He made her smile. She even laughed several times, something she thought she'd forgotten how to do. She was grateful to him. And she loved this house, along the lines of the one she had just taken, but larger, with a fire burning at each end. The space where her bed would be was here a dining area, a scrubbed pine table with six painted chairs in front of one of the fireplaces; on the table a cobalt glass bottle held the florist's red poppies she had brought with her. Along the wall a narrow stairway led up to two small bedrooms. At the other end, books lined the walls, and two low armchairs, one upholstered in blue and one in yellow, faced the fire across an oval rug. A desk on one side of the room, a long, narrow work table on the other; footstools and baskets of magazines, tiny tables with reading lamps found what spaces they could.

Eve could not move into her own place until Saturday and found she was reluctant to go back to her hotel room, so chilly the bedclothes always felt slightly damp. It wasn't only the warmth of this house that held her. She felt unexpectedly at ease with her fellow American and when Dolores pressed her to stay and offered to drive her back into town later, she'd sunk gratefully into the blue chair and sat absorbing the heat from the fire while she listened to the icy rain pummel the windows, as if someone were tossing fistfuls of sand.

She and Dolores hadn't talked an hour before Eve, who had vowed not to reveal anything about herself to this loose-tongued woman, had told her nearly everything: how her husband of more than twenty years had left her for another woman; how her brother, her twin, her other half in the only real sense of the word, had been shot to death in the parking lot of one of Dallas's better restaurants while on a three-day business trip; and how her father had soon afterwards suffered a second and fatal heart attack.

'There are a lot of things I could say.' Dolores set the tray on a footstool. 'All of them true. But you wouldn't believe me. So I'll just keep quiet.' She kicked off her shoes and curled herself up in the yellow chair. Eve turned to face her.

'Say one of them.'

'All right. You *will* get over it, all of it. It may seem like the end of your life to you right now, but it's not. It's just one stage, and you'll get past it just like you did the good ones. Believe me, I speak from experience.' She added a splash of water to one of the glasses and indicated that Eve should help herself. 'I thought *I* was only going to have one husband, if I thought about it at all. One house, one life. One *country*. It didn't work out that way. I learned that nothing is for ever. Nothing. And,' she went on after a pause, 'you'll find it's not an entirely bad thing, to cut the bliss. That sounds like a cruel thing to say at the moment, I know, but contentment smothers a lot. You'll be surprised what can emerge when it's stripped away.' After another pause, she laughed. 'See? I told you you wouldn't believe me.'

She waited until Eve had fixed her drink and settled in the blue chair opposite her. 'But that's all I'm going to say. I didn't ask you here to lecture you.'

The two women contemplated the fire and sipped their drinks in silence for a while before Eve said, 'Why did you ask me here?'

'Do I need a reason? I ask everybody. Everyone who interests me. And I must admit that being Martin Oliver's wife you interested me right off the bat. Then when you walked into O'Gorman's and said you were going to live out at Derrymore, I was really fascinated.'

'Why?' Eve turned to look at the other woman, whose round, dark face was alive with curiosity.

'It just seems like an odd place for you to choose, that's all. I wouldn't have thought you would want to go back there.'

'But going back there was the whole point. Not just getting away.' She described how she had come across the photograph taken at Derrymore, how she'd been possessed by a desire to be there again.

'And the Hope-Rosses?' Dolores cocked her head sideways. 'Did they seem pleased to see you again?'

Eve said nothing.

'Excuse me' – Dolores leaned forward and cocked her head – 'but you did read your husband's book?'

'Of course I read it.'

'I just wondered. I thought maybe you hadn't read it.'

'Why? What was wrong with it?'

'Your husband said – well, *conjectured* – that Evelyn Hope-Ross was a lesbian. You didn't miss that, did you?'

'So what?' Eve was surprised. 'What's wrong with that?'

'Not a thing, if it's true.'

Eve just looked at her.

'I know it must seem a small thing to you whether or not a woman who was your age a hundred years ago was gay or not, but, frankly, the Hope-Rosses were certainly pissed off.'

'What do you mean, *if it's true*? There isn't any question, is there? All those quotes from her diaries and –'

'*Mis*quotes. Or, more accurately, partial quotes.'

Dolores got up and knelt in front of the fire, jabbing at it with the poker, keeping her back to Eve as she spoke.

'The point of research is to get at the truth about your subject, not to go hunting for sentences you can cut to fit your own preconceived pattern. If the fact doesn't fit the theory, you throw out the theory, you don't bend and twist and cut the fact to fit the theory. That's what we're talking about here. The words he quoted were all her words, yes, but were often taken out of context, giving things an entirely different slant.' She brushed her hands against each other and got painfully to her feet with much cracking of joints.

'How do I know?' she went on. 'I've seen the original sources, the ones your husband used and the ones he did not use.' She sank back into her chair and picked up her glass, then set it down again, leaving her hands free to gesture.

'All her life this woman kept an annotated daily diary, what we would call an appointment calendar, with the difference that at the end of each entry she always scribbled in a couple of sentences or paragraphs about what had happened during the day. These were what your husband –'

'He's actually someone else's husband,' Eve reminded her.

'Sorry. You probably don't even want to hear this.'

'Oh, but I do. I do.'

'The fact is that, in addition to those diaries, for one very pivotal year Evelyn Hope-Ross also kept a journal with much longer entries, sometimes five or six pages for a single day and, I'm afraid, it renders the notion that she was gay ridiculous. Now, your husband did not have access to it, but –'

'Why?' Eve cut in. 'Why didn't he have access to it?'

'Because it only came to light when Peter got the idea of letting that cottage you're moving into as a holiday house and went down to clean it out. No one had been inside for decades, even the way down to it was completely overgrown. He had to cut a new path with a back hoe, or whatever they call it, and a scythe. He thought it was empty except for a lot of useless trash, because, when she gave up going to the cottage, she had all her things moved to the house. But in one of the half-dozen or so tea chests –'

'Why would anyone leave a half-dozen tea chests behind?'

'You're thinking steamer trunks or sea chests. A tea chest was just a wooden box that tea was shipped in. People held on to them for storing things in, the quintessential Victorian garbage can. Anyway, Peter was so discouraged by all the debris as well as the dirt and mould and cobwebs he nearly locked the door on it all again. It took him days to clear everything out. But in one of the boxes he found, wrapped up in a protective oilskin, an old, leather-covered manuscript book. And when he started reading it, he –'

'Wait,' Eve interrupted again. 'How did it get down there in the first place? I thought she lived in the house.'

'She never *lived* in the cottage, no. But when Peter's parents came and took over the house, she started using it as a kind of retreat. The house was left to her brother Francis, who was in the navy and away most of the time. *She* was the one who ran it. Then, after Francis was murdered –'

'He was murdered?'

'He was shot on his own doorstep. In fact he died in her arms.' Dolores raised her eyebrows. 'I thought you read your husband's book.'

'Seven years ago.' Now, Eve thought, someone's brother being shot was not the kind detail that would escape her memory. 'What happened?'

'It was during the Civil War. He was a very vocal supporter of the Free State, even met with Michael Collins once. One night when he was home on leave, they were playing cards and there was a knock at the door. He went to answer it. The servants were all conveniently out, given the night off for some local fête, so he opened the door himself and was shot point blank four or five times. Evelyn and Anne came running, but whoever it was had disappeared into the night.'

'How awful.' It came back to her then, the memory of having read of the one woman's brother dying in her arms while the other woman went on horseback to fetch a doctor, picking her slow way through a moonless, starless night for three miles.

'Anyway' – Dolores dismissed that part of the story with a wave of her hand – 'Derrymore went to the next brother, Dominick, who never came back to Ireland because of what had happened to Francis. He died in England, while she kept the house going through absolutely the worst time here. But she wouldn't give it up, wouldn't give in. She loved Ireland and she loved that house. Her cousin Anne had lived with her for about ten years, but she died not that long after Francis. There was a farm manager who lived in the yard, and someone in the front gate lodge, but she was often alone in that huge house, answering every dead-of-night knock at the door herself, giving up whatever was demanded: guns, horses, silver. After Dominick died in England, Derrymore went to his eldest son, who did decide to come to Ireland and take up residence.' Dolores spread her hands wide.

'So his wife becomes the mistress of Derrymore, after Evelyn has been de facto mistress for decades. Naturally, they didn't get along any too well. How could they? Evelyn travelled a lot, of course, she got away for months at a time, but Derrymore was her home, and this corner of Ireland was where all her best paintings were done and where her fiction was set. She had a studio in the house, a space she'd created when she was very young, but she wanted a place to escape to that was outside the house, a place where she could be on her own to read or write or to see her friends without her nephew's wife barging in at will.' She turned in her chair to face her guest. 'Years later when she started losing her sight and could hardly walk any more, her left leg was so badly deformed from riding side-saddle for fifty years, she had all her stuff moved back up to the house, and locked the door on the cottage. So it was clearly *her* decision to leave that journal behind. She had used material from it for at least four novels; two of them – *Conversation in Oils* and *Two Sisters* – were, I think, her best. And she probably didn't want Peter's mother throwing it into the fire after her death. She wanted it found.'

'But it's hardly Martin's fault, is it,' Eve said, after a silence, 'if the journal wasn't available to him? Why did they wait so long to look inside the cottage, anyway, if they knew she had used it?'

'Derelict cottages were not always the prime bit of real estate they are now. And even when Peter saw that he could bring in some income by letting it out, he assumed there was nothing of any value inside. He remembered very well when his great-aunt gave up the cottage, remembers her being down there personally overseeing the removal of her things up to the house.'

'But when he found the journal, why didn't he inform Martin?'

'Why on earth *should* he have? He was furious with him. No matter what he didn't have access to, the fact remains that he butchered quotes from the diaries.'

'In what way? Can you give me an example?'

'For one, he quotes every single time Evelyn Hope-Ross mentions sleeping with another female, from the time she was a small child until she died. It never meant anything. Women used to share beds all the time. It was quite common. A question of space, a question of *warmth*. Completely innocent of sexual overtones. But he doesn't supply that context. And the way he selected which phrases to quote, the way he piles them up. *Charlotte crawled into my bed during the night. Slept with Anne again. Spent another wretched night in Celia's bed*. That kind of thing. And he quotes from the entry the day her cousin Charlotte, who at the time was her closest friend, became engaged. *Inevitable Black Day. A tearful C. confessed her engagement. We embraced and wept, but I shall never, never forgive her.*

'She didn't say that?'

'*Yes*, she said that. But there are enough previous references to a certain "B." to make anyone suspect it was not the loss of "C." she was so upset about. *And* there was the letter from Virginia Woolf. In that case, it was what he failed to quote that was so –'

'But why?' Eve could not believe it. 'Why would he do that?'

'What I said before. He bent the facts to fit his own preconceptions. And probably to fit a book proposal he had a contract for.'

'He did have a contract,' Eve admitted.

'Look.' Dolores held up each finger in turn as she enumerated. 'Here is a woman who never married. Who went to a great deal of trouble *not* to get married. Who had very close lifelong friendships with women. Who lived with another woman for ten years. Who, as an old woman, had a fondness for wearing men's hats and masculine-looking suits and who could do anything a man could do – shoot, hunt, fish, break a horse.' She turned both palms up. 'So your husband assumes, Ah, undiscovered lesbian writer. Juicy. He writes a proposal, gets a contract –'

'It wasn't that kind of book,' Eve broke in.

'It was sensational enough around here, believe me,' Dolores snorted. 'No. What I mean is, juicy for him, for his career. When your husband wrote his book – not to mention when he conceived the idea of it – it was just *beginning* to be sexy to write about gays. I mean, in an unprejudiced, neutral way, without any of that not-that-there's-anything-wrong-with-it sanctimoniousness.'

'But he's not that kind of person,' Eve insisted. 'He's not an opportunist. He really isn't.'

'This is the crumb who left you for a younger woman?'

'She's not that much younger.'

Dolores hooted, but Eve stared into the fire. The other woman abruptly stopped laughing, reached over and touched her arm.

'You're right about the kind of book it was. It was a sensitive, tasteful portrait of an extraordinary woman who because of her upper-class background never got her due in her native land. But it was not *that* extraordinary woman. That's what upset Peter. It was as if he'd commissioned a portrait of his great-aunt, a woman he remembers very fondly, and got back a complete stranger. And your husband didn't have the courtesy to tell him what slant he was giving the book. That's what really hurt. Peter was not only shocked, he felt used. *He* thinks your husband is an opportunist of the first order.'

'But Martin would have assumed that Peter *knew* his aunt was a lesbian.' Eve had given up trying to get Dolores to stop referring to Martin as 'your husband'. 'Why should he have brought up the subject? I can't even imagine discussing anyone's sexual preferences with Peter Hope-Ross. Can you?'

'Obviously' – Dolores gave another hoot – 'I've had the pleasure. Anyway, when this journal turned up, he came to me to see if it would be excuse enough for another book and to ask for suggestions about who – *whom* – to approach.' She snorted again. 'We've never been *friends*. They think I'm pretty bizarre, I know. But I've had this house for fourteen years now and I often go to their church when I'm here, just to swell the ranks, you know, and that counts for a lot with them. I said, sure, I'd look at the stuff. I never thought of taking it on myself. To tell you the truth, I was never much interested in Evelyn Hope-Ross. My field is Irish literature and I've always thought of her as more Anglo than Irish. You know. Full of the prejudices of her time and her class. And

George Eliot she's not, believe me. The novels, with two or three exceptions, are fairly mediocre, strictly commercial, written to support the painting. But this journal is really something, and reading it, or *trying* to read it – her writing is hell to decipher – I found that a lot of my own assumptions about her were completely wrong.'

Her phone rang then and she went out to the kitchen. Eve could hear her laughing and apologising, that she thought it was *tomorrow*, and making arrangements to meet the next afternoon.

'I take it you've met Henry Cole,' she said when she returned. Eve nodded, thinking that must have been who had phoned. But, apparently, there was no connection.

'Now there's a strange bird. I can't really get back in there until he's gone. But when I do, I'll show you some of the journal entries.'

'No.' Eve held up a hand as if to ward off the idea. 'I don't even want to hear Evelyn Hope-Ross's name again, ever.'

'She could be just the person to help put things in perspective for you.'

'What do you mean?'

'I mean that you're falling apart, if you don't mind my saying so, because you are suddenly forced to live without the men in your life. Am I wrong? Please tell me if I'm wrong. And *here's* a woman who struggled and fought for the *privilege* to live as you are now being forced to live, without men. Don't get me wrong.' She made a sideways gesture with her hand. 'She was no man-hater. Quite the contrary. She adored all those brothers, particularly Francis. She just arrived at the decision that she didn't want to get married. A married woman was simply a baby-making machine. A baby a year, until you wore out. Some women gave birth as much as twenty times. Can you imagine that? I mean, *can* you?'

'No. Two were as many as I could handle.'

'I'm not even talking about raising children. I'm talking about giving birth to them. I'm talking about being pregnant for twenty years of your life. Elizabeth Bowen's great-grandmother, I was reading just the other day, gave birth twenty-one times. And fourteen of them *lived*. Evelyn Hope-Ross wanted to do other things. She wanted to paint. You two have that in common, too, the painting. And my God, her brother dying that way. I really think you two should become better acquainted.'

'I really think I should leave.'

'Don't be silly. The Hope-Rosses certainly wouldn't hold anything against *you*. It's your husband who —'

'Oh but they do.'

Eve described her meeting with Peter in the bank.

'But he would have assumed that your husband was here with you. And he certainly does not want to see *him* again. No wonder he hurried away; he probably expected your husband to walk in at any moment. The idea that you two were divorced would never have entered his mind. These people mate for life.' She broke off and fell silent a minute. 'All that's needed,' she went on, 'is a word dropped in the right direction, and I'm going to do it for you whether you like it or not. I'll write to them tomorrow. I have to anyway, to let them know I've decided to take the book on.' She gave a shake of her head. 'Not that it will do *me* any good professionally. It's very *un*sexy to want to try to prove that somebody *wasn't* gay.'

Saturday she woke feeling none too well. But moving into the cottage was just a matter of lugging her two huge suitcases down to the car. She made a third trip up to the fourth floor of Ballard's for her shoulder bag and carry-on, then left the car behind the hotel while she bought a set of sheets and some towels, food and laundry detergent. The price of sheets, two or three times what she was used to paying for them, made her think with longing of her packed boxes at home. By the time she'd trudged back to her car for the fourth time, she would have given anything to be able to dip into those boxes for five minutes and take what she needed.

Not that she any longer had to worry about money. Evan had seen to that in naming her his sole beneficiary. The multinational corporation on whose business he had been engaged in Dallas had seen to it that the double-indemnity clause of their generous life insurance policy had been honoured, even though his death had not been accidental. She had benefited in other ways as well: stocks and savings, his condominium, his car, his furniture, his extensive collection of prints and drawings, old records, tapes, compact discs. She was also, now, sole beneficiary of her father's will, of his life insurance policy, his stocks, savings, house, car, furniture. She did not yet know the details, nor wished to. It made her feel guilty.

Following the coast road, as Máire O'Gorman had shown her on the map, she turned off onto the long narrow track that had recently been forged to the Hope-Rosses' cottage. Still, she could not drive right up to it but had to park an inconvenient distance away.

She was glad now that she had kept the hired car, but if she stayed for any length of time, she would have to look into buying one. She certainly wouldn't want to be living out here without one, having to walk into Clonmere for everything. The way the weather changed so fast, clouds blowing in from the Atlantic, she might start out walking under a sky of brilliant blue and be beaten to death by hailstones ten minutes later. And there were winter storms, she remembered, violent ones. And what if she needed to get herself to a doctor or hospital? What if she had a heart attack? At this moment, lugging these suitcases, it seemed a distinct possibility. There was heart disease up and down both sides of her family. Her mother had died when she was sixteen years younger than Eve was now.

Relieved to see the turf she had paid for yesterday stacked outside the door, she carried one bundle inside and hauled the rest round to the shed at the back. She got a knife from the kitchen to cut the plastic bands and piled the turf beside the fireplace. Only then did she realise that she had no idea how to make a turf fire. The briquettes were like stone, concrete. How could they possibly burn? She didn't have any newspapers and, damn it, she had forgotten to buy matches.

She hauled the last of her bags in from the car and went through the pockets of jackets, jeans, her coat, went through her bag again. She opened the fridge to put away the food and was reminded by its dark interior that she'd also forgotten to arm herself with two-euro pieces for the meter. She went back to her bag, went through her pockets again. It was so cold inside the cottage it didn't matter whether the fridge was on or not. But she would have to have light, and soon. The bank wouldn't be open again until Monday. And she had to have matches. And newspapers. And someone had to show her how to start the fire.

Slamming the door behind her, she strode up the narrow path. A fierce west wind had risen, coming straight off the sea, rolling black clouds before it. Overhead, three grey gulls floated inland, wings motionless, like surfers riding a wave. At the top of the climb Eve stopped to catch her breath. Looking down at the churning water, she took a handkerchief from her pocket and mopped at her nose, then set off again, wetness seeping through the soles of her useless leather boots with every step. It got dark so early now, if she didn't hurry she would never find her way back down.

Henry Cole, she saw as she passed the drawing-room windows, was at the piano again. She imagined him a highly structured person, his days regimented by self-imposed schedules. She tapped at the window three or four times before he heard her. Through the glass she watched his long fingers fumble with latches and bolts.

'Hello, hello. Come in,' he said, bolting the door again behind her. 'How are you? All right? Will you sit down?'

'No, thanks,' Eve said. But she was exhausted, and so cold. 'Well, yes, I will, thanks. Just for a minute.' She took the chair closest to the fire and leaned forward chaffing her reddened hands together gently. Her fingers were ice; she imagined them snapping off under pressure. Henry stood over her, wringing his own hands.

'And how are you settling in?'

'I forgot to bring matches. And newspapers. And two-euro pieces. And I don't know how to light the fire.'

'Goodness, all that?' He looked down at her. 'Would you like a cup of tea? I was just about to put the kettle on.' This time she did not refuse, and when he asked if she preferred India or China, she said she did not know the difference.

'India then,' he said, as if she had answered his question. When he was gone, Eve leaned back in the deep chair and propped her feet on the fender for a moment to dry her boots, her eyes drawn up to the serene features of the female Hope-Ross ancestors whose portraits hung too close to the ceiling all around the room.

There was the sound of running water, splashing, dripping. A snap, crackle, the fire spat angrily. She opened her eyes with a start and swung her feet away from the sparks. Rain whipped the windows. She sat up, moved stiffened limbs carefully. It was completely dark outside. A lamp glowed behind the chair opposite hers, making the white wallpaper shine like satin, raising the diamond pattern that receded in the daylight and throwing sombre shadows up across the family portraits.

The door opened and closed silently. Henry Cole peered round the Chinese screen positioned squarely in front of it to block arctic draughts from the upper regions of the hall. 'Ah, there you are.' He spoke as if she were the one who had gone away. 'Sorry tea was so long in coming. I did bring it, but ah, ah –'

He rushed to the nearest window and drew the curtains. There was a screeching of invisible rings dragging across rusted poles concealed by the brocaded pelmets. He moved on to the next window. 'Would have shut them before but didn't want to ah, ah . . .' He tossed his hair. 'I say, would you mind stepping next door to the library? Tray's in there. I'll nip down to the kitchen for that kettle.' Then he was gone. Except for that first glance, he had not looked at her.

Eve stayed as she was for a while before reluctantly hauling herself out of the chair. It wasn't until she was on her feet, dizzy and light-headed, that she realised she was coming down with something serious, something rapid. Galloping pneumonia. Was there such a thing? She couldn't think. Her head was hot, her hands ice. She still wore her coat but was shivering, and ached all over. There was a scratchy furriness in her throat and a heaviness in her chest. She held her coat closed with one hand and went out of the room.

A number of doors opened off the tiled hall, identical, heavy, intricately carved. She could not remember which was the library. Boot heels clattering on the tiles, she paced to keep warm until a door slammed at the back of the house and Henry Cole, carrying a steaming kettle, came rushing up the dark passage from the kitchen. He shut the door to the drawing room that

Eve had left ajar, and opened the one into the library, nodding her towards a large hexagonal table near the fire. A tray full of china and silver gleamed in the firelight. Cups and saucers, plates, spoons, knives, teapot, milk, sugar, a platter of buttered slices of brown bread, a bowl of preserves, an empty jug. He filled the teapot and replaced the lid with a crash, then filled the empty jug with hot water.

'Bread and butter, jam. Adele's crabapple, remarkably good. Sit here, won't you?'

He occupied himself with ceremoniously handing her a plate, knife, cup and saucer, crested spoon, then offering the bread and butter, the jam, pouring the tea, bringing sugar, milk. At last he sank into the chair opposite her, his long legs stretched in front of him and crossed at the ankle. Holding his plate near his chin, he devoured the thick slabs of buttered bread with wolfish bites.

The library was smaller and warmer, with dark curtains drawn over shuttered windows. Every inch of wall that was not window or door was lined floor to ceiling with bookcases whose glass fronts gave back the firelight from a dozen angles. Other large tables, round, oblong, square, were covered with papers, ledgers, books. One of the glass doors in the bookcases stood open, a key dangling from its lock. Eve had never been in this room where Martin had worked. Henry Cole, following her eyes, waved a long-fingered hand.

'These shelves tell quite a story. Latin and Greek poetry, a complete library of hunting literature, *Punch* from day one, every solitary volume.'

He set down his plate, picked up his cup, drained it. He wore, Eve saw, a woollen jersey and a cardigan under his tweed jacket. 'Journals of the first antiquarian society in Ireland, lists and measurements of every rath and tomb and standing stone. The first archaeological studies in this county, the first written histories, the first photographs. The first *maps*. Mountains of picture albums full of studies and experiments with light and chemicals and tints and double exposures. Gardening diaries full of discoveries about the composition of the soil and new strains of fruits and vegetables and new breeds of cattle. They used to dabble in these things, once upon a time, and all at the same time: archaeology, botany, photography, medicine. Do you think they were smarter than we are? More intelligent? I do. I think that evolution came to a peak in the nineteenth century and we've been spiralling back towards the apes ever since.'

Eve merely blinked at him.

'Now we specialise. Now we can do one thing and nothing else. I, for example, am an historian. And I presume that you do something?' He had never used her name. Eve had no idea if he knew what it was.

'Well, I – I've done some painting.'

'Painting!' He slapped his forehead with the heel of his hand. 'They *all* painted, they wrote books, they had their own darkrooms, developed their own photographs. Evelyn Hope-Ross, for example, published books, exhibited paintings in three or four countries, ran a farm, bred and sold horses, cured all the local ailments, mended broken furniture, sang on the stage and played the church organ. And on a horse, was a match for any fabled warrior.'

He stopped to refill their cups. Eve became aware of the scrutiny of another pair of eyes and turned to find a dun-coloured Persian cat perched on the small table at her elbow, cold blue eyes fixed on her face. She started, rattling her teacup in its saucer. But the cat remained unmoved and continued to stare.

'Penelope. Rather attached to that chair, I'm afraid. Adele dotes on the beast, now that the last of the dogs has gone to his reward. Neither had the heart nor the energy to break in a new pup. I say, are you all right?'

Eve, who had been listening as if from a great distance, found she could not control her shivering and pulled her coat more closely round her as Henry regarded her with mounting concern. After a moment he got up and, stopping to knock the cat from the arm of Eve's chair, he took up the kettle and hurried from the room, banging the door shut behind him.

She took in a series of deep breaths to try to stop the

shivering, but it only made her cough. Inside her boots, her socks were still wet from walking through the sodden grass, and she began to focus on them feverishly as the source of all her misery. If she could only get her boots off, all would be well. She tugged and tugged, then worked at the heel of one with the toe of the other, but they had tightened too much drying by the fire and would not budge. She struggled a while longer, then gave up and sank back into her chair.

Henry was not gone long, returning this time with a smaller tray, on which were several glasses containing various shades of liquid. He handed her first a tumbler of water and a paper of white powder, which she obediently poured onto her tongue and swallowed with the water. She was then handed a hot whiskey, on the surface of which floated a thin slice of lemon studded with four cloves symmetrically arranged, a detail that touched her through the gathering fog of fever. Henry picked up the other glass, a darker shade of amber, and sank back into his chair.

They both knew that unless he simply put her – like a cat – back out the French windows she'd wandered in through, she was about to put him to a good deal more trouble. He would have to drive her down to her cottage, dash through the rain along the muddy track, then fumble in the dark to turn the electricity on, light a fire.

'Look here' – he leaned forward in his chair – 'in the circumstances, I think you had best stop here tonight.'

'Oh, no,' Eve said. 'No. I couldn't.'

'Quite.' He slumped back in his chair and stared sullenly into the fire. There was another silence until she spoke again.

'Would it be less trouble if I stayed?'

'Would, actually,' he said, quietly.

The hot whiskey having done its work, Eve had dozed off again when her compulsory host woke her to say that a room was ready. She did not want to move. She'd had visions of spending the night in this cosy chair by the fire, drifting in and out of sleep.

She had to drag herself out of the chair, out of the room, through the hall, up the stairs, round the gallery, through the arch, down a corridor. She was dimly aware of striped wallpaper, pictures hanging, long windows on two sides, a corner room. It was not warm, and had a damp, musty smell, but a new fire burned in the fireplace, and near the bed the bars of an electric fire glowed promisingly. The duvet had been turned back, or thrown back in a hurried search for a bed with sheets. She sat on the edge of an armless boudoir chair and asked Henry if he would mind helping her with her boots. 'I tried downstairs. I can't get them off.'

He looked at her a little frantically, then advanced and turned his back to her, bending as if to receive a pass. Eve lifted a foot into his waiting hands. He grasped her boot expertly by the heel and tugged, but it was not until she had planted first one foot and then the other firmly on his bony backside that she was released from her boots, each one coming away with a force that sent Henry staggering a few steps. With the second boot came the sock hanging out of it like a drunken tongue. Eve had already pulled off the other one. 'Wet,' she explained.

Henry fled from her naked feet, across the corridor to another room and switched on a light, returning with a pair of thick, grey, hand-knitted socks, each as long as an arm.

'The geography. Down the passage, three doors, on the right.' He backed out of the room. 'I've left the light on. I'll be just across the way, later, should you, ah . . . Don't hesitate.'

Eve gratefully pulled on the woollen socks. They would go neither over nor under her slim-legged jeans and bunched at her ankles. She imagined Henry's elderly mother knitting them for him in the intimate knowledge of the full length of his foot and the tremendous scope of his bony heel.

After a trip to the unheated bathroom she found that the bed – she had prepared herself for sheets of ice – was as warm as Arabian sands. The secret was an electric flannel sheet that lay beneath the cotton one. Between that and the winter-weight duvet, she slept alone as snugly as in a shared womb.

In the morning, she was far worse: fever, chills, coughing. Her chest was aching; it was painful to breathe. She went down the icy passage to the bathroom and barely had the strength to get back to bed. She lay there, head burning, teeth chattering, sweating. It seemed hours before Henry tapped at the door. Dressed in the same clothes he'd worn the night before, he went first to the windows and drew back the heavy drapes, letting in the grey light of another wet and gusty day.

It was a beautiful room, she saw now, the walls papered in wide stripes of dark green and white that had yellowed to cream, the carpet bloomed with faded cabbage roses. Four long, white-framed windows took up the two corner walls. Watercolours and oils filled nearly every other inch of available wall space. Henry straightened several of these before he came and stood by the bed and looked down at her.

'Lord!'

Cheeks flushed and shivering so she could hardly speak, Eve asked if he would phone Dolores Depriest for her. 'I don't know her number, but I know she has a telephone. Would you ask her to come here?' Henry was so relieved he was at the door in two strides, then came back.

'Who –? Who, ah, ah, shall I say is –'

'Eve.'

'Eve,' he repeated, and it seemed to her that he took the name on his tongue as reverently as a communion wafer.

She dozed and slept and dreamed, and then he was back again, ushering in Dolores and another man. Standing next to each other, the two men could have been a textbook illustration of ectomorph and endomorph, one too tall and thin, the other too short and stocky. But once Henry had withdrawn, the other man seemed average in every way.

'This is Bob Kilpatrick, my neighbour,' Dolores said. 'From what Henry told me, I thought I'd better wait until the Kilpatricks got home from church and talk one of them into coming with me. Irene is a doctor as well.'

'She is of course. I believe in equality in marriage.' The doctor talked cheerfully while he opened his bag and took out a stethoscope. 'Doctors should marry doctors, teachers, teachers, poets, poets.' He threw back the duvet, sat close to Eve and unceremoniously pulled up her sweater. 'Old men should marry old women. Bald men should marry bald women.' He listened to her heart, lungs, rolled her over, thumped her back, ordered her to breathe deeply while he moved the stethoscope, like an ice cube sliding across her back. Then he had her sit up, breathe again, cough. He felt her pulse, took her temperature. The whole thing took less than three minutes.

'Pneumonia.' He pronounced the word with immense satisfaction as he removed the stethoscope from his ears. 'You'll need a strong course of antibiotics. I'll give you an injection now and a prescription for tablets. You'll take one every twelve hours for ten days. You'll be feeling a bit better in a few days but you must take every last tablet regardless. And you must have complete bed rest. That goes without saying.'

'I can't stay here.' Eve moved slightly away from his thigh, which was pressing against her side. 'I have to go – home.'

The doctor got to his feet. 'You'll go home in a pine box if you're not careful.' He administered the injection, swabbed at her backside with something cold and astringent, then snapped his bag shut. 'I'll just have a word with your man below.' He winked at her from the doorway. Dolores, who'd been standing at the window during the examination, came to the bed and looked down at Eve with a mixture of amusement and concern.

'Well, look at you. Three days ago you didn't want to hear Evelyn Hope-Ross's name again. Now you're sleeping in her bed.'

'I can't stay here,' Eve said. 'You know I can't. You'll have to drive me down to the cottage.'

'Don't be an ass. Who would take care of you there? I'm going to Dublin. I have an appointment in the morning I really can't change. And I'll be gone at least a week.' She shook her head again. 'No. You stay right where you are.'

'Dolores. Please.'

'No.'

She was adamant, but Eve still pleaded.

'Just drive me down there. That's all you have to do. I'll be all right. I'll be fine. There's food —'

'You're wasting your breath,' Dolores cut in. 'Literally. Listen to yourself.' She put her hand on Eve's forehead. 'You're burning up. It's raining like hell. You want to go down there where there's no telephone . . .'

But she did offer to drive down for whatever Eve needed, and when Eve had trouble thinking what she might need, Dolores said she could figure it out. As soon as she was gone, Henry returned with a breakfast tray: tea, buttered toast, a boiled egg, salt and pepper.

'I'm so sorry for landing myself on you this way,' Eve said.

'Nonsense.' He tossed his hair. 'My ah, ah — Nonsense,' he said again, and was gone.

Dolores was back in less time than seemed possible, carrying Eve's shoulder bag, sketchbook and pencil box. Behind her, Henry carried one of Eve's two giant suitcases. He set it down like a porter and departed without a word. Dolores unzipped it and took out underwear, pyjamas, dressing gown, slippers, socks, some sweaters, a pair of jeans, a pair of shoes, toothpaste, toothbrush, shampoo. The shoulder bag she deposited on the floor near the bed and laid the sketchbook and box of pencils on the bedside table. Everything else she stashed away in the chest of drawers, then zipped the suitcase and stood it next to the wardrobe, out of sight. The room looked exactly as it had before.

'I packed up that food you bought and gave it to Henry with the whiskey and wine. Looks like you're going to be stuck with each other for a few days.'

'Oh, God,' Eve groaned. 'Who is he, anyway?'

Dolores sat on the edge of the bed, lowered her voice. 'A nephew or godson or something. In any case, he spent a lot of time here as a child. When he was a university student he was the holiday tutor for the Hope-Rosses' children. You know, he picked them up from their schools and brought them back to Ireland for the summer, did lessons with them, and he helped in the garden. He came every year, for years, long after the kids needed lessons. They had two children, very close in age, a boy and a girl. Henry was evidently in love with one of them.' Dolores paused for effect, then smiled. 'All right, he was in love with the girl. She died very young, at twenty or twenty-one, I don't know what from. It was Adele who was telling me all this and I didn't like to ask. Probably pneumonia.' She laughed, a low squawk. 'Anyway, Henry's working on a catalogue of the house at the moment. He's an historian.'

'So he said.'

'But I know from Adele that this is also a big favour he does them every year. He comes and takes care of the house so they can get away for a month. They stay in his place in Cambridge. It's a sort of vacation for them, and they miss the worst of the bad weather here.' Dolores looked at her watch. 'I'd better get Bob back to his Sunday lunch.'

She started to walk towards the door, then came back. 'I forgot to look around for something to read, but there's a whole library downstairs. Ask Henry for something. Ask him for that journal, like I was telling you.' She gave another squawk of a laugh and went to the door again. 'I'm off now. Take care. I'll come see you when I get back.'

She shut the door, then opened it and put her head back in. 'By the way, this was Evie's room too.'

'Evie?'

'The daughter. The one who died. They named her Evelyn, after the great one, but called her Evie.'

She slept most of the afternoon, drifting in and out of sleep and from one dream to another, like a patient being wheeled into a series of different rooms, each one a mistake, each worse than the last. In one room Lily and Rose were quite small, no more than five. They lay side by side, dead. Beside them, Peter Hope-Ross sat with his head in his hands. Eve rushed to her children, but unseen hands gripped her shoulders. She struggled, screamed, woke herself up.

The long windows were filling themselves with bright dusk, as if all the light from the room paused there before departing. Outside one window, an intricate black branch wavered close to the wet panes. She imagined herself sketching it but made no move and soon fell back to sleep and dreamed again, cried out again, woke again.

She lay there trying to regain consciousness. It was like trying to climb out of a pit, trying to climb out of the fog and confusion of her dreams, where everyone was alive, and at all ages. Her father was a young man, her mother a younger woman than Eve was now. Evan was a child, a boy, an adolescent, a man, a corpse. Eve was a child, her children were adults. Martin was always her husband.

'I would never leave you,' he said.

She woke to a low, rasping, grating sound. Henry Cole was on his knees in front of the fireplace shovelling ashes into a bucket. Eve watched as he quietly swept the hearth and laid a new fire with logs he had carried up in a basket, and papers he had already torn and twisted. He added a few pieces of firelighter and set a match to the paper twists. He went to the windows and drew the curtains. Then he picked up the bucket and moved silently across the room, stopping near the bed to switch on the electric fire.

'Thank you.'

'Ah!' He straightened, startled by her voice. 'Thought you were . . . Hope I didn't . . . Let me just –' He moved closer to the bed and turned on the lamp. He took a watch from his pocket and replaced it, then took out a small brown vial. 'Afraid it's time for this. Found a chemist open on Sunday.'

Removing the cap and cotton, he tipped a white tablet into her hand, then poured some water from the jug into her glass. It was hard for her to sit up, her chest was so sore, and the action jarred something and started her coughing again. She had got into her pyjamas after Dolores left, winter-weight flannels, but it was cold outside the covers; she had been sleeping with the duvet up to her nose. Henry crossed the room to the wardrobe and pulled open a deep bottom drawer, rummaging in it until he came up with a grey knitted shawl that gave off a strong odour of camphor. Eve wrapped it round her shoulders.

'Thank you. You're a good nurse.' She plunged ahead so he wouldn't have to respond. 'Don't let me forget to reimburse you for that prescription.'

'Oh, I didn't pay. When you can. Doherty's chemist. No hurry.'

He retrieved the basket and bucket and went out, shutting the door, but not all the way. In a few minutes the cat pushed its way in and lounged confidently towards the bed. It stopped by the electric fire to stretch, then leapt all of a sudden, a great long leap, onto the bed and curled itself on top of Eve's thighs. It was, she decided now, a beautiful cat, beige and sleek, with chocolate paws and face. Curled up, with its heartless eyes closed, it seemed almost capable of affection.

'You miss Adele, don't you, Penelope?' Eve tried to make friends, stretching down a hand to stroke the cat's neck. 'You can stay with me. But I wish you'd shut that door.' Wide open, it let in draughts of frigid air. Eve contemplated getting out of bed to shut it but, as with sketching the branches against the failing light, accomplished nothing beyond imagining herself walking across the room. When Henry returned with a bowl of soup and plate of bread on a tray, he kicked the door shut behind him and hissed at the cat. He set the tray down on Eve's lap and went after the startled animal.

'Don't,' Eve said. 'Please. She's company.'

'I say, are you —?' Henry looked around. 'You've nothing to read. Would you like something?'

'Yes, thanks, I would. But don't make an extra trip. Just next time you're coming up.'

'And what would you like?' he asked patiently, after they had regarded each other in silence for a moment. 'What sort of thing interests you?'

'I don't know. What is there?'

Henry just looked at her.

'Do you think I might look at Evelyn Hope-Ross's journal?'

'Good Lord!' He looked as if she'd suddenly pulled off her pyjamas. Dolores, Eve realised too late, had been joking when she suggested it.

'It's just that the other night Dolores Depriest was telling me —'

'The hand is not at all easy to decipher,' Henry interrupted.

'Forget it,' Eve said. 'Really. I'd like a mystery. Are there any mysteries?'

'I'll bring it up,' Henry said, turning on his heel.

31 March 1882
London

This day I attained the great age of three and twenty, for which occasion Mama has made me the present of some very harsh words, accusing me of ingratitude, selfishness, and idleness. She says I have become slipshod in my habits and slatternly in appearance, I make no effort to amuse the men who condescend to make themselves agreeable to me, and sometimes speak to them in an inappropriate manner. I have, she fears, all but ruined my chances of getting a suitable husband.

When I retorted that I had no wish to get a 'suitable' husband, she flew into one of her celebrated rages and informed me that my wishes were of no consequence in the matter. She reminded me of all the debts incurred by poor Papa in financing my five failed seasons out thus far, providing carriages and horses and dinners and dresses, all of which she kindly enumerated for me from my first year's white muslin to this year's rose toile, and every yard of corded silk in between.

Given her high state of indignation, I refrained from pointing out that I should have been quite happy to spare Papa the entire expense, that I should far prefer to have passed these last five springs at Derrymore, going about barefoot and riding through the countryside with my hair blowing free. Not that I am any longer permitted either to go barefoot or to let my hair blow free. All such freedoms ended with the approach of my coming out. Why it is called coming 'out', I cannot say, when what it signifies is every form of constriction and confinement. The hair is twisted round pads and pins, the feet squeezed into slippers of the smallest possible size, the body cinched into suffocating stays and tortured with stomachers and improvers and bustles. One is constantly exhorted to come indoors out of the sun, or, if indoors, to move away from the comfort of the fire and not to blotch one's complexion with exposure to the heat. One's very tongue is tied up in artifice, one's whole being caught in a web of cunning and design.

1 April

Tried to make peace with Mama.

Much as I miss the light-filled rooms of Derrymore and much as I miss my brothers and cousins and the dogs and the horses and all the confusion of home, and much as I loathe this atmosphere of intense husband-seeking, I apologised and promised to try to conform more closely to Mama's notion of the demure yet determined debutante, so that I might be allowed to continue my drawing and painting lessons at the South Kensington School of Art.

It hardly seems fair, given the enormous outlay during the months of the Dublin and London seasons for extravagant frippery and for activities so hateful to me, that I should have to beg to be allowed to absent myself a few hours each day, to don a grey serviceable dress and indulge myself in an interest entirely my own. It is the only thing that has made London bearable for me, the only thing that has made it possible to endure the endless round of visits and lunches and teas, dinners, parties, balls.

Mama melted at my apology and assured me that I really am lovely enough and clever enough and that, although I have no fortune and am no longer young, there is no reason, if I will only put my mind to it, why I should not still make a brilliant enough match. Did I want to waste my life, as did my poor Aunt Netty, in lonely idleness, guided by no star of duty, a burden on the shoulders of my brothers and their families, an unwanted, unloved and resented maiden aunt? It was not that difficult to get a suitable husband. Men wanted only to be flattered. Why would I not try? Why would I not do and speak just as she did? She had always known how to talk to a man. And look at cousin Charlotte, exactly the same age as I and already three times a mother.

She broke off there, as well she might. I nearly flew at her. 'Really, Mama,' I said. 'You go too far. How could you mention Charlotte's marriage to me? How *could* you?'

2 April

Crawled exhausted to bed at two this morning but could not sleep. I could only lie awake thinking of Charlotte, my own old Charlotte, and of him I am now forced to think of as her husband.

I was seventeen and he twenty-two when Henry Brooke, spending some summer weeks with his uncle at Carrigleagh House, first came to Derrymore. Our interests and inclinations, even our talents, corresponding one for one, our attraction to each other was strong and immediate. An accomplished rider, crack shot, and able tennis partner, Henry Brooke was much in demand. He was also a fine painter, particularly in the medium of watercolours and on the subject of seascapes. As Derrymore commands the best views of the harbour and headland, and as the Irish light changes by the hour, if not by the minute, Henry was to be seen riding up our avenue at all hours of the day and evening. Laden with painting gear, we would set off through the garden to the grass point beyond the orchard and paint together in companionable silence, until a barrage of brotherly and cousinly banter would drive us back into the heart of the family festivities.

There, too, his presence was much in demand. Trained from an early age as a pianist, he could play a great variety of pieces and was a generous performer. We often played together and sang many duets. He was an excellent and tireless dancer, as am I, and, as girls are in rather short supply in our family, we danced together often.

When the summer was over, we could not of course, without impropriety, write to each other, but he had stolen away with him a carte-de-visite photograph of me, while I had hidden at the back of my bedroom cupboard several sketches of him, drawn rapidly and in secret during our few uninterrupted hours of painting. And, I dare say, that in the course of those so long intervening months he found as many excuses and opportunities for contemplating my likeness as I did his, for we found at the very start of our second summer that our open-hearted affection had already deepened to love. Our comportment remained largely what it had previously been, but there entered into our rendering of the mournful lyrics in our duets a new warmth, and sufficient significant glances were exchanged as we faced each other across the piano as to leave me in no doubt of his sentiments, nor he, indeed, of mine.

As the months progressed we began to spend more and more time together, walking and talking and consulting on everything, from the degree of blue pigment necessary to capture the green of a meadow immediately after a heavy rain, to the sort of hat required to produce a necessary ecclesiastical effect in a masquerade or family theatrical. And returning from a picnic or some other outing, we often walked home circuitously, evading the others. But my family, especially when combined with that of my uncle's, is numerous, noisy and active; there are always many visitors and guests. And there being so many brothers and cousins and everyone therefore accustomed to seeing me in the company of young males, Henry's discreet attentions to me went unnoticed, until Lady Beresford came to visit.

It did not take that officious person long to decide that there was something between us. She was not two days at Derrymore before having a quiet word with Mama. My mother, who had been in a state of complete ignorance on the subject, burst immediately into my room, an ominous redness spread upon her countenance. That something more than the ordinary was going on, she informed me, was a fact perfectly obvious to everyone, and she demanded to know what I intended by this most disgraceful flirtation with a young man who was absolutely without expectations.

I was thrown into confusion by the suddenness of this attack and could think of no response other than that I had always assumed it was the gentleman who was questioned about his intentions in such matters. But this seemed only to further incense my parent. 'A young man of fifty pounds a year has no business having intentions of any kind,' she said, and stormed off to speak to Papa.

I well knew what the result of such an interview would be, as Mama has a way of compelling acquiescence in such matters, and slept not at all that night, and shed many tears. I was unable to go down to breakfast and my appearance had not much improved some hours later when Papa sent for me to come to him in the library.

'Evelyn,' he said abruptly and without preamble, 'I have paid your luckless suitor the courtesy of questioning him upon certain financial matters, the particulars of which were already well known to me, and was forced to inform him that he must be refused.'

'Papa!' I was horrified. 'Henry has not asked me to marry him.'

'Ah, but he has asked me,' my father said, wagging a finger at me, as if I'd been caught out in some piece of mischief. 'As he has been refused most unequivocally, it seemed best to ask that he refrain from calling at Derrymore for the present. I am sorry, my dear.' But he did not seem at all sorry and looked very blank as I sat before him sobbing with the force of a sentiment most likely beyond the power of his failing memory to recall.

'Your mother agrees absolutely with me in this,' he said at last, as if I should find some measure of solace in the information.

'I cannot believe,' I said, when I was able to speak, 'that Henry has been dismissed without even consulting me. What God-given right have you and Mama to choose my husband?'

'That is quite enough, Evelyn.'

My father walked to the window and stood looking out for some minutes while I continued to sob. When I had regained a measure of composure, he returned and stood next to my chair and laid a hand on my shoulder. 'There, there, this is nonsense, my dear. You will be over it in a day or two. What has happened? You have had your first suitor and he has been refused. That is all.'

There were several more interviews between Papa and myself in the succeeding days, but I was unable to move him in the slightest. And then Mama would come flying after me, chiding me, insisting that I really must not worry Papa any more on the subject, that he was at his wits' end trying to know what to do for my five brothers – whom to put into the army and whom into the Church, and whom to put to sea. Derrymore would go to Francis, of course, but how he was to keep it nobody could know, with capital steadily dwindling and rents in arrears. It was time I was made to see more clearly my part in the general scheme of life and accepted my responsibility, my sole responsibility, which was not to waste time on frivolous flirtations but to set my mind to finding a *suitable* husband, one equipped to provide adequately for me and for my children.

These interviews I was able to bear with equanimity only because I had, on the second evening of Henry's banishment, received a note from him, delivered to me by my cousin Charlotte, to whose house he quite naturally repaired upon being barred from calling at ours. In it he told me what had transpired between himself and Papa, an account which largely coincided with that of my parent. He ended with a declaration of his love and a plea for some indication that it was returned, for only if it were would he be able to bear our cruel separation.

As I read his note a second time, a thrush poured forth his soul into the evening and I looked to the window where Charlotte stood in profile, waiting for my reply, her small foot moving impatiently. Although confused by emotion, I could not be insensible of the effect of her appearance, unusually well turned out as she was for a summer evening at home, her gown a light blue cashmere with a dark coquettish cape attached to the shoulder by a bow. Her pale hair was beautifully dressed and there was a bloom on her cheek and a sparkle in her eye which contrasted keenly with my own haggard and tear-ravaged countenance.

The impression registered on me with an acute thrill of pain, and I knew, even as I penned my pledge of love to Henry, knew even as I took Charlotte's place at my window and followed with mingled hope and despair her preoccupied progress through the garden, knew even before Charlotte herself knew, that she would win him from me.

3 April

I made myself absolutely unwell yesterday with such long brooding on those sad events now five years past, with the result that I did not go to South Kensington and further my slow advance along that one way in which I see a real opening, daylight and freedom. What is more, at the end of the day's unhappy brooding, coming as it did upon the heels of a sleepless night, I was so neglectful of my appearance that Mama, who casts all blame for any physical disarray on my association with the freewheeling world of art students, once again threatened an end to my lessons.

I vow therefore never again to dwell on Charlotte's treachery or Henry Brooke's inconstant heart, or on that black time following their betrothal when merely living seemed to require more effort of will than was within my power to produce. I have since recovered, thanks to a merciful God. And as I know that all blame in the matter must be laid at the door of my own complete dependence, I hereby pledge my troth, and indeed am already secretly wedded, for better or worse, to my own heart's freedom and to the resolution that no one else shall ever again hold in their hands the absolute power of my life.

'I have to talk to you.' Martin shut the bedroom door behind him. He sat, not on the edge of the bed, but on the chair across from it. He was dressed in chinos and corduroy jacket; he had not come to bed at all. He clasped his hands, leaned forward. 'I don't know if this will come as a surprise to you or not.'

Eve, crushed by sleep, flattened by a dead weight of dreams, closed her eyes a moment, then slowly – she knew she should not take this lying down – hauled herself into a sitting position, leaning against the headboard Martin had made from knotted-pine planks the year they were married.

'I can't go on like this.'

She looked at him, really, for the first time in months, since he had started running away from her, and was shocked by the change in him. The lines on either side of his mouth had dug in deeper, as if whatever he'd been struggling with had sunk in its claws and would not let go. His eyes had grown older than the rest of his long, handsome face and were deeply pouched now, with brown smudges underneath, like bruises. If she had been sleeping too much, he had been sleeping too little, staying out of bed until he was sure she was asleep and slipping out again before she was awake. The phone ringing sent him leaping down the stairs to answer it, although there was a telephone next to the bed.

'No,' she agreed, although she herself would have put off this moment as long as possible.

In retrospect it would have been better if he had gone right then. If he had said goodbye and simply left. Their marriage would be behind her, the door locked, curtains drawn; she would miss it, but it would have been left intact, something familiar for her to look back on. *I know that place. I used to live there.* But the talking went on for days, like a wrecking ball swinging relentlessly at what they had spent twenty years building, until there was nothing left, their marriage in ruins, levelled, and she recognised nothing. It was her fault. She had wanted to know why, wanted to understand. She wanted time.

So now she heard all about Susan – she had known it must be Susan, had intuited that it might *be* Susan the first time they met – how Susan had liberated him, freed him, saved him; how he had thought his life was over and she too, Susan, was mired in a stagnant marriage; how the first time they made love they had cried out in surprise, because they had forgotten it could be that way; how he had discovered the real meaning of the word *mate*; how when Eve had taken Lily and Rose on a college visit to California, he and Susan had gone away too, had spent five days and nights together, working together, cooking and eating and sleeping together; how since that time, three months before, there had never been a day when they had not been together for some part of it, the only part of any day that mattered to him any more.

Eve held up a hand to stop him.

'So, you've been having an affair for three months? Four? And now you want – '

'We're not having an affair. I want to marry her, Eve. She wants to marry me.'

'I want to marry you, Eve. You want to marry me. We want to have children sometime anyway. It's just what we wanted coming sooner than we wanted, that's all. It's not a tragedy. I would never leave you. How could you think I would leave you?'

She'd been in despair when she realised she was pregnant. She couldn't believe it. One slip-up, one lapse of memory, just one, and she — just two months into her junior year in college — was pregnant. It was a mistake, she thought. This was meant to happen to somebody else. She could think of worthier victims; there were people she knew who'd been sleeping around since high school, indiscriminately, while she had waited for love. And she and Martin had been so careful. Except for that one lapse, she'd taken every single pill, regardless of bloating, bouts of black moods and even dangerous blood-clotting in her legs.

She'd just been reading about the Depression, how thousands of people who'd furnished their houses on the instalment plan and had been paying religiously for years would miss one payment, *one,* and the repossession men would come and take away everything a family had, leaving them destitute. There was no credit at all for their years of conscientiousness or for what they had already paid. Eve couldn't believe what she was reading. How were these things allowed to happen? Was there no justice?

Martin was in his first year of graduate school and already living in abject poverty, already up to his neck in debt. He had miles to go, years; then he would have all those loans to pay off. She was afraid to tell him. She was afraid to tell her father, afraid to tell her brother, afraid to go to the doctor, afraid of an illegal abortion. For weeks she was afraid, sick and afraid. But the night she told Martin, all that burden of grief she had lain trapped under for nearly two months was suddenly lifted. He kissed her belly, her breasts; he held her face between his hands, looked into her eyes. 'I would never leave you,' he said.

She tried to finish the year and almost made it, but went into labour during her very first final exam. She didn't mind; it didn't seem important in the least. In fact, it seemed the least important thing in the world. She had assumed she would get some kind of a job, she didn't know exactly what. She'd been concentrating in English and studio art but had no idea what they might lead to.

Then she had twins, two babies instead of one, and so stayed home with them. How could they afford childcare for two infants? Martin didn't want them left to strangers any more than she did. They agreed: Eve should stay home with them, since he could not. But he, too, put them first, playing with them, teaching them how to tell the time and tie their shoes, reading to them, taking them with him whenever he could, wherever he went, giving Eve a break, time to rest. As soon as the twins were old enough to sit up straight, he bought child seats for their bicycles and every summer night after dinner he and Eve would take long bike rides with Lily, named for Eve's mother, and Rose, named for Martin's, behind them, nodding their heads like sleepy flowers.

They moved across the country several times as Martin tried to find his rung on the academic ladder, and changing schools, changing friends, was difficult for the girls. They depended on Eve more and more, rather than less and less. She invited children in to play, she invited Martin's colleagues to dinner, but essentially they were an insular, self-contained family. Instead of going out to a movie or a restaurant on weekend nights, she and Martin tended to stay at home with their children. Eve, twenty-five years old, never wondered if there might be another way to live.

She grew nearly all their vegetables and herbs. She loved to paint, loved to read. There was never enough time for everything she wanted to do; her days were never empty but too full. Later, there were classes – clay, watercolours, oils – tuition-free classes at the university where Martin happened to be teaching. And there was a series of jobs – she worked in a bookstore, in the campus admissions office, did proof-reading for the university press, painted a mural on a neighbour's patio wall, another in a local restaurant – always part-time; she was always there when the girls came home from school.

She and Martin were at one in their shared goal: to provide their children with an unshakeable sense of security.

He remembered things differently.

Their marriage was a dull habit of domestic routine, and unbearably claustrophobic; for years he'd been suffocating. Eve was entrenched in a world of her own making, a dream world, daydreams, night dreams. The outside world meant nothing to her, but he needed it. He needed to take part in it, to meet more people, make more contacts, have more adventures, more *excitement*. He was an extrovert, it seemed, caught in an introvert's web. Now Susan had freed him.

The last night of their endless talking, Eve dreamt she was a prisoner in a small room, discovering by accident that the door had been unlocked all the while. She wandered out like a madwoman or an invalid in a white nightgown and men's socks, feeling along the walls, peering into other rooms. She woke – why did she have to wake up? anything was better than waking, anything – not only to an overwhelming sense of doom, but to confusion. Who had been the prisoner here, after all?

'I see only your faults now,' Martin said the next morning. 'And that's not fair to you, Eve. You deserve more than that, you deserve to be loved.' The way he was loved now. The way he loved Susan.

'Don't.' For the first time, she was enraged. 'Don't pretend you're in any way doing this for *me*.'

Then he wanted credit. Credit for what Susan no doubt deemed his tremendous sacrifice. 'I stayed with you until the twins were grown. I didn't leave you with them.'

No. He waited until they were gone; he was leaving her with no one.

'Get out,' she said. 'Go, if you're going.'

And so he went.

Much of what he said was lies, rationalisation, revisionist history. He *had* loved her, really loved her, and he *had* been happy. Going through drawers and boxes, she came across endless pieces of evidence. Snapshots, even a fairly recent snapshot, taken by Rose of her and Martin out behind the house, face to face, nose to nose, arms around each other's necks, laughing. Letters, cards, messages, whose words all ran together. *Happy Anniversary, my love, my life, my . . .*

But much of what he had said was true. She wasn't blind. She had noticed him becoming increasingly moody, discontented, irritable. She also had gradually become aware of the circumscription of their world. She wasn't working any miracles of self-deception; she just hadn't known what to do, how to go about changing things.

But their chance was coming. When the girls went away to university in September, she and Martin, left alone, would have no choice but to break old habits that had centred around their children, to start over, make a new life. The only other time they had been away from the twins for an extended period was those months in Ireland when they had had their first real honeymoon, twelve years after their wedding, and they had done very well on their own, extremely well. They could do it again.

But their chance had come too late.

11 April 1882
London

I have had the unexpected pleasure of becoming re-acquainted with the novelist and critic Mr Stephen Clarke, whose books and articles have created such a stir, yet whose recent succession to the ownership of some thirteen thousand acres of the County Mayo had last season nevertheless altered the battle plan of many a mother, including my own.

When he finally deigned to make an appearance at the end of last season, indeed at the very last of the Castle balls, he impressed me as being of an extremely cynical cast of mind and voiced such a great number of caustic remarks about everyone and everything he saw that I could not refrain from asking why, if he despised Dublin society so very much, he troubled to subject himself to it. He thereupon confided that he was there for the purpose of observing others, not of amusing himself, that he had come solely in the interests of a book he was engaged upon writing. And when I enquired, as I was so clearly expected to do, as to the subject of his book, he fixed on me a pair of cold blue eyes and said, to my astonishment, that his book was about me.

'In that case, Mr Clarke,' I replied, when I was able to find my tongue again, 'I can only hope that you will manage to contrive a more felicitous conclusion to your present work than you did for your last.'

'Alas,' he said, 'it is, I fear, destined to be a tragedy.'

I was naturally intrigued, and when he returned in an hour's time to claim me for the second waltz for which we were engaged, I asked if he would not consider granting me a reprieve. Would he not revise the plot, or at least the ending, of his book?

'I would most certainly contrive a happier conclusion, Miss Hope-Ross, were it in my power to do so. But I am afraid your doom is sealed.'

I demanded to know his meaning, expecting a smile, an end to his joke, but he was perfectly serious.

'You do not see that you are dancing on the edge of a precipice, Miss Hope-Ross. You' — he gestured to include the whole assembly — 'you continue to dream only of your dresses and your husbands while —'

'Mr Clarke,' I cut him off. 'You cannot possibly have the slightest idea of what I am dreaming.'

He apologised and said he hoped he had not offended me, as that had certainly not been his intention. I myself was not to blame, he said, for I was just as powerless as any peasant, and just as deliberately kept so. He felt nothing but sympathy for all intelligent young women who deserved better, but for whom this yearly herding to the marriage mart was the only answer.

'I cannot speak for all of my sex, Mr Clarke,' I said, with some acid, 'but as for myself, I can assure you that marriage is the question, not the answer.'

That is the entire history of our acquaintance. Yet when I encountered him in the entrance to this hotel some days ago, he greeted me with a degree of enthusiasm I should not have expected from him. Indeed, I should not have expected him even to know me at all, dressed as I was in my drab grey art student's attire. For he had seen me only in white Surat silk and a turquoise broché train, and that more than a twelve-month ago, and had seen me then not as an individual person but as one of a vast herd of cattle driven to market by our mothers.

Consequently, I was charmed by his very genuine pleasure in meeting me again, and by his voice, which, when divested of those sardonic overtones I found so repellent, is really quite pleasing. I see now as well that, despite a pair of decidedly sloping shoulders, he is a nice-enough-looking man, perhaps a year or two past thirty, with a soft brown beard and brown moustache, and an intelligent, expressive mouth.

He had been on his way out of the hotel when we met in the entrance, yet turned back and invited me to step into the ladies' drawing room, which, unusually enough for that hour, was entirely deserted. As it was a miserably raw and wet day, he moved a low chair somewhat closer to the fire and urged me to sit and put my feet upon the fender to dry my boots. He then turned another chair to face mine, and, as I was in possession of a rather conspicuously large sketchbook, we soon began to discuss my slow progress at the South Kensington School of Art. This is a subject about which he is extremely knowledgeable, for he himself passed some three or four years in a Paris atelier, and, although he soon gave up any idea of painting, he continues to follow the work of others with the keenest interest and has written numerous articles of a critical nature, some of which I have read, on the subject of contemporary French painting.

Rarely presented with so sympathetic an ear, I soon found myself confiding to him that I feel myself severely limited by the School's misguided efforts to protect my innocence and long to draw, as do the male students, from life. Because we women are kept separate from the men and confined to drawing from half-draped plaster casts and from medical textbooks, our work consequently suffers from a general lifelessness.

'May I?' he said, holding out a hand for my book, which I had no choice but to surrender, then sat red-faced and anxious, staring into the fire, while he turned its pages.

'London will never allow you to draw from life, Miss Hope-Ross,' he said, upon closing the book at last. 'You have, in any case, already learned what little this staid city knows of art.' At this my face grew hotter still, but I had hardly begun to digest this unaccustomed morsel of praise when he declared with surprising vehemence, 'You must go to Paris, that is what you must do.

Everything new and exciting that is happening in the world of art is happening in Paris.' He then spoke with a great deal of animation about the work of several French painters with whom he is well acquainted. 'You must go and see them. I will write letters for you.'

'I shall never get to Paris, Mr Clarke,' I said. 'Not for the purpose of studying art.'

I described to him my state of utter dependence, how I have no money of my own except for the few coins given me occasionally by my mother; how my lessons at the School must be begged for yearly and are constantly under threat of being terminated if I do not behave exactly as my parents wish; how they expect me to find a husband, and regard my passion for art merely as an amusement, perhaps on a par with but not quite as acceptable as my passion for hunting; how they would never agree to send me to Paris for the purpose of becoming an artist.

'Then you must become independent of them.' He examined his fingernails for a moment or two, then looked up at me again. 'Miss Hope-Ross, did you not once inform me – and most energetically – that for you marriage is not the answer, but the question?'

I assented a touch hesitantly, as I could not tell if he meant to be serious or sardonic. But he nodded his grave approval, and I was encouraged to add that the intervening year had only increased my reluctance to marry and that, while I had begun the study of art chiefly as a possible means of attaining independence, I now find that I crave independence chiefly as a means of pursuing a more serious study of art, something I feared might not be compatible with marriage.

'You need have no doubts upon that subject, Miss Hope-Ross,' he said, with a rather superior smile at my naïveté, 'for it is a well-known fact that matrimony soon extinguishes a woman's creative ability. Indeed, only the most ineradicable kind of artistic talent can continue to exist side by side with the qualities of self-abnegation, patience and submissiveness that must be cultivated by the satisfactory wife and mother.'

It emerged that he has given a good deal of reflection to the matter, as it is the chief theme of the novel he finished writing a year ago, yet which he has been forced to revise and revise again due to a fundamental disagreement with his editor.

'My heroine is a highly spirited young lady and I would far prefer to provide her with trousers and cigars and a villa on Lake Como. But as a purely pragmatic response to commercial demands, it seems that I must provide her with a husband instead.'

He looked at me with eyebrows raised in what could only be described as a mischievous expression and I confess that I blushed to the roots of my hair and did not know where to look, for I could not forget that he once jested that the book he was writing was about *me*. I cannot express my relief when he returned to the contemplation of his apparently fascinating fingernails.

'I should like to make my heroine a self-reliant person who relishes her freedom, who cherishes the opportunity to come and go as she pleases, to travel the wide world, if she should so desire, untrammelled by husband or children, and who, above all, enjoys that calm that is so essential to reflection, that self-sustained calm, alone out of which the imagination can take wing.' He then fell silent for a moment or two before training on my already overwarm countenance the full force of his penetrating gaze.

'So you see, I mean to encourage you, Miss Hope-Ross, if not to incite you. For I too rebel against society's matrimonial prescription.'

I cannot begin to put into words the salutary effect on my mind and spirits of that so absorbing half-hour's conversation. Had I passed from the room bearing aloft a blazing torch, I could not have felt more enlightened, nor more imbued with purpose.

What's more, I feel myself much changed since we spoke. My work has improved with my spirits, as even my very grudging tutor admits, and I am heartened and cheered by a new lack of awkwardness I feel in company, for I find that I can converse quite easily with the other sex now that my resolve to reserve myself has been so substantially strengthened that I need no longer fear incurring the unfavourable opinion of a possible suitor.

Mama has not known what to make of it. She is much pleased with my sociability and commends me for making an effort to be amiable but continually cautions against a too easy familiarity of tone which may give the impression that I invite an unwomanly spirit of comradeship to enter into my conversation with a gentleman. While she concedes that he may possibly be bored by a lady whose thoughts and feelings are constantly running to love, she insists that he will certainly be put off by one who ventures beyond the bounds of her natural sphere of topics.

28 April

Three days ago, Mr Clarke came to the hotel for the express purpose of offering me employment.

'You must have money of your own,' he said, 'and if no one will give it you, then you must earn it, and the surest way I know of for a lady in your position to accomplish that end is by writing.'

I began to protest my lack of competence for such an endeavour, but he held up a silencing hand.

'You write many letters, I presume, Miss Hope-Ross?'

'Yes, of course I do,' I said. 'I enjoy a rather wide correspondence, but –'

'And you keep a journal, a diary?'

When I replied that at present I keep both a diary and this journal, he was kind enough to say, as if the conclusion were self-evident, 'As you are an intelligent and articulate young lady and have practised writing daily, I feel quite confident of your ability to manage something for publication.'

'Mr Clarke –' I began again to protest, but he went on to say that he had been just that morning on the point of refusing a request from the *Pictorial* for an article about the Dublin season, when he thought of me.

'That is a subject with which I know you are acquainted with the intimate knowledge of an insider, yet which I strongly suspect you would be able to treat with the objective eye of an outsider. Am I mistaken, Miss Hope-Ross?'

I could scarcely conceal my eagerness to accept the challenge. Indeed, I have long wished to share with a single sympathetic soul my opinion of the Dublin or London season, and here I was being invited to tell the world and to actually be paid for it as well. I had only to consult my own diaries in which I have recorded over these past five years all necessary details about the Lord Lieutenant's Levee, the Drawing Rooms, the Castle balls, the State dinner parties, the private dances in the Throne Room, the glitter of Patrick's Hall and the grandeur of the Vice-Regal procession.

'I see you have already begun,' he said, unable to conceal his amusement.

I have been working on this article for several days now, by the last of my candle at night and by the first rays of morning's light, and although I find it a much more difficult task than I would have imagined possible, I feel sure that another day or two of labour shall bring it to its conclusion.

5 May

I have shown my article to Mr Clarke, who, on the whole, finds it satisfactory. However, he insists upon the expansion of a certain theme introduced near enough the beginning as to necessitate copying again the entire twenty pages. Yet I delay, for I am thrown into confusion by the nature of what I am now asked to include.

The passage in question opens with a description of the presentation to the Lord Lieutenant and Her Excellency of the year's Irish debutantes, beginning with the terrible heat and fatigue of the blue drawing room, where the young women and their mothers or presenters are crowded (herded, yes) together to wait, sometimes for hours and nearly fainting from the heat, for the chamberlain to call out their names. When a girl is summoned, two aides-de-camp, stationed at the door for the purpose, take her train from her arm and spread it behind her, and she walks, with what courage and poise she can muster, into the Throne Room through a most critical-eyed human corridor to the throne itself. After the hundreds of white dresses assembled in the ante-room, she is nearly blinded by the sudden blaze of colour: the scarlet coats of the guardsmen, the brilliant silks and satins and the glittering jewels and diamonds of the ladies of honour, and of Her Excellency. Upon her arrival at the throne, she genuflects, as the Lord Lieutenant, dressed in ceremonial knee-breeches and white hose, leans forward and kisses her upon each cheek. She then rises, curtsies to him once more and proceeds to the door leading to St Patrick's Hall, where another pair of aides gather up her train and return it to her arm.

I have never given a moment's thought to the reason for the Lord Lieutenant's kiss and have always regarded it simply as a matter of ceremony and tradition. But Mr Clarke, with a great deal of embarrassment on both sides, explained to me that the origin of this tradition is rooted in the custom known as *droit de seigneur*, a most vile custom indeed, one practised in Ireland up until the end of the last century and which concerns the right of a landlord to claim the first night with any girl on his estates who announces her intention to marry. According to Mr Clarke, this heinous custom, long after it had largely fallen into general disrepute, continued to be practised by some degenerate few well into the present century, usually in secret and often under the guise of a girl being summoned to the landlord's house as a servant. It is essential, he insists, that I at least hint at the origin of this customary kiss bestowed upon the debutante by the Lord Lieutenant, who, by dismissing her, grants his permission for her to go and find her husband – if she can! – in Patrick's Hall.

19 May

After a fortnight's silence, Mr Clarke has called again to say that since the Phoenix Park murders in Dublin he has been very much occupied with writing opinion pieces for various newspapers both here and in America. I said I hoped that I might have the opportunity of reading his articles, so that I might begin to understand what it all means.

'I can tell you that simply enough,' he said. 'It means that our way of life is coming to an end.'

'That is as I had feared,' I said, for it does begin to seem that his prophecy of a year ago, that we were dancing on the edge of a precipice, may prove to be all too accurate.

'Why should you fear it, Miss Hope-Ross? Have you not spoken of your own wish to rebel? To escape?' Then, without waiting for an answer, he proceeded to contradict himself.

'You are quite right to be afraid. There have been grievous injustices done and retribution is about to fall. Ten thousand landlords dwelling like an army of occupation among millions of the enemy. Even armed to the teeth, what chance do we have? None. The Irish will not rest until the yoke of English rule has been thrown off. Ireland is no longer fit for us to live in.'

'But I am *not* English,' I said with some indignation. 'I am Irish. I was born in Ireland. My father, my grandfather –'

He interrupted. 'To the Irish you are and always have been English.'

'But Mr Clarke, not a day passes in London that someone does not allude to my Irishness, to my Irish voice, manner or customs. I do not even like the English, if the truth were to be told.'

'Nor do I, particularly,' he rejoined. 'And I too am thought by them to be Irish. But the fact remains that to the Irish peasants we have the voice, manner and customs of the English.'

I bristled at this. 'I wish you would not use that word. *Peasants*.'

He seemed both startled and amused. 'And which word would you prefer that I use?'

'We were taught to say "the poor people" when –' But here I was interrupted by a brief, rather scoffing burst of laughter.

'I fear you will find that "the poor people" will not thank you for your nice distinction.'

'But you speak of them as the enemy, of being armed to the teeth against them. I must say that you speak only for yourself, Mr Clarke. My father has no more need to arm himself against his tenants than against his own children. He comes and goes freely among them. They all know him; they know all of us; we know all of them.'

And knowing Stephen Clarke's – and his father's – reputation as an absentee landlord who leaves his estates in Ireland in the hands of an agent while he lives abroad on the income wrung from them, I proceeded to describe how for my father's tenants – and for all the poor people of the district – Derrymore is the centre of the world, where they come not only to pay their rents or to work but for medical treatment and advice on their personal affairs, how any of them are free to call upon my father at any hour of the day, and how he has never employed an agent to act on his behalf.

'Perhaps you can give up your country so easily, Mr Clarke, because you do not live there, but it is my home, my only home, as it has been for my family for over two hundred years.'

'I am grieved to see that your heart is so deeply engaged, Miss Hope-Ross,' he said, moving his head in a maddening gesture of sympathy, 'for it will certainly be broken.'

He leaves tomorrow for Dublin. Mama leaves tomorrow as well, for Derrymore, while I am to remain a month with Aunt Gort in order to continue my lessons.

It was the end of the week before she made her way downstairs again, feeling much better, though not really well yet, and now Henry was down with, as he put it, a stinking cold and it was her turn to play nurse. Fires first, she decided. There was plenty of firewood. Henry had carried it up from the basement and had made a run into Clonmere for more food, tea and whiskey before taking to his bed.

In the library she pulled back the heavy curtains, holding her breath against the puffs of dust released by the motion, and folded back the shutters. Wind-blown rain thrummed horizontally against the windows. It had rained all day yesterday, and the day before, but there had been at least three rainy days, maybe four, when the sun had come out late, just in time to set. The doctor had come on Sunday and the very next afternoon, she remembered, the room had been briefly flooded with rosy light. Three days of that, maybe four, starting on Monday and followed by two days of steady rain would make this Saturday, or maybe Sunday. She had no idea what the date might be. She was beginning to feel as if she and Henry Cole were the marooned sole survivors of a shipwreck, or the only chance passengers on a runaway train without engineer or conductor, passing through countless tunnels of darkness and flashing stretches of light.

She tore up old newspapers and crushed and twisted them, as she'd seen Henry do, and added them to the basket of wood to carry up to his room. She thought of Mr Keneally saving her

Irish Times and made a mental note to call him. She would have asked Henry to pick up the papers for her if she had known when he was going into town, or the village, as he called it.

She set the basket down in the hall, holding the door open for Penelope, whose food bowls and cat-box were in the kitchen. But this daytime fire was an unaccustomed luxury; the cat eyed her resentfully and refused to budge from the leather chair. Eve went alone down the dark passage to the kitchen, but a distinctly audible scurrying sound from several directions sent her back to the library to scoop up the enraged cat. She carried her back to the kitchen and let the door swing shut behind them.

An enormous black range, fronted by a number of steel-latched doors of varying sizes, occupied one side of the room. She had admired it when Adele had first shown her the kitchen and had often seen it again when she, or she and Martin, had been invited to informal lunches at the long white table. But the prospect of using it, of making a small pot of soup, made her feel something of an acolyte pressed into service at the high altar. Against two other walls stood two monumental white deal dressers, each with tier upon tier of dinner services, hundreds of pieces, and their counters littered with packaged food Henry had bought, and with what Eve saw upon closer inspection were the droppings of many mice.

The table was strewn with soiled plates, mugs, knives, forks. She carried them into the scullery and washed them up along with the pile of crockery already there. She cleaned the work surfaces with soap and boiling water, then took Penelope's empty food bowl to the scullery and cleaned that as well. 'If you want to eat,' she informed the cat as she shut her into the kitchen, 'you're going to have to work for it.'

The telephone was on a table at one end of the drawing room with its forbidding assemblage of female forebears dressed in gowns of satin, velvet, silk, hair elaborately coifed. Their cool eyes met each other's, glancing sideways or across the room, so that they seemed to whisper to each other from portrait to portrait about this trespasser from another time who dared wander into their drawing room in pyjamas and a man's haircut, uncombed, unwashed.

The directory listed two dozen Keneallys, but no newsagent. He most likely didn't have a telephone in that tiny closet of a shop. He would have to wait. But she hated the thought of disappointing him day after day, making him wonder each morning if he should write her name on yet another newspaper and add it to the stack already taking up too much space. He'd been so kind to her since that day she had fled his shop, talking to her the same way he did to the children who swarmed around him like bees. *Now, my lovely, will that be all for you this morning?*

She was standing right next to the phone when it rang, a euphemism for the ear-splitting sound it made, more like a smoke alarm than a telephone. She jumped, then picked it up before it could make its awful noise again. 'Hello,' she said, and when no one spoke she said again, 'hello?'

'Is this 6-8-4-2-3?' a woman's high magisterial voice clearly enunciated. Eve's heart sank as she recognised the voice.

'This is Adele Hope-Ross. Who is that?'

Eve was completely silent; she could not even breathe. The voice at the other end called, 'Hello, hello. Are you there?' Quietly, carefully, as if the receiver might break, Eve put the phone down.

In the library she stood clutching her elbows, staring into the fire, stunned by the stupidity of what she had done. And how pathological, being unable to say her own name. If Adele had asked a question requiring any other answer, if she had said, May I speak to Henry? Eve could have handled it. But she could not say her name, she could not say to Adele Hope-Ross, This is Eve Oliver. She stood there, overwhelmed with remorse, until the muffled buzzing of the telephone in the next room sent her flying up the stairs.

'Henry.' She used his name for the first time that week; he had yet to use hers. 'Henry! The phone is ringing.' He had been sleeping and eyed her with drowsy apprehension.

'In the drawing room,' he said warily.

'I know, I know, but you won't believe what I did.'

She was right; when she told him, he could not believe it. Reluctant to give up his sleep, he pulled himself into a sitting position. 'But why?' he said sternly. 'Why did you not *say* you are the new tenant?'

It occurred to her only then that Henry did not know who she was. When she had grabbed his arm that day he had shown her the cottage, when she told him she wanted to take it, he had sent her to the estate agent's office to sign the lease; other than showing the cottage to prospective tenants he had no other role in the transaction and had handled none of the paperwork himself. As she had told him her name was Eve when he was phoning Dolores for her, the opportunity for proper introductions had never presented itself.

'Henry.' Once she had begun to use his name she could not seem to stop. 'Henry, I'm sure you've heard of Martin Oliver. Well, I am Eve Oliver. I was married to Martin Oliver until nearly a year ago. When I met the Hope-Rosses, I was his wife. When he was here writing that damn book, I was his wife.' She stood some feet from the bed, far away from Henry's long, thin form, and described as best she could the chain of events that had brought her to Derrymore. When she had finished, he looked at her in silence and with no expression whatsoever.

'I know what you're thinking,' she said. 'If Evelyn Hope-Ross knew I was here, sleeping in her room, in her bed, she would turn over in her grave.'

Henry smiled. 'No,' he said, 'I believe she would have liked you.' And when Eve, staring at the carpet, appeared not to have heard, he added, a little lamely, 'Yes, one — one feels quite sure that —. Look here,' he said, 'I'll just go down and ring Adele. She'll be concerned.' After a pause, he added, 'She's rather a fan of yours.'

Eve looked up at him.

'Not only of your work — which, by the way, ah, ah — I'll just speak to her, shall I?'

Eve went back to the kitchen to make some soup for lunch. Halfway down the passage a thin shriek reached her ears over the sighing and moaning of the wind. She'd forgotten Penelope, forgotten the mice. Cautiously, she pushed the door open, but saw nothing. Then she heard the shriek again and, following the sound, found Penelope stretched full length on the scullery floor, lazily and almost playfully swatting with one paw at a mouse she held down with the other, as if she didn't want to kill it, not quite yet. Annoyed by the interruption, Penelope regarded Eve coldly for a moment, as if to say that this was none of her business and she would not understand. The mouse continued to writhe, drops of bright blood splattered round it. Eve had not counted on this when she ordered the cat to catch mice. It had seemed a perfectly natural and logical thing to do. But this, what she was seeing, was torture.

She took a metal flour-sifter from its hook on the nearest dresser and threw it at the cat. It struck the floor and clattered away, but Penelope merely got to her feet and started to drag the mouse by its tail out of the line of fire. Eve took hold of a broom and swatted at the cat until she let go of the mouse and made a dash for the door into the passage. It stood open now, Henry poised there, astonished at the sight of Eve sorrowing over a wounded mouse. He was wrapped in a woollen dressing gown that seemed to conceal many layers of things. His hands thrust deep into the pockets of his dressing gown, he tossed his uncombed hair.

'Best put it out of its misery, no?' he said, when she had explained. 'Can't very well shoot it, can we? A bit small for that.' He suggested either drowning it in the scullery or tossing it outdoors.

Eve was all for putting it out, where it might at least have a sporting chance. She found a dustpan, which Henry slid under the tiny body and carried it to the kitchen door. She opened it for him to a sharp scent of the surging sea and the rain coming straight at them in sheets. The wind seemed to have thundered across the ocean for the sole purpose of flattening them with the door as soon as the bolts were drawn back. Henry shouldered it shut again after disposing of the mouse, then set down the dustpan and shook the rain from his hands, which he plunged back into his pockets.

'No shortage of them, you know,' he said. 'These old country houses. Overrun with mice.' He lounged against the table while she made a pot of tea. 'Used to be rats. Lived in the walls, under the hearths. They'd put down poison, and the things would rot under the floors. Quite a stench.'

Eve's nostrils flared and would not unflare themselves. She put a mug of tea into Henry's hands. 'Take this up with you. I'm going to make some soup.' Then she remembered. 'Henry, what did she say?'

'Nearly forgot.' He touched a hand to his forehead. 'Have to ring up the rector. February is her month to do the flowers. Slipped her mind. Thank God. Wouldn't have liked to go out in this. The wind's shifted round to the northwest. Afraid we're in for a bit of a blast.'

'But this is January,' Eve said.

'First of February, actually.'

'Is it? What's today? Saturday?'

'Sunday. That's what reminded her.' He looked around, as if for something to write on. 'Must remember to bring mimosa in to the church on Saturday.'

'Where are you going to find mimosa at this time of year?'

'In a sheltered corner of the walled garden. Next to the glasshouse.' He shuffled towards the door with his tea, but Eve stopped him.

'Henry. What did she *say*?'

'Oh. Oh, ah – Perfectly all right, as I expected. 'Fraid I said it was a bad connection, that you could hear her while she couldn't hear you. Happens all the time here. She was quite sympathetic. About the pneumonia, and ah, ah – Looking forward to seeing you, actually. She was always rather a fan of yours, you know.'

'Was she?' Eve was inordinately pleased to hear this.

'And of your work. Which I also – ah, ah. Didn't care for your husband, though. Not after – ah, ah –' He escaped, backing out of the kitchen as he spoke, and letting the swing door slap shut behind him.

Eve found the carcass of the chicken she had bought over a week ago and which Henry had roasted just the day before. He'd left it uncovered, but at least it was in the fridge. She put it into a pot, covered it with water, then sliced in onions, potatoes and carrots. She'd found a slice of Brie in the refrigerator, too, and a piece of cheddar. She put them on the table to come to room temperature and took a box of soda biscuits from the pantry and set it next to the cheese.

After a sudden violent attack of coughing used up the last of her meagre energy reserves, she poured herself a mug of tea and decided to wait for the soup so as not to have to make the long trek up and down the unheated passage. She sat with an elbow propped on the table, her chin cradled in the palm of her hand. She only gradually became aware that the box of biscuits, just inches from her nose, was moving, vibrating the way things do in an earthquake; a shuddering, rippling, shifting of molecules. Or was it? Now it was still again. She sat up straight in her chair and watched it, like a cat. Nothing. Hallucination, she thought, imagination. She touched a hand to her forehead, then jumped to her feet as the box started shuddering again and fell over on its side. This time she felt not a qualm as she hurried with it to the door and hurled it out into the storm.

When the soup was ready, she brought a bowl of it up to Henry, along with the cheeses and some bread, then ladled out another bowl for herself and took it into the library to sit by the fire.

She wrote two letters, one to Lily and one to Rose, then spent the rest of the afternoon sketching: the dense, dark shelter belt of conifers across the lawn, all stretching to the east as if trying to flee the storm, the spiky branches of the chestnut tree swinging and straining against the leaden sky, the wedge of empty sea visible through the trees, white-capped all the way to the horizon. She drew Henry's head from memory, several times. They were the most pleasant hours she'd known in a year.

The storm raged on through Monday and into Tuesday. Eve came to think of it as a living thing, a dragon or nine-headed Hydra that howled across the Atlantic and scaled the cliffs. She thought of her cottage from time to time and wondered how it was holding up. Despite the two-foot walls, she was very glad not to be alone there now. Even Henry finally admitted that this was the worst winter weather he could remember.

'I've never actually seen lightning here,' he said. 'Nor heard thunder, for that matter.'

He spent most of the time in bed, but late in the day would come down to the drawing room to play the piano for an hour. Eve, lying back in a chair in the next room, listening to the storm of Beethoven drowning the sound of the wind, stopped feeling a fool for landing herself in the lap of a complete stranger, and felt instead only gratitude for the chain of circumstances that had brought her to the safety of this house, at this time. She knew that, had the Hope-Rosses been in residence, she would have caused them no end of inconvenience. They would have felt the need to provide breakfast, lunch, drinks and dinner all at their appointed hours. They would have felt the need to *talk* to her, and she to them; it would have been a strain on both sides.

It was so easy sharing the house with Henry, easy to lead their separate lives, easy to avoid unwanted conversation, or even each other. She never felt that she was impinging on his privacy or preventing him from doing what he would ordinarily be doing were she not there. Of course, the fact that they had fallen ill by turns meant they were rarely downstairs at the same time, except for his hour at the piano, an hour she came more and more to look forward to.

But on the last day of the storm the roaring of the wind began to tear at her nerves. It circled the house like something deranged trying to get in, trying to beat down the doors, howling and moaning. The rain drummed so hard against the windows she thought they would break; sometimes it splattered down the chimney and made the fire spit and sizzle. Little puffs of smoke blew back into the room. She closed the shutters and drew the curtains, but the house was filled with sounds she hadn't noticed before. Loose-fitting windows rattled; picture frames shifted on the walls of the hall so full of draughts; somewhere a door banged shut, and then banged again; outside the window, water spilled from the gutters and splashed non-stop onto the flagstones. It sounded as if the whole world were filling up with water. Every now and then there was the crash of a falling bough.

The library door opened suddenly. Eve leapt to her feet.

'Henry!'

'Sorry.'

'It's the storm.' She pulled the lapels of her dressing gown closer together. 'It's making me jumpy.'

He walked to the window on the west side, drew back the curtains and opened the shutters. Eve went and stood next to him. But aside from the shapes of the nearest branches, there was little to see but their own wavering reflections lit by the glow from the fire. In their nightclothes they could have been an old married couple.

'I've always rather enjoyed a good storm here,' Henry said. 'Perched on the western edge of Ireland, the western edge of Europe, two hundred feet above the sea, one gets the feeling of being suspended on the very brink of chaos.' Eve, who had not considered this point of geography before, was silent.

'In one of Evelyn Hope-Ross's novels there is a passage about the age-old warfare between the Atlantic and this outpost of Europe, how the sea has clawed out of the hills the most dramatically ragged headlands and long, winding inlets. And caves,' he added, after a moment. 'There are the most marvellous caves in those cliffs below.'

'Not under this house, I hope.' Eve had an image of the ground beneath them a mere shell concealing a vast network of long, deep hollows full of the seething sea.

Henry smiled. 'Not to worry, Eve,' he said, speaking to her reflection. 'People have stood in this same room listening to these same sounds for more than two hundred years.'

His use of her name for the first time, and the way his voice dropped into a lower register when he said it, made her feel as if he had reached out and touched her. She felt unexpectedly flooded with warmth. Their eyes met and held in the glass for a charged moment, as if a switch had been thrown. Then there was a tremendous rolling crack of thunder and almost simultaneously a blinding flash of lightning that lit up the world and knocked them both back from the window. Henry glanced at her a little sheepishly, then closed the shutters and curtains against the strangeness outside. He switched on two lamps and opened the drinks cabinet.

'Bit early. But in the circumstances . . .'

She packed her suitcase and stripped her bed, then walked silently past Henry's door and went down the stairs, her arms full of sheets to launder. There was no electric clothes dryer, but the sun was out and there was still a strong enough wind to dry the sheets in an hour.

When her bed was made up again, she would ask Henry to drive her down to the cottage. They could go by way of Clonmere, as he was supposed to deliver the mimosa to the church; she could buy matches and more food, pick up her newspapers, get change for the meter, pay the chemist for her antibiotic. Henry could show her how to light a turf fire. Dolores might be back today. She would ask her to dinner. In a day or two she would invite Henry.

She would buy a table. A small round table, four or six ladder-back chairs, an oval rug would create a third area in the space between her sleeping and sitting quarters. She would ask the O'Gormans to come. She would cook them a joint, whatever that was.

This voluntary glimpse into the future was like a window opening in what had for too long been a blank wall. As she stepped out into the fresh, bright air for the first time in more than ten days, she knew that she was recovering much more than her physical health. She was beginning to feel less like someone forced to enter a race too late, with a couple of limbs lopped off.

The wind was brisk and cold. She was struggling to get the

second of the laundered sheets attached to the line behind the kitchen when she was startled by Henry, in muddied wellingtons, coming round the side of the house from the direction of the yard. She had assumed he was still in bed, but the way the doors to every room were always kept shut against draughts it was difficult to know where anyone was unless you knocked, or opened a door and walked in.

The hand-made sheets were more like royal-family size than either king or queen; wet, they were quite heavy and difficult to handle. Henry, stung in the face by a flapping corner Eve had lost hold of, caught it with the speed and agility of a dog catching a fly on the wing and nailed it to the line with a clothes peg. He rooted among the fallen debris in the grass for a forked pole and hoisted the sheets high into the wind, like vast, blue, snapping sails.

'Thanks.' Eve dropped the bag of clothes pegs into the laundry basket. 'I didn't know you were up. Are you feeling better?'

'Much.' He tossed his hair. 'And you?'

'Yes. I'm going to try to move into the cottage again today. I hope I have better luck than last time.'

'Ah,' Henry said, in an entirely different tone. He dug his hands deep into his pockets and looked away from her, an artery throbbing visibly on the side of his neck. He seemed hurt, as if he thought she'd considered it bad luck to have been shut up with him for the past couple of weeks. She could have bit her tongue. The fact was, she was really going to miss him, miss living under the same roof with him. She didn't actually want to go at all, but now that the storm was over she no longer had an excuse for staying.

'Did you go for a walk?'

He gave a snort. 'Been feeding the hens.'

She remembered now Adele once taking her to see her prize bantams. 'You mean, they haven't been fed all this time?'

'Oh, they've been fed. Rang up the boy from the farm down the road. Does odd jobs now and then.' He pawed at the ground with the toe of one boot, like a horse. 'Damn fool left the door on the latch.'

'Well,' Eve said, 'who would steal them?'

Henry looked at her as if she were mentally unsound. 'Fox? Mink?'

'Oh.' Eve turned towards the house with the laundry basket under her arm.

'I was just going for the mimosa,' Henry said. 'If you'd care to come along. Put on some wellies, why don't you?'

The ground was littered with fallen twigs and huge, hollowed-out tree limbs covered with silvery scales of lichen. Henry sighed and clucked over several slates from the roof. The trees and shrubbery were still wet and dripping; chill drops blew at them from all directions. Walking between the walls of laurels, the ground carpeted with leathery yellow-spotted leaves the rain had beaten down, Eve saw herself three weeks earlier, rushing after Henry on this same path, thinking how bizarre he was. It seemed to have happened years ago, to another person, to two other people.

He led her all the way round the outside of the garden wall, inspecting for damage, before inserting a key into the lock of a red-painted door. How far would that be, the perimeter of a three-acre garden? She knew she had once had the tools for working that out, but had lost them somewhere along the way. Whatever the distance, it seemed interminable in oversized gumboots.

'We'll go out the other way,' Henry said, locking the door behind them.

He led the way across the garden to the glasshouse. Eve, who had never been inside the walls before, stopped to look. The garden was divided into six sections intersected by five wide brick paths. Six narrow paths sliced diagonally across each section to provide access to the large triangular plots. But only the path they were on, cutting straight across the centre, was relatively clear; the rest had been long overrun by weeds.

It was so calm, the quality of sound inside the garden so

completely different from that outside, it reminded Eve of *The Secret Garden*, Lily's favourite book. *How still it is! How still!* Henry, when she caught up, was dragging out of the path a long, moss-covered limb from one of the beech trees outside the garden. Beneath it lay the shiny black body of a rook, as big as a cat.

'Lord!' Henry nudged the carcass with a foot.

But damage to the garden was minimal. And with the wind walled out, it was several degrees warmer inside than outside, and almost eerily silent. Eve commented on the calmness. 'Is that why these gardens were walled? For protection against the wind?'

'Winds and thieves, yes, but principally rabbits. Absolutely rabbit-proof, this garden. The walls are not only ten feet high, they're sunk four feet deep.' Pointing with a long finger, he explained what kind of things had grown where. Gooseberries, raspberries, currants, loganberries, potatoes, carrots, peas, onions, rhubarb, cabbage, lettuce, beans. Flower borders edged each plot: carnations, heliotrope, pinks, dahlias. The skeletons of espaliered apple, pear and peach lined the walls like starved and crucified trees.

'What did they do with it all?'

'Oh, it was all used, once upon a time.' Henry started down the path towards the glasshouse. 'Designed to feed thirty, forty people. Family, guests, staff. But with no one to work in it, it's gradually dwindled. They grow only what they need.'

'What a shame,' Eve said, 'to let it go.'

'They have plans, it seems. They've been looking for a couple to come and live on the premises in exchange for help. As you've seen, one thing they can offer is accommodation.'

Eve could tell from his voice he didn't think much of the idea. 'If they got it going again, they could supply the restaurants, the bed-and-breakfasts, the hotels.'

'Adele's been thinking along those lines,' Henry said. 'Although not so, ah, ah – ambitiously. The only replies they've had have been from England. One of the things they're doing there now – interviewing.'

He disappeared into the potting shed and came out with a

long-handled shears, then began to cut a number of branches
from the mimosa, whose spiked heads of tiny yellow blossoms
were just coming into bloom. He cut carefully, Eve noticed,
diagonally, just above outward facing buds, handing each branch
to her as it was cut.

'You've done some gardening yourself.'

'A bit.' He turned to hand her another branch, smiled. 'Quite
a bit.' Then he disappeared into the shed to put away the clippers.

'Where was Duneske House?' Eve asked, when he emerged
again. 'Where Charlotte lived.' This was something she hadn't
known to ask about seven years ago. But now she could see
Charlotte, in a blue cashmere dress, making her way through the
dusk to steal her cousin's lover. Henry took them out through
another door, locked it behind them, then relieved her of the
mimosa and nodded to the south. 'Straight through there. It was
visible from here. A charming house, by all accounts, long and
rambling and full of windows, doors, light.'

'What happened to it? Burned during the Troubles?'

'No.' He drew out the word in a long sigh, then started
walking towards where the house had stood, talking as he went.
'A far greater number of these houses were pulled down by their
owners.'

'Why?'

'Disappearance of gardeners, for one,' he said over his
shoulder. 'Live-in staff, resident carpenters, odd-job men. *Income.*'
Several hundred feet short of where the house would have been,
he veered off to the left and picked his way through the trees and
undergrowth.

'Maintaining places like these. Even when the land has been
sold off, there are the gardens, the house and contents to care for.
The rates to pay. Some had no choice but to pack it in.
Charlotte's eldest brother' – he nodded at the clearing in the
tangled wilderness ahead of them – 'couldn't afford to live here,
the way things were going. Sold the house to an American, but
the American's English wife was afraid to live here. The way
things were going. They couldn't afford to keep it, couldn't sell

it, no one would buy, and they simply could not pay the exorbitant rates on it. So they pulled it down.' He shook his head. 'One would *think* the government would have rushed in to buy these houses, to save them from destruction.'

'I don't know,' Eve said after a moment. 'If I were a former slave, I don't think I could have cherished an antebellum plantation house, no matter how beautiful it was.'

Henry looked straight ahead in silence for some time, his jaw working and the vein in his neck throbbing again. 'One could never be convinced that such wanton destruction is not utterly pointless. Look at France. French peasants were every bit as oppressed as the Irish. But come the revolution, did they burn Versailles to the ground? Did they tear down the chateaux of the Loire? Or let them fall down from neglect? Of course not. They knew their worth.'

'They may have held on to the chateaux,' Eve pointed out, 'but they butchered everyone who lived in them.'

The historian let out a bark of laughter. He moved ahead, and seemed to be looking for something, then stopped before a straggling myrtle, all but one of its branches dead.

'This was planted from my great-grandmother's wedding bouquet. It was a tradition to plant the wedding bouquet in the garden. To see what came of it. That branch still puts out pinkish blossoms every spring.'

'Your great-grandmother?'

'Charlotte.'

Charlotte. It made sense now, Henry's having spent all those summers here. It made sense too, his bitterness about the house. They stood in silence for a few minutes, lost in their separate thoughts, Eve contemplating the scene suggested by this remnant of bouquet: the wilderness that was once a garden, full of people, Charlotte radiant in her wedding white, Henry Brooke in dove grey and tall hat, Evelyn Hope-Ross hovering on the fringes, hollow-eyed and broken-hearted.

'Henry.' She turned to him. 'Is that who you're named for? Henry Brooke?'

'Henry Brooke Cole, actually.' He smiled, then led the way back to the house. They walked in silence, again pursuing their different trains of thought, Eve musing about Henry being Charlotte's great-grandson, about his connection to the Hope-Rosses, about how it was to his house or flat they went in England, and how it was he who had charge of Derrymore in their absence, not their own son.

'Don't the Hope-Rosses have a son?' she called to his back.

'They had a son,' he said after a pause.

'But —' Eve thought Dolores must have got it wrong, 'I thought it was the daughter who —'

Henry stopped and turned.

'They had a son and a daughter and have sadly lost both. The daughter many years ago, the son just five years ago. A motoring accident.'

They had reached the edge of the lawn. Shifting the armful of mimosa to Eve, he bent to retrieve the slates blown from the roof as they went heavily over the grass in silence.

She put the clean sheets back on the bed and finished her packing. Lugging her suitcase down the stairs, she could see from the landing that Henry was standing in the hall doorway, looking out as if in shock. He did not turn as she crossed the hall. Coming up beside him, she saw; it took her breath away. Completely uprooted, the huge oak that had stood in the curve at the top of the drive had fallen across the gravel sweep, where Henry's little Morris, caught by the upper branches in a grisly embrace, lay crushed and mangled.

They went down the steps to survey the devastation. The Morris's roof was flattened and the windscreen smashed, but Henry was not concerned about his car. It was the tree he mourned. 'The last of the first planted.' He reached up to lay a hand on the trunk, as if it were the flank of a fallen animal. And with its great girth and length, its bark deeply ridged and scaled, it did have the tragic grandeur of a dying beast, a last dinosaur.

Where it had stood yawned a crater wide enough to bury three of Henry's car.

He got on the telephone, first with the Hope-Rosses, who rang back three times, and then with the O'Gormans, who referred him to someone else. Eve made sandwiches and coffee. While they ate, she said she would walk down to the cottage and get her car. Henry said he would have to wait for the tree-removal people. But before lunch was finished the men arrived and, having passed on their instructions, he said he would go with her; they could carry the mimosa down and drive to the village from the cottage.

Their arms full of branches, and shoes to change into, they retraced their steps the length of the littered lawn, through the wet laurels and along the garden wall. Only this time the air was split by the relentless buzzing of power saws. They veered off to the narrow path through the sheep meadow and, rather than climbing the cattle gate, unravelled the tangle of rusted wire that kept it latched, then retied it behind them. The meadow was full of moist black pellets and black-faced sheep that skittered away as they approached. The cold, fresh air was full of ozone, the harbour below calm and blue. White sea birds swooped and swirled. Descending the path that angled down the slope, Eve was relieved to see that all the slates on the cottage roof were intact; she could so easily have been inside during the storm. They were at the door before she realised that anything was wrong.

Water lay in a pool just outside the door, although the path to either side of it was already drying. Her eyes moved up from the pool to its source: water seeped under the door from inside. She and Henry exchanged a glance before he opened the door she had neglected to lock ten days before. More backed-up water came out in a little rush over the threshold. He went inside ahead of her. 'Lord!' he said, and then again, 'Lord!' Eve stepped inside.

Both windows facing the sea, the windows that Adele had had cut into the thick end walls to provide more light as well as a view, had been smashed with a violence that shot shards the length of the room. The surface of the far wall was cut and scarred, the mirror over the chest of drawers had shattered; broken glass lay all over the sodden bed. Eve's second suitcase, still unpacked, lay open on the floor, full of broken glass and water that had ruined exactly half her things, including the journal Lily had given her. Eve stooped and fished it out. Its covers peeled off in her hands. Inside, her thoughts had all run together into a dark muddled stain. She dropped it back into the suitcase, stood and looked at the unslept-in bed, strewn with long fingers of glass.

'Good thing I ran out of matches.'

Henry was standing close behind her, and when she turned to face him, he put a hand on her shoulder; his lips moved, but before they formed any words there was a sound at the door, a shadow was thrown across the floor, and they moved apart.

'Oh, my God!' Dolores, in her tweed hat and trench coat, stood in the doorway, taking it all in without needing to ask any questions: the unused bed, the unpacked suitcase, everything told her that Eve had not been in the cottage. She looked from the windows to the wall to the floor. 'Oh, my God,' she said again. 'I phoned the house a couple times this morning,' she said to Henry, 'but there wasn't any answer. So I assumed' – she turned to Eve – 'that you were here. Oh, my God,' she said a third time.

'The windows must have blown in,' Eve said. 'The wind was incredible. I never heard anything like it.'

Henry, his hands joined behind his back, addressed the ceiling. 'I should think it was a wave.'

Eve's car would not start, so they followed Dolores down the track to where hers was parked. A clunker, she explained, an old banger that had already saved her so much in car hires she figured that, if she came back one day and found it gone, she would still have come out ahead. She left it parked outside her cottage while she was away and the grass always grew up round it before she returned. Last spring she'd found a bird's nest nestled next to the radiator, a perfect nest with three tiny spotted eggs.

'No mother, though. She must have been away when I started the car. And it was three weeks before I had the oil checked. The eggs would have been hard-boiled by then. You should have seen the mechanic's face when he opened the hood.'

One of the car's idiosyncrasies was that the passenger door would not open. Eve climbed into the back seat with the mimosa. Henry, whose legs were judged too long to fold into the back, got in on the driver's side and climbed across the gear lever.

Dolores backed out of the lane and onto the road at top speed, and talked nearly as recklessly as she drove, all the way into Clonmere. At one point Henry, who'd been keeping his eyes on the road, risked a sideways glance at her. He seemed stunned, as if he hadn't believed it possible for anyone to string so many words together. When Eve leaned forward to ask Dolores where she might buy a table, Henry turned and glared at her, as if to say, Don't ask her *anything*.

'I bought mine in Kilcreene, at Donlon's.' Dolores laughed. 'I have to take you there sometime. It's a wonderful place. They own half the village. A big pub, a funeral parlour, a furniture store, all in a row. Their hearse is always parked in front of the pub. I can't imagine that could be very good for business.'

In no time, they were at the church gates. Dolores volunteered to bring in the mimosa so Henry could go to the O'Gormans to report the damage to the cottage and arrange for a clean-up, while Eve went into Egan's to restock their depleted stores of food and wine.

The cat lay sleeping with her back pressed against the fireguard. Eve sat next to Dolores on the sofa, Henry sprawled in a chair across from them. On the table between lay a plate of crumbs. It had been dark for an hour. The curtains were drawn, the lamps lit, one bottle of wine was finished and a second opened. Dolores was talking about her time in Dublin, the plays she had seen, the various people she'd had dinners and drinks with, her research, her days in the National Library. When the telephone shrilled, all three gave a start. Even Penelope rose up and blinked, before curling herself down in the opposite direction. Henry crossed the room in three strides and snatched up the receiver. Dolores turned to face Eve and dropped her voice to a confidential tone.

'Look. I have a proposition for you.' She spoke quickly, as if she'd just been waiting for a chance to speak to Eve alone. 'A job, of sorts, if you're interested. I had this idea in Dublin that you might like to help me with the art part of the book. Track down the paintings, select the ones to be reproduced, say a few words about them.' Her heavy black brows shot up, warding off some imagined protest. 'I have to get somebody. Why not you? Why not? And when you said in the car earlier how much you were enjoying reading the journal, I knew I was right. What do you think? Will you think about it?'

'And what about the Hope-Rosses? How would they like it?'

'I think they would like it just fine. I was right, by the way. I had a note back from Adele; it was waiting for me when I got home last night. They don't hold anything against you personally. They never blamed you. How could they? And now that your husband –'

She broke off as Henry came back to where they sat and took up the wine bottle. He filled Eve's already half-full glass then reached towards Dolores's, but she covered it with a hand. 'No more for me. Designated driver.' He sloshed some into his own, sat back in his chair and looked at Eve.

'They were extremely upset. About your losses. And about the possibility that you might have been – ah – injured. Adele was beside herself about having put in those windows.' She'd said that, if she wanted to, Eve was welcome to move into Mrs Matt's, one of the two flats in the yard. It had been redecorated recently for the couple they had hoped to find but hadn't, and it was fully furnished.

'No, ah, bedclothes. Just at the moment. Tomorrow, if you –'

'Well, that's settled then,' Dolores cut in, getting to her feet. She pulled on her coat, said to Eve, 'We'll talk,' and was out the door before anyone could stop her.

It was ten o'clock. Having opened another bottle of wine, they sat near each other on the sofa, lounging inebriately, Henry telling Eve about the house in the yard he had not yet taken her to see; when he had opened the kitchen door and turned on the outside light, it was raining again, a hard, driving rain with fat white drops, like snow, and they decided that Mrs Matt's could wait until morning.

There were two Mrs Matts, he explained. The first was the wife of Matt Kane, Evelyn Hope-Ross's farm manager. Their oldest son, also named Matt, lived his whole life at Derrymore, working as jack-of-all-trades. His widow, the second Mrs Matt, survived him by fifteen years and had continued to live, rent-free as was the custom, in one of the two flats in the stable yard. It had been the Hope-Ross children who had begun calling the place Mrs Matt's Cottage.

Eve had made an omelette full of cheese, which she and Henry devoured. She had eaten more eggs in these past two weeks than she had in the past ten years; eggs, cheese, butter. Why did these lethal things not seem to count here? Henry had grilled thick slices of bread and cut up some oranges. They had also fed each other selected portions of their pasts, Eve telling Henry about Evan, and Henry telling her about his summers in Ireland as a boy and then as a student, about the lessons he gave to Peter, the son, and then to the daughter, who had later died of complications from scarlet fever at nineteen years of age.

Eve pictured a raven-haired beauty in a tweed skirt and a string of pearls, white teeth, shining eyes and the poise and certainty of one bred in a great slate-roofed house rising out of a wealth of lawns and laurels, gardens and specimen trees, at least two of which had been brought back from India as saplings rolled in carpets by one's great-great-grandfather. On Monday she had come running down the stairs in tennis whites, and on Friday was carried down in her coffin. Or so Eve imagined.

'Gave me my first drink, Mrs Matt.' Henry smiled at the memory. 'Used to call on her my first day back, a tradition of sorts. Always gave me tea and buns. A marvellous baker. She evidently judged me man enough one year. Never touched it herself, only for callers. Hadn't the least notion what to pour, like all non-drinkers. Gave me a tumbler full of whiskey.' He held one hand above the other to indicate a very large glass. 'Not sure how old I was. Just out of school. It was pouring with rain, of course, and I made it to – there.' He turned and pointed over his shoulder to the French windows, shuttered now, the curtains drawn. 'Nearly drowned before I was discovered by one of the children. I can still hear her. "Mummy, Mummy, something's terribly wrong with Henry!" Then Adele, bending over me. "Oh *dear!* I'm afraid Henry's rather *drunk.*"'

Eve smiled, then pictured the scene and laughed out loud. Henry, flushed with pleasure at his success, poured more wine into their glasses. When Eve reached for hers, he said, 'You should have been a pianist. You have such long fingers.'

'I did take lessons for six years.'

'And?'

She sat back with her wine. 'No sense of time.'

'Time!' His own laugh was a short bark.

'That's how Miss Haynes, my instructor, put it.'

'Stupid woman. To discourage you, that is.' In leaning back again, Henry shifted closer to her, his shoulder all but touching hers.

'She also said she didn't think that I had anything to say in music. I had no idea what she was talking about, and my father thought it was the most pretentious thing he'd ever heard. He used to joke, "Tone deaf, I understand. But deaf and dumb?" Now I know what she meant, and she was right. I really didn't have anything to say.'

'You mean, as you do in your painting?'

'I was thinking more of your playing.' It occurred to her just how much she would miss this – she'd come to take it almost for granted, hearing him play every day – and she asked if he would play something, then immediately wished she hadn't. He waited a moment, then, as if dismissed, got up without a word and went to the piano.

Stupid woman, indeed, she thought. I don't know how to do this. I don't remember.

He played a Chopin nocturne, and then another. She had never heard him play anything so moving before and gave herself up to it. The piano was behind her, but behind Henry was a lamp that magnified and flung his shadow ahead of them both. She lay back against the sofa watching this immense shadow move on the wall, looming as he leaned back, and crouching as he bent to caress the keys. She let the music wash over her, completely seduced by it. Even Penelope, she saw, lay on her back, her head to the side, eyes closed.

When he finished playing, Henry went first to the fireplace and took up the poker, stabbed at the dying fire, then put on another log. He poured the last of the wine into their glasses, then fell onto the sofa, spent, as if he had run ten miles.

'Thank you,' Eve said, reaching for her glass. 'I love Chopin.' Rather drunk herself, she made a slop of the word.

'He was a great Romantic, Chopin, in every sense. Dazzling showman. He made countesses swoon.'

Eve considered several comments on his own performance, but Penelope opened her eyes just then, looked straight at her, and yawned. No need to be spectacularly stupid, she decided.

'Was he?' she said instead, then jumped as the telephone shrilled again. Henry looked at the clock on the mantelpiece as he got to his feet. It was nearly half eleven.

'They must be very upset indeed,' he said drily. But a moment later his tone was very different when he turned to Eve.

'It's for you.'

She got up and went to the phone as if to the gallows. She had given Lily and Rose this number but had told them to use it only in an emergency, and now one of her daughters was calling to tell her that something had happened to the other. Henry had put the receiver next to the phone and she picked it up as if it were a snake, she was so sure that this was going to be bad news. And when she heard the voice at the other end, she was certain of it.

'Eve. I'm so sorry. I know it's late there.'

'Martin.' She gave Henry a little wild-eyed glance, at which he turned and went considerately out of the room. 'What's happened? What's wrong? Are the girls –'

'The girls are fine,' he hastened to assure her. 'I just talked to them both two minutes ago. I called them to ask them how to reach you.'

'I can't believe you actually called here,' she said, with the irritation that often follows in the wake of needless worry. 'What if the Hope-Rosses had been here?'

'Aren't they there?'

'They're in England.'

'Then what are you doing there?'

This she couldn't easily answer, so said nothing.

'Who was that who answered the phone?'

'Their nephew,' she said. 'Or cousin. Or second cousin. What difference does it make? Why are you calling?'

'Are you all right, Eve? You sound – I don't know – not quite yourself.'

'I've had pneumonia. And I just drank a couple of bottles of wine.'

'Look, I really have to talk to you, but obviously this is not a good time. I'll call you again tomorrow. Will you be there?'

'No. I'm renting one of the houses in the yard. I'm moving in tomorrow. I doubt very much if there's a telephone.'

As she was saying this, Henry came back into the room, bringing in a little rush of cold air from the hall. She caught his eye and raised quizzical eyebrows. He shook his head, then moved towards the table and started gathering up the empty bottles.

'No, there's no phone.'

'Eve, don't move in,' Martin said, his voice full of urgency. 'You have to come back.'

'Come back?' she said numbly, as Henry moved past her again, his arms full of bottles, and went out of the room.

'The trial starts on Tuesday,' Martin said quickly, as if afraid she might misunderstand. 'You have to be there. They need you.'

'No!'

'You have to, Eve. You're his only living –'

'No! I told them no. I can't do it. I won't do it.' Weeping now, she slammed the receiver back into its cradle. After a moment, she lifted it again and laid it next to the telephone.

Before leaving Boston, she'd had a letter from the Dallas District Attorney's office reminding her of the trial dates for the two boys arrested for Evan's murder, and when she wrote back and said that she would not be there for either trial, that she would be out of the country, the DA herself had phoned her. It was essential for Eve to be there, she'd said, essential for the jury to put a face to the bereaved, and essential for Eve herself, in order to achieve closure.

This arrogant assumption, that a perfect stranger would know what was essential for her, had only angered her. Achieve closure. She loathed both the easy phrase and the concept, as if anything – least of all helping to send two teenagers to their deaths – would somehow put a lid on her brother's death, make her miss him any less or give her, who had always opposed the death penalty, some sort of grim satisfaction. Though she knew that, if she actually saw her brother's killers, she would probably want to tear them limb from limb. Which was why she did not want to see them. Above all, she did not want to sit in a courtroom day after day and hear all the unbearable details, a sure way, she sensed, of turning the bereaved into the permanently bereft.

Henry had left his own half-full glass behind, as well as hers, but he did not come back. She had cried herself out, she had finished her wine, the fire had died down, more than an hour had passed, and still he did not appear. She went out into the hall, where her suitcase no longer stood at the foot of the staircase, then went up.

A faint bar of light was visible under the door of the room she had come to think of as hers. She pushed the door open; her suitcase stood next to the bed, the lamp on the bedside table was lit, and three bars of the electric heater glowed. Down the passage, another sliver of light shone under the bathroom door. Henry's own door across the way was shut.

Unable to believe he meant to go to bed without a word, she unzipped her bag and took out what she would need for the night, hurried out of her clothes and into her dressing gown, then opened the door again and walked round the room, taking another distracted look at some of the pictures she had come to know so well; a shawled old woman, a young girl with black hair and black Spanish eyes, a fleet of exotic-looking fishing boats in the harbour.

She heard the bathroom door open. A few seconds later Henry's bedroom door was opened, then shut; she held her breath, minute by minute, until she understood that the door was not going to be opened again. He had to have seen that she was there, yet hadn't even put his head in to say goodnight.

What on earth was wrong? Or was this some exquisite degree of Anglo niceness or reticence her more blunted American perceptions could not appreciate, or even perceive?

In the bathroom she filled the tub with hot water. Henry had left her plenty; in fact the water was so hot that when she first stepped in, she had to leap out again, so hot that when she had managed to ease herself back in she nearly lost consciousness. After long minutes of lying in a stupor, her eye fell on a tiny black curl of hair, not hers, caught at the edge of the overflow vent. She leaned forward and lifted it onto the tip of a forefinger, then lay back again, the curl resting on her stomach like a microscopic cat.

'Henry, Henry, Henry,' she murmured.

She had thought him so odd at first, so strange, and he may well have felt the same way about her. But she had come to like him, really like him, and he, she knew, had come to like her. But these last two days, they had taken another step closer. The attraction was almost palpable, and it was mutual; she was sure it was. It was hard to be mistaken about such a thing. All those charged moments were no less real for having been interrupted. By that spectacular jolt of electricity, by Dolores, by her own bad timing, by Martin.

Was that what was wrong with Henry now?

She heard his voice say, so tonelessly, *It's for you*, and saw his face when she said Martin's name. It was completely expressionless, as if he had shut down, closed up.

Did he think she was still in love with her husband?

Was she? She was certainly not unmoved by his voice on the telephone. She may not have sounded like herself to him, but he sounded exactly the same, his voice still that low, gravelly baritone that had first attracted her to him. She had always loved his voice.

Her feelings for him confused even herself.

She had been so *angry*. And for so long. She had wished him all manner of misfortune. She had wanted him to suffer.

She had not invited him to Evan's funeral, not even informed him, taking an almost grim sort of pleasure in imagining some future circumstance in which he might casually learn that his oldest friend had been dead for weeks or months. But she had reckoned without her daughters. She should have known, had she been capable of thought, that they would let their father know within minutes of her phoning them, and that he would attend the funeral.

She was aware of him across the aisle, stealing sideways glances at her. To see how she was taking it, to judge if she could cope, or just to make sure she knew he was there. She had no way of knowing. But he knew what her brother had meant to her; Evan had meant almost as much to him. Then at one point in the service he leaned forward suddenly, his hand over his eyes, and it was this detail – oddly enough, considering all she had endured in Dallas – that had made her brother's death real for her. It was a simple gesture of Martin's that had shattered her.

Weeks later when her father died without warning, keeling over in his kitchen one Saturday morning after struggling without success to come to terms with his son's murder, she had been alerted by his next-door neighbour that, although his car remained in its usual place, he had not emerged by nightfall to bring in the morning paper, nor had he answered the doorbell or the telephone. Without even trying to reach him herself, Eve phoned the police.

She had taken the neighbour's call on the telephone that stood on a small table at the bottom of the stairs and she was still sitting on the second step from the bottom, the telephone in her lap, when the call came from the police, and she remained there to talk to her daughters.

This time when Lily and Rose, calling from California, woke their father to give him the news, he didn't hesitate. He still had his key to the tall grey Victorian house he had painstakingly restored over the past several years and that now had an accusing 'For Sale' sign planted in its front yard. When Eve failed to answer the door, he let himself in and was taken aback to find her sitting right there, still on the steps, the phone still in her lap.

He brought her a glass of brandy and made her a pot of tea. He made the funeral arrangements, notified everyone who needed to be notified, phoned the obituary in to the newspaper, drove her from Boston to the small town in western Mass-achusetts where she had grown up, arranged for their daughters' flight, picked them up at the airport and brought them back to their grandfather's house. And he helped her through the awful funeral itself, walking and standing and sitting beside her.

She knew he felt somehow responsible for all that had happened to her after he left, and she had wanted him to feel that way; she too had blamed him, as if his extracting himself from her life had started a landslide, an avalanche. And while she was grateful to him for rushing in to help, she had felt his subsequent absence even more keenly.

It had been so much easier to be angry.

When the bath water had gone tepid, she stepped out of the tub and rubbed herself dry, put on her dressing gown and went back down the passage. She didn't know she was going to tap at Henry's door until she did.

She heard what sounded like the creaking of a wooden ship at sea, which she knew from the bed she had been sleeping in was the groaning of an old mattress suspended on even older ropes; she thought he was getting out of bed and couldn't think what she would say when he opened the door. But he did not open the door. She waited a moment, then went across to her room, shut the door and leaned against it, so mortified she could hardly breathe.

There was no possibility of sleep. She didn't have to get into bed to know this. She got dressed again and turned off the electric fire. After all the trouble she had taken with the sheets that morning, it wasn't worth using this bed again just to lie there sleepless, her mind in turmoil, thinking about Evan and about Martin, fretting about the trial and about the long arm of the Dallas District Attorney, fretting about what was wrong with Henry.

If she had learned nothing else in the past year, she had learned that the only successful way to court sleep was by pretending to avoid it. She would go downstairs, put another log on the fire, and read.

3 June 1882
London

Left to my own devices today, as I am in disgrace, Francis off visiting old school friends, and my packing done.

Two things of note have occurred. It came to Aunt's attention – it was, I believe, maliciously *brought* to her attention – that my name has headed a petition presented to the South Kensington School of Art, demanding that female students, like the men, be allowed to draw the human figure from life.

Aunt Gort, following a discussion with my uncle, who has not since then bestowed upon me so much as a single glance, wrote at once to my parents, and my orders were not long in coming. I leave for Ireland tomorrow in the company of Francis, who arrived last evening for the purpose of escorting my unworthy carcass home. My admirable brother kept up an impressively stern and sober aspect in the presence of Aunt and Uncle, but the moment we were left alone, he opened his arms and we fell upon each other with much hilarity on both sides. Aunt and Uncle being engaged to dine away from home, our solitary meal gradually acquired all the characteristics of a nursery tea, with a degree of high spirits, loud laughter and bad manners that shocked the servants.

My present disgrace naturally led us to recollections of earlier instances, most notably the punishment I incurred for commandeering a leaking rowing boat from Uncle Charles's quay and piloting it full of screaming brothers and cousins through a series of holes drilled by the sea into the cliffs, and, as I had failed to calculate the effects of the rising tide, nearly decapitating the entire crew.

It is a rare occurrence indeed to have an evening alone with Francis and I must admit that, although at first I resented his being sent to fetch me, as if I were not capable of walking aboard a perfectly seaworthy vessel and disembarking on the other side, it is remarkably good to see my favourite brother again. He was good enough to say that I had been sorely missed at home and that the hunting this spring was not the same without me. But I had to hear also of the stupendous courage and competence in the saddle exhibited by a visiting female cousin of ours, whose acquaintance I have yet to make, but whose tiresome name has for the past month appeared in every letter sent from within a thirty-mile radius of Derrymore. Francis says I am sure to love Anne Morgan, which means that I am sure to hate her, especially as I find myself already indebted to her.

But I go before myself. The second thing of note that has happened is that I have received payment for my article on the Dublin season, along with a letter from the editor praising the 'freshness and originality' of its style. He says that the piece is 'clever and full of life', that it contains some 'superior sketches' and bright bits of dialogue which lead him to suspect that my real talent may be for fiction, and that if I should try my hand at a story, he would be happy to read it.

I cannot begin to say what were my feelings when the cheque fell out of the envelope. To be shown, all in an instant, that I can do something for myself, that I need not beg for every penny but might make my own way, was nothing short of a potent drug that turned my blood to wine and made me quite drunk with happiness.

As to being indebted to my as yet unknown cousin, Francis assures me that this prodigy has gone a good way towards rescuing me from my present shame by means of what is either a very primitive or a highly developed sense of humour, aided by Mama's habit of reading the morning letters aloud at breakfast. I myself never write her a word that could not be heard at once by Papa and my brothers, as well as a number of house guests and servants. But Aunt Gort, who is not unaware of this practice of her sister's, must, in her haste to warn my parent of her offspring's depravity, have forgotten to draw her usual black box round the section not to be read out and Mama, knowing that any news of me would be of special interest to the family, read it in as clear and loud a voice as she possesses, up to and including the words 'live nude', at which point she faltered, leaving the dreadful words hanging in the air in what Francis described as the most appalling silence ever, in his experience, to have fallen upon that table.

They all sat frozen, paralysed, he said. There seemed no way out of it, except for the earth to open up and swallow them all, when the silence was suddenly shattered by stifled sobs and coughs and everyone's attention shifted to Anne, who appeared to be at once weeping and choking to death on her toast. However, upon closer examination she proved to be merely laughing, which word, my brother says, is a very poor representation of such tearful ecstasies as she was exhibiting.

Her mother, Madeleine, who is my second cousin, apologised for her daughter's inexcusable behaviour and attempted an explanation of Anne's peculiar sense of humour, or sense of the absurd, which she claims afflicts her like an illness. But Madeleine, Francis says, is similarly afflicted by these attacks of *fou rire* and she too soon collapsed behind her handkerchief, from whence emitted squeaks and gasps of stifled anguish. From there, he said, it was not a moment before the laughter was general, with even Papa and Mama roaring. Now, as Francis wisely pointed out, having once given way to laughter on this topic, our parents can never again regain their high ground of moral indignation.

I am not sorry to be going home in any case. London is a miserable place, crowded and noisy and dirty. This house smells of the river and what passes for a large garden here is really a mean little space like a prison yard; so many paces this way, so many that. I miss the incomparable Irish air and light, and the openness of Derrymore ranged along its cliffs, the sheep meadow and the orchard high over the sea. Reminiscing with my old comrade-in-arms last evening, I could actually smell the wet seaweed and feel the hot slatey rocks beneath my feet. And I have only to close my eyes to look down on the fishing boats and the white-sailed racing yachts in the harbour below, and out through its mouth to the broad white Atlantic rolling in from the horizon.

No, I am not at all sorry to be going back. I am as determined as ever to earn the money to go to Paris and learn all I can, but it is not escape from my home that I crave; it is the freedom to be allowed to remain living there, and to come and go as I please, and, above all, to be allowed to paint in peace. Now I have been thrown a lifeline, I shall seize hold of it with all my strength.

I will write. I will paint. I will work.

20 June
Derrymore

Have been much occupied, and much disturbed.

I was scarcely through the hall door when Mama served me notice of my having been assigned to sing, in just two weeks' time, the part of the bumboat woman in the charity performance of *Pinafore* she has got up. Quite aside from the fact that I happen to be the only contralto she knows well enough to conscript into service, I feel certain Mama meant to strike a bargain: Do this and we'll forget about *that*. What I did not know when I agreed to take on the role of Little Buttercup, but learned soon enough, was that the part of Captain Corcoran was to be sung by none other than my 'cousin' (as Mama now refers to him) Henry Brooke, he and Charlotte and their three children having been with Uncle Charles and Aunt Emmeline at Duneske for some weeks now.

This arrangement could have been devised only by someone as thoroughly righteous as Mama. She believes, I have no doubt whatever, that as it would be *wrong* of me to think of Henry

Brooke, it is therefore *impossible* for me to think of him, that the moment he became betrothed to my cousin, I would naturally have routed all thoughts of him from my own mind. Mama has obviously routed all such thoughts of him from *hers*, as she now remembers only how well we two sang together. Consequently, she has thrown me quite literally into his arms and has gone so far as to prod a completely stupefied Henry with such stage directions as, 'Captain Corcoran, I really must insist that you place your arm around Little Buttercup's waist.'

This is naturally not the first I have seen of Henry since his marriage to my cousin, but it is certainly the first we have been together for hours and hours on end, and I find that the constant proximity of his person, the embraces we are pushed into, and the words the script forces us to say to each other severely tax what small stores of self-possession I have managed to lay by. It is a strain, both physical and mental, such as I have never before been made to endure.

Yet not a single member of my entire family seems to have the slightest inkling that the source of their entertainment might be a cause of pain to me. I have had to fight back a good deal of rising gall as I remember how the mawkish lyrics of our old duets used to move them all to tears; yet our very real suffering moves them not at all. They simply do not see. The first rehearsal was nothing less than excruciating. My nerves were in shreds. I funked line after line. Henry, too, capable actor though he has always been, dropped lines or left them unfinished, stuttered and stammered and spoke as if choking on sawdust the first time he had to say to me, 'I am touched to the heart by your innocent regard for me, and were we differently situated, I think I could have returned it.'

One would think that Charlotte, at least, would be on the alert. But Charlotte, who has confided to me that she is yet again with child, is completely absorbed by her own unhappiness. She has even had the neck to solicit my compassion, as if her present tribulations must cancel all past treachery.

It is all too abundantly clear that hers is a marriage (who could have foreseen it?) of little common sympathy and less respect, of little talk and no discussion. She is much occupied by her children, it is true, having already too many to entrust to the care of the single (and singularly young and inept) nurse they are able to employ. What's more, her last confinement damaged a nerve in her left leg, which causes her to hobble after she has been seated for any length of time, and she has grown quite plump, I might even say fat, which is a constant source of misery to her. She has grown rather dull as well and will speak of nothing but her children, who do not seem to *me* to be so remarkably interesting. That a lithe and lively girl should have been so quickly and utterly transformed is indeed a grievous thing, but somehow I cannot find it in my heart to pity her.

24 June

I find that I am already forced to swallow my own words and to pity Charlotte from the bottom of my soul.

Returning long past midnight from Duneske House and an evening's celebration of the success of *Pinafore,* as well as of Charlotte's and my own birthdays, I found myself stranded alone with Henry in the dark and the rain in the seclusion of the laurel path. I blush now to remember how he outmanoeuvred my (I now realise) all-too-cognisant brother for the honour of holding an umbrella over my miserable head. There was no need for Henry to have come at all, as Anne and I were perfectly willing to lend each other an arm through the dark. But in the end, after a great deal of noise, Francis took Anne, Dominick escorted Madeleine, Mama got Gerald (Papa as usual having gone on ahead) and I fell to Henry. Then, just as all were setting off, he found that he must return to the house for his cigarette case, with the result that by the time we set off in earnest, the rest of the Derrymore party was well in advance of us.

Yet I know in my heart, had they all been well within hearing, I would not have raised the alarm, and I know too that I must have suspected something of what my cousin's husband intended, and that I willingly allowed it to occur. There had been that evening, in addition to genuine conversation for the first time in nearly five years, a certain unspoken sympathy between us, as is always the case with fellow survivors of a catastrophe, and there was as well something of a mutual thrill of triumph, for we had managed, despite being subjected to all the torments of hell, to acquit ourselves rather well. Our performance had been a great success; we each alone knew what the effort had cost the other, and, as for me, Henry's fortitude had certainly won back a measure of my former respect and regard.

At the same time, I swear that no one could have been more surprised, more shocked, than I when I found my hand seized, and my waist encircled by his arm.

And yet, I waited. I allowed some thirty seconds, a minute, to pass — it seemed an eternity — before breaking free. I allowed myself to savour (it is not too strong a word) the pressure of his arm straining me to him, his lips seeking mine. I allowed myself to feel the keenest stab of regret. *That I must live without this!* I allowed myself, too, the bitter triumph brought by the thought, *and so must he.*

At last I found the strength to wrench myself free, and ran blindly from him to the end of the path into the garden, kept on my feet by some power other than my own. I already knew I would speak of this to no one, not even to Anne. But how was I to get into the house and up to my room unnoticed in such a distraught condition, panting like a hound after the chase, my hair wet through and falling down round my face?

My heart nearly stopped when I saw a small glow in the dark that was certainly someone smoking in the garden. I was in terror that it would be Papa enjoying a last cigar. But it was Francis who called to me in a low voice and we moved towards each other in the dark, I aided by the glow from his cigarette and he by my gasping sobs. He sheltered me under his umbrella and put his cigarette into my hand. I inhaled it deeply, and gratefully.

'Now pin up your hair,' he said quietly, and waited in silence while I did so, then took my arm and led me round to the hall door and, once inside, walked me straight to the foot of the staircase and, for the benefit of the ears gathered in the drawing room, called after me that I should dry off and get straight to bed so as not to catch my death.

I'm not sure what made me weep the more, that I had for a second time had to wrench myself, and my heart, from Henry Brooke, or that my brother had taken the trouble to understand me, and without passing judgement had come to my aid. But of one thing I am certain: I would not for the world exchange my life for Charlotte's. Nor, for that matter, for Henry's. This night we are all three of us plunged into misery. Yet they are fettered, while I am free.

5 July

I have been engaged in painting Anne's portrait, which has gone a long way towards soothing my mind and fending off thoughts of my other cousin and her husband. While I usually prefer an unlovely subject to its reverse, I find Anne an uncommonly good sitter, with the patience and endurance of a professional model.

However, although she is kind enough to pronounce both it and me brilliant, I am not at all satisfied with my study of her. I have got the chestnut wealth of her hair, but am unable to fully capture the subtle shadings of her complexion, and my palette seems incapable of producing the peculiar brown of her large eyes, although that is not a matter of pigment so much as it is the compensating charm of expression frequently bestowed upon the acutely near-sighted. For so afflicted she proves to be, and this handicap only deepens one's appreciation of her pluck in the saddle, which, now that I realise she is as good as blindfolded when facing walls and leaping ditches, seems to me the most extravagant kind of fearlessness.

And I have discovered that I am not the only scribbler under this roof, for she writes as well, and has herself published many essays of a political nature, she being an advocate of the separation of Ireland from England's rule. This I learned when she, perusing one of my sketchbooks, came across a series of caricatures I had done in London of various notables, including, I am almost ashamed to say, Her Majesty. She very much admired them and suggested I might think of getting work not only as a writer but as an illustrator for magazines and journals.

When I confided in her my desperate need to earn enough money to study in a Paris studio, she did not seem to regard such an ambition as being in any way extraordinary but rather as in the natural course of things and offered to write immediately to several publications where her name is known. I then told her about the piece I wrote for the *Pictorial* and about the editor's request for a story I had yet to attempt. She says that when I do submit a story I should consider making a set of drawings to accompany it, as there could be no better way of making my 'talent' as an illustrator known.

10 July

Anne and I have been working together these past five days on a story which has been growing, almost of its own accord, to nearly novel length. It takes place against the background of the current land disputes and we are making it, at Anne's suggestion, as shocking as we are able. Indeed, we refer to it as our 'shilling shocker'. An old woman and her daughter are boycotted by their neighbours for their occupation of the farm of a relation who's been evicted for failing to pay his rents. No one in the village will sell food to them. No one at the fair will buy their cattle. Two nights ago we slit the throat of one of their lovely heifers and last night set fire to the hayrick that was to see the cattle through the winter. And such a fire! It blazed high into the night at the very edge of the sea, and not a soul to lift a finger to put it out.

The weather has been very fine, even hot at times, and we have been working out of doors, lying in the grass of the sheep meadow or sitting in the shade of the crabapple orchard, I with my MS book and pen and Anne her plate-camera for capturing a feeding curlew or a steamer on the horizon bound for America. She is an intrepid photographer and has made studies of everything, from the family at charades to the beggar women in the village streets to me painting in my studio and out of doors. I have never had such a nice companion.

15 July

If Mama only knew I have not only clamoured for the privilege of drawing from an unclothed model, I have myself become one!

In one of the journals to which she holds a subscription, Anne discovered an advertisement by a French publisher offering to pay handsomely for photographic studies of female nudes for an 'artistic' volume he is compiling. At first this was a cause of much merriment as we speculated upon photographing various female members of our household. But then the thought occurred to us: why should we not photograph each other? We both possess rather fine figures, and if photographed from the rear, our faces not visible, who could possibly recognise us?

But how were we to find a suitable place for such compositions? Every room in the house is constantly subject to unannounced invasion. Our usual spot in the sheep meadow would have been most aesthetically pleasing, yet that too is easily accessible to spies. We needed a place full of light, yet secluded enough to allow us adequate time to disrobe and to carefully compose our portraits and to dress again. This is where my intimate knowledge of the surrounding inlets and coves proved useful. I selected the most isolated of these coves, the most difficult of approach, yet which affords a thin band of strand.

This morning we rose at five, dressed by the first rays of light and took several large towels to provide the excuse, should one be required, that we had gone for an early morning bathe, and successfully made our silent way down the back stairs and out through the kitchen unobserved. It took three-quarters of an hour to reach the strand, as the way down is much overgrown now with brambles and clumps of gorse. Also, the last time I had made that same clandestine journey I was not so impeded by the style of skirts I must now wear. I was only too happy to be rid of them when we reached our destination.

We quickly shed the rest of our garments and spread them carefully upon the rocks, timid at first, demurely avoiding each other's eyes and rather shamefacedly dodging about. But such false modesty soon gave way to a fundamental pride in the beauty of our forms, our own and each other's.

The day could not have co-operated more fully with our purpose, the morning mist lifting to reveal a sky of so intense a blue it seemed almost to have been painted with a broad brush; the air was blessedly still, and though the water was quite cold, we were on the whole not uncomfortable.

Anne stood directly behind me while I posed, stretching one foot forward into the water, the other behind, my whole body reaching forward, one arm outstretched behind, the other shielding my eyes, as if I were looking out to sea for a lost lover. Would he not have been surprised to find me thus! Anne, who has not undergone such a rigid regime of stays as I, and therefore has not quite so small a waist, was seen to best advantage lounging on the strand, one leg drawn up, the other submerged to the knee; propping herself on an elbow, she threw the other arm languidly behind her head. A most fetching wanton.

Who, seeing us erectly seated at breakfast, our hair pinned up, our high starched collars fastened severely at our throats, our ties tied, our boots laced, could have guessed that not an hour before we had been disporting naked as sea nymphs on the strand?

20 July

If I may quote Little Buttercup: My amazement! My surprise!

Thanks to both Anne and Madeleine, who have somehow convinced my parents that the far wiser course to pursue with respect to me is that of indulgence rather than denial, I have been granted a studio.

It is, to be sure, a hideous place, a narrow room over the scullery with a strong scent of routed rat and leaking windows. But there are a number of advantages, not the least of which is privacy, and that is all but ensured by the ugliness and coldness of the place. Also, it is quite long, nearly forty feet. It has been cleared and cleaned, an old stove installed, but otherwise left as empty as a cave, and with Anne's help I have furnished it from the attics with unwanted rugs, a couple of large tables, small chairs, and all the painting paraphernalia collected by me and various daubing ancestors. We have also hung the walls with my accumulated efforts, most of which have until now been stashed beneath my bed.

When all were hung, Anne announced that my first exhibition was an occasion to be celebrated, and drew from her pocket two slightly crushed cigarettes. Tobacco has not been forbidden me, for the sole reason that my parents could not conceive of a female person committing such a heinous act. They would as soon think of forbidding me to plunge a kitchen knife into their hearts. Occasionally Francis or Dominick or Gerald will allow me a secret puff or two, but this was the first cigarette I have ever had to myself, and I must say that when we collapsed into chairs and lay back in perfect comradeship with our boots propped upon the stove, exhaling smoke at the water-stained ceiling and discussing various ways of murdering one of the more prominent characters in our shocker, I enjoyed that cigarette as I have few other pleasures in life thus far.

Henry awoke badly in need of a glass of water and a paracetamol. Extracting his earphones, he laid his CD player on the nightstand and looked at the clock. Half past four. The string quartet that had sent him off into a troubled sleep would have finished hours ago. He got out of bed, shoved his feet into his slippers, pulled on his dressing gown and went out into the passage.

He was surprised to see the door of the bedroom across the way standing wide open. Eve often failed to shut doors, coming into the library or going out of the drawing room, leaving the door open behind her so he would have to get up and shut it. But he hadn't yet known her to leave her bedroom door open all night. He moved noiselessly across the carpet to look in, and was surprised again to see that the bed had not been slept in. Yet she had certainly been in there when he went into his own room. A glance down the passage showed him that the bathroom, the door of which she had also left ajar, was unoccupied.

He had come upstairs in a disappointed, disillusioned sulk, sure that, despite what Eve had told him the day she'd hung up on Adele, there was still some strong bond between her and her husband, if not a legal then an emotional one.

And what had she and that Depriest woman been talking about when he interrupted them? *And now that your husband –*

Now that her husband what? Had changed his mind? Was sorry? Wanted her back?

He was well acquainted with the photograph of Martin Oliver on the jacket of the book he'd reread fairly recently when Peter had asked his advice about this new project. He'd taken it out and looked at it again after Eve had told him who she was. The man's handsome features sprang all too easily to mind when he heard her say his name, her voice so full of feeling he had been hit and quite knocked off balance by an unexpected wave of jealousy, a feeling he recognised instantly, having been caught in its clutches before, having once been so jealous he was sick with it, sick and ashamed, but for all his shame, none the less able to rid himself of it. It had taken him years to break free and he would not let himself in for it again. He *would* not.

He'd come so close to making an ass of himself.

Now he felt something very like panic course through his veins. Where could she have gone in the middle of the night, in the rain, on foot? Or had someone come for her? He had assumed that her husband was phoning from America, but he could just as easily have been phoning from the village, or from a car down the road. Had he put her up to something? Academics, he knew from experience, could be just as cut-throat in their methods as the ambitious in any other profession.

Not a suspicious person by nature, Henry also knew from experience that lovely women did not usually make themselves quite so agreeable to him. And so quickly. Nor had she wasted a minute getting her hands on that journal. And she had seized the opportunity of living at Derrymore, snatched it from those other Americans. *I'll take it!* She obviously hadn't feigned pneumonia. That was real enough. But she might deliberately have neglected matches and newspapers — *Good thing I ran out of matches* — and whatever else she claimed to have forgotten. For that matter, it was easy enough to make oneself ill in this wet climate, where a little neglect went a long way.

These thoughts chased through his mind, one on the heels of the other, as he hurried down the passage, round the gallery, down the stairs. Relieved to see the light under the drawing-room door, he opened it, peered round the screen and saw that the phone was off the hook. Puzzled, he replaced the receiver and went to the sofa. The lamp behind it was still lit, but the fire had been reduced to a heap of useless grey ash and the room was quite frosty. Eve, her arm around Penelope, who lay curved against her, slept curled up on the sofa in her coat, Evelyn Hope-Ross's journal safely on the table beside her.

Looking down at her, Henry was first struck by the openness of her face in repose, and then by the fact that she had obviously done a lot of weeping – her eyelids were pink and slightly swollen, and one hand held a clutch of wadded tissues.

The emotional roller-coaster that had caught him up in its crazy pattern of steep inclines and sudden dips and bends now plunged him into remorse. She must have heard some worrying news; perhaps one of her daughters was ill, and he had not even waited to ask if all was well. Completely self-absorbed, his only thought had been for his own preservation, and he had shut himself away from her without a word.

But if there had been some emergency concerning one of her family, she would hardly have left the phone off the hook, would she? Henry considered this for a moment before arriving at the only conclusion possible: whatever she felt for her former husband, whatever had transpired between them over the telephone, she did not want him to phone again.

How mistaken could he have been? He could not understand his own ambivalence, how two such completely opposed and conflicting emotions could take possession of him at the same time.

His hand on her shoulder, he tried to wake her. She could not stay there, sleeping in the cold; she would have a relapse. He gave her shoulder another little shake, to which there was no response, then touched her hand and was alarmed by how icy it was.

Taking her by the arms, thereby knocking Penelope to the floor, he raised Eve to a sitting position, then got her to her feet and held her with one arm while he switched off the lamp. He led her carefully through the dark, out of the room and up the stairs, where he hesitated before leading her into his room. His bed was warm. He would see her into it, then go across the way himself.

He took off her coat, sat her on the bed, struggled with her bloody boots. She was awake now but he proceeded as if she weren't, lowering her against the pillows and pulling the duvet up to her chin. He reached out to switch off the lamp, but she looked up at him just then.

'Henry, what's wrong?' she said, her voice muzzy and nasal with sleep. 'Why wouldn't you answer when I knocked?'

Stricken, he sat on the edge of the bed. 'Did you knock? When? I didn't hear.' He waited, but she said no more. 'What did you – ah–? Was there something –?'

'No. I just wanted to – I just wanted to say goodnight.' This was said with a small smile. But at the same time her grey eyes welled with tears.

'Goodnight, Eve,' Henry said after a moment, and leant forward to kiss her forehead, and then her lips.

She was alone in the middle of the bed with the sun in her eyes and a terrific headache. Waves of turquoise light shimmered up one wall and across the ceiling; she watched until, feeling a little seasick, she reached for Henry's travel clock and held it at arm's length: it was past noon. She hadn't slept so late in years, or drunk so much wine. Replacing the clock, her eye fell on the portable CD player with its dangling earphones.

She smiled, stretched and lay back against the pillow, letting her senses return gradually, letting her eyes wander round the room, the twin of the one she had been using: a large, square corner room with windows in two walls, the same carpet of huge faded cabbage roses framed by the same slim margins of black-painted wood floor. But its walls were papered in dark blue and held only two prints, both hunting themes. Books and clothes, including her own, were scattered over the carpet, and on two of the windows the heavily lined curtains, meant to block draughts of cold night air, had been pushed all the way open, had been left that way all night, she surmised, because Henry would want to wake to those jewel-like reflections of sun on water.

But where was he now?

Gone to feed the hens?

When it was clear he wasn't coming back, she decided to get up, rolling over to the open-curtain side of the bed to take a look out of the window, and stepped a bare foot into a pool of Henry's twisted pyjamas, warm from the bright shaft of sunlight in which they lay. She leapt, as from something live, snatched up her clothes and boots, retrieved a button sprung from her jeans, and sprinted across the unheated passage.

She found him in the kitchen. He had gathered a basket of eggs, several of which he had also cleaned. They sat on the table near a rag and a small heap of feathers. Eve looked into the basket and turned quickly away. For a moment she thought she was going to be ill. Then Henry handed her a small glass of watery-looking orange juice.

'Just a splodge of gin,' he said, 'It *does* do the job.'

Both a little self-conscious, as if unsure of their footing on this unfamiliar ground, they ate breakfast – eggs, bacon, toast, tomatoes – hungrily and largely in silence, but worked together companionably enough cleaning up the kitchen then selecting armloads of sheets, towels and blankets from the locked linen cupboard and lugging them across to Mrs Matt's.

The complex of yard buildings was more extensive than the house itself. Next to the ones Eve was to occupy, another set of rooms, identical – two up and two down – but unused for years, was all dust and cobwebs and cracked windows. Directly across loomed the coach house, its doors eaten away at the bottom by time and rot, or perhaps by rats. Then came the row of horse boxes, most of them also unused for years, their doors shut and latched, hinges rusted; yet over each door was a small, perfect fanlight, panes by some miracle of chance still unbroken. At the entrance to the yard a pair of iron gates twice Henry's height stood open beneath a Georgian arch; a clock in the cupola over the arch, its time once told in Roman numerals, had stopped permanently at twenty-five minutes past eleven on some long-ago morning or night.

Upstairs in Mrs Matt's was a narrow bathroom with the longest tub Eve had ever seen – she could lie flat in it – and two bedrooms, both fairly large. She could bring Lily and Rose over for their holidays, a possibility she had not considered when she impulsively took the cottage, when she hadn't been thinking ahead more than a day at a time.

Downstairs consisted of a small, dark sitting room and a large bright kitchen with a tiled fireplace taking up most of one wall. The ceiling was high, the woodwork painted white; light poured in through a row of windows above the double sinks. Against the opposite wall sat a long oak table, perhaps made from another fallen giant, its surface scrubbed over many years to a pale satiny finish. She knew this was the room where she would live.

But it was a bone-chilling cold. She wanted to retrieve the turf she had stored in the shed behind the cottage and get a fire going. She wanted to see if her car had dried out enough to start. She wanted to go back into Clonmere; she still hadn't claimed those newspapers or paid for her prescription and, in this new place, she needed a whole new list of things. She wanted some paints, paper, canvas. And she wanted to get away from Henry. The silence was becoming a strain; it was beginning to make her self-conscious and irritable.

'I'm going down to see about my car,' she said, thinking to give them both an out, but Henry went along with her almost as a matter of course, though they walked single-file and exchanged hardly a word the whole way down.

Was this simply a natural retreat into English reserve, or was it serious regret for having taken too large a step too soon? Last night had felt to her more like love than sex, he had shown her such absolute attention and care, waiting for her, guiding her, at every step of the ascent. Now she wondered if it wasn't just alcohol. If only he hadn't slipped out of bed while she was still asleep, if only he'd stayed, held her again, she would know it wasn't just something that had happened in the night, in the dark.

But except for her headache, she now felt much as she had before he sat on the edge of the bed – completely confused.

At least the Nissan responded, starting right up this time. She unlocked the boot and Henry transferred all the turf to it. They carried out everything that could be salvaged from the cottage, filling the car with sodden rugs, seat cushions, bedding, then drove up to the house, draped, hung and spread things to dry, then again exchanging hardly a word, went down for a second load.

'Well now, there she is, there she is. Thought we'd lost you. Thought that dirty weather'd sent you flyin' back to America.' After spending the morning with Henry, Mr Keneally's voice was like the sun breaking through a grey winter sky.

'It wasn't the weather. I had pneumonia.'

'Pneumonia!' The shopkeeper's voice was a whisper. It was pneumonia that had carried off his father, he told her, after just five days of it. 'And just look at you, not only up and walking again but looking fit as a fiddle.' It was the drugs they had now. It was the drugs.

Several people had come in behind her, crowding the tiny shop, curtailing the conversation. Eve said she wanted to collect the papers he had saved for her, or at least to pay for them, but he wouldn't hear of it. He took that day's paper from the reserve stack, her name scrawled across the top, and handed it to her. If it was back issues she was interested in, she would have to take it up with the *Irish Times*. Knowing it was useless to argue the point, she glanced round for something else to buy, but not immediately seeing anything and recalling him say, *It'd be a help to the business*, asked for ten instant-winner lottery tickets.

She settled up with the chemist, then went into Logan's for a cappuccino. The dark-haired girl behind the counter, the blue of whose eyes always caused Eve to look into them longer than was polite, seemed mildly puzzled to see her again but said nothing beyond what was necessary.

A card pinned to the notice board near the cash register caught her eye: a grey 1999 Volkswagen Polo, 'used, not abused'. She thought about it while she drank her coffee, then on her way out tore off one of the telephone numbers that fringed the bottom edge of the card.

In a bright new shop that had not been there seven years earlier, it took her an hour to make her selection, fingering the fat silver tubes, examining the coloured labels, savouring the names: cerise, crimson, cobalt, sapphire. She settled on white, black, Payne's grey, raw sienna, burnt umber, cadmium yellow, ultramarine, Windsor blue, and also a new sketchbook, paper, charcoal, and brushes, although – before all work had come to a halt – she had been applying paint as often with sponges and empty spray containers as with brushes. She contemplated the materials for stretching canvases and admired an expensive easel for some minutes, but shied away from them for fear of being intimidated by their professional presence and flooded by feelings of inadequacy. She would have to approach this quietly, sneak back in by a side door.

The young man busy with paperwork behind the counter paid no attention to her until she was finished, when he made eye contact for the first time; yet another shade of blue. He was about the age of Lily and Rose, she guessed; his clean-shaven face had a scrubbed look.

'Setting up shop?'

Eve nodded. 'I couldn't bring it all over with me.'

'American?'

She nodded. 'Sorry.'

He smiled then, a winning grin despite narrow, crooked teeth. 'Yez are not the worst.'

'Glad to hear it,' Eve said, 'I think.' Then, to change the subject: 'This is a wonderful shop you have. I thought I'd have to go to Dublin.'

'It's not mine.' He seemed surprised she should think it was. 'I'm only the current slave.'

'Whoever owns it, I'm happy to see it. It wasn't here the last time I was here.'

'Lady from Holland opened it nearly a year ago. She paints as well.'

'I'd like to meet her.'

He said nothing, simply raised his dark eyebrows so that Eve wondered if the Dutch woman was his point of comparison for saying, 'Yez are not the worst.'

It was almost dark by the time she got back to Derrymore. Henry was not in sight but had laid a fire for her and left matches and a packet of firelighters on the mantelpiece. At first she was touched. But her confusion was such that within minutes she was worrying if he had laid the fire so that she wouldn't come looking for him.

So she would know how to do it the next time, she crouched to examine the precisely arranged pyramid of briquettes before holding a match to the chunks of firelighter and twists of newspaper sticking out here and there.

In the small sitting room, featureless and bleak, were two upholstered armchairs she tugged and pushed into the kitchen, a braided rug she carried out to lay in front of the fire, and a small side table she placed between the two chairs, creating an inviting, and warm, place to sit.

It was fully dark by the time the food was put away, the beds were made up, the towels hung and her suitcase unpacked. Exhausted, she soaked in the long tub, stretching out full length to wash her hair. Dressed again, she pulled on some wool socks, so thick and heavy that not even her commodious fleece-lined moccasins would fit over them, and padded from room to room, a towel wrapped round her head, turning lights on, acquainting herself with her new house, then settled in front of the fire with the newspaper.

She was asleep in her chair when a knock at the door made her heart thud. She pulled the towel from her head and crossed the floor in her stockinged feet, running her fingers through her hair. Expecting Henry, she was amazed to speechlessness to find Peter Hope-Ross standing there, removing a flat tweed motoring cap.

'Hope I'm not disturbing you.' He fished a rumpled handkerchief from his pocket and daubed at a drop of moisture clinging to his narrow grey brush of a moustache. 'It seemed all right. I saw your lights.' While distributing her things among the rooms, she had inadvertently left on nearly every light in the house.

As if the encounter in the bank had never happened, he was delighted to see her again, solicitous for her comfort, apologetic about the loss of her things, the inconvenience, the danger, and, when she stepped aside to let him in, approving of her rearrangement of his furniture. 'What a good idea!' Then, taking in the painting paraphernalia spread out on the table, he approved that as well, delighted to see she was still at it.

His tall, lean figure was even leaner than it had been seven years ago and his kind blue eyes seemed a shade paler and slightly misted, she noticed, as they wandered from the table to the walls and ceiling, checking, from long habit, for signs of damp or dry rot.

'Come in and sit down,' Eve said, mortified by her shoeless, wild-haired appearance.

'No, no, I won't interrupt any further. Just wanted to see how you were settling in.' Removing his cap from the overcoat pocket where he had stashed it a moment ago, he added: 'And to ask you to come to lunch tomorrow. Welcome you properly. Half one?'

She was certain Henry would drop by, at least for a minute or two, but he did not, not that night and not the next morning, and she found herself feeling anxious and apprehensive, even more of her equanimity draining away. The games people play; he was better at this one than she would have thought possible. In this state of uncertainty, she felt disadvantaged having to see him in the presence of Peter and Adele, and changed her clothes three times, finally settling on black wool trousers and a white silk blouse.

Judging fifteen minutes the least amount of leeway to allow a host – she'd always thought it slightly rude when guests turned up on the dot – she waited until a quarter to two to set off across the yard, but didn't even have a chance to ring the bell when the door was opened by Adele, who must have been on the lookout for her and who touched each of her cheekbones briefly to each of Eve's.

She seemed unchanged, tall and thin and so physically like her husband Eve found herself wondering again, as she had before, if they were not related; distant cousins, or not so distant. The same long fierce noses, high cheekbones and pale blue, bird-like eyes, intently amiable. Even their hair was the same shade of gunmetal grey, although Peter's waved and curled while Adele's hung perfectly straight to within an inch of her shoulders. She led Eve into the drawing room and sat beside her.

'Now. How have you been? In the wars, according to Henry and Professor Depriest. I can't tell you how sorry I am about the cottage.'

Before Eve could respond, the door opened and Peter came round the Chinese screen with a tray: a decanter of sherry and three, finger-slim glasses. Only three, she noticed, her heart skipping like a stone across the surface of a lake. Just a week ago Peter and Adele's unexpected kindness would have made her happy beyond belief, yet now the absence of a fourth glass made her feel nearly the opposite and she accepted hers with an unsteady hand. Penelope, who had slunk into the room on Peter's heels, chose that moment to leap into her lap, upsetting her sherry. Much fuss was made mopping at Eve's trousers, getting her another drink, scolding the cat, who lapped greedily at the spilt sherry on the carpet. It gave Eve time to collect herself.

Adele looked up at her husband, who stood with his back to the fire. 'Won't Henry be joining us?'

'I gave him his drink in the kitchen. He's having a bit of trouble synchronising things. Henry is giving us lunch,' he added for Eve's benefit.

To hide her pleasure, she bent her head to the unrepentant

Penelope, who had leapt back onto the sofa and forced her way under Eve's arm. Stroked and petted with unwonted attention, the cat began to purr like a well-tuned motor.

'She has no loyalty,' Adele said a little crossly. 'I don't believe she's missed me in the least.' She got to her feet. 'I'll just go and see.'

'I say, Eve,' Peter said, when she was gone. 'The other day. In the bank. Dreadfully sorry. Running late, you know. Boat to catch.' Then, as the dinner gong sounded a single basso profundo note, he set down his glass with a small thud, as if declaring the subject closed. 'Now. Shall we go through?'

Henry was divesting himself of an apron when Peter brought Eve into the kitchen, which the ancient Eagle range kept a good deal warmer than any other room in the house. He pulled on his tweed jacket over a grey cardigan, then rushed to adjust Adele's chair as Peter seated their guest. This same man sending a button flying from her jeans now seemed all but unimaginable.

There was smoked salmon and brown bread, followed by beef roasted with potatoes, parsnips, and carrots, and peas with mushrooms. Henry carried each dish round to each of them, quite literally giving them lunch, a courtesy to which Eve had never grown accustomed. Used to friends helping themselves from a sideboard or simply passing the serving dishes to each other at the table, it made her uncomfortable to be waited on, except in restaurants. And Henry's obvious agitation did nothing to put her at ease. Each time he bent beside her with a new offering, the platter or bowl shook a little. She in turn rattled the serving fork, the spoons, and flipped a pea into her lap.

The talk was general – the weather, the traffic, the state of the economy, the world – until Henry asked about the Hope-Rosses' search for a couple to help in the garden.

'Rather bad luck there, I'm afraid.' Peter came round with the wine bottle again before pouring the last drop into his own glass. 'Two couples seemed quite suitable, but they turned us down. Two others were quite keen, but one proved a bit shaky on their pins and the other —' He broke off and went to the dresser, where another bottle of wine stood open and ready.

'I *liked* the Mortons,' Adele addressed his back, then turned to Eve. 'But she creaked and cracked, poor thing. She would have been helpless in a year.'

'And useless.' Henry said, hovering near Eve with a plate of cheese. 'Do try the Irish blue.'

'And the other couple?' Eve asked. Having successfully transferred a slice of the blue from the serving plate to her own, she assumed Henry had moved away and, looking up again, brushed his sleeve with her nose .

'Brie?' he croaked, causing Adele's eyes to sweep quickly from Eve to Henry, back to Eve, who struggled to cut a slice of the Brie Henry now inadvertently held slightly out of reach.

'They were much younger. And quite able-bodied. But there was something unsavoury about them. The way they kept glancing at each other, so —'

'Furtively,' Peter put in as he sat down again.

'And something about the way they were dressed,' his wife went on. 'Pointed-toe shoes. A surplus of jewellery.'

'*He* wore a large ring on his little finger,' Peter added, spreading a water biscuit liberally with creamy butter.

'Not that they were *criminals* —'

'They might well have been.' Henry, off duty at last, sank with relief into his seat again.

'We decided to pack it in,' Peter said, topping the buttered biscuit with a wedge of Brie. 'Fact is, if we did take on a couple who proved to be unsuitable, we might not find it quite so easy to dislodge them.'

As if the word reminded her, Adele reached over to cover Henry's hand with her own. 'I wish you didn't have to rush off.' Turning to Eve, she said, 'Henry is leaving us tomorrow.'

'Not by choice,' he muttered.

'The water in his taps froze solid and then exploded.'

Peter chortled. 'Hardly *exploded*.'

'There was quite a bit of damage by the time we managed to

get it shut off. We did what we could, of course, and had some men in. But only Henry can —'

'I heard only this morning,' Henry cut in, looking directly at Eve.

'I know we ought to have told you over the telephone,' Adele said. 'But we thought it best not to worry you beforehand. After all, there was nothing you could do about it from here.'

Eve offered to drive Henry to the airport in the morning, giving the excuse of wanting to return the hired car; she would take the bus back. But Peter wouldn't hear of her 'pigging it out' on the bus. He would go with Henry to the airport; Henry could drive the hired car and Peter his own.

Eve, who would happily have sacrificed the car in exchange for a few hours alone with Henry but wasn't otherwise willing to give it up until she had found another, said nothing.

It was after five and pitch dark by the time they finished coffee in the drawing room. When Eve got up to leave, all three of her hosts walked her to the hall door. She thought she would never have a minute with Henry. Then Adele opened the door and looked out — it was a starless, moonless, frosty evening — and turned to Eve.

'You'll need a torch.'

'I'll get one.' Henry hurried off and returned with one the length of a truncheon.

'Did you think I would get lost in the dark?' Eve said, as they rounded the edge of the house and turned into the lane. Henry switched off the torch, leaving them in utter blackness; they ran into it like a wall, stopped in their tracks.

'You see?'

Eve nodded, then realised he couldn't see her and said, 'Point taken.'

They followed the narrow beam of light down the lane and into the yard. Eve, though holding on to Henry's arm, kept stumbling on the mossy, rounded cobbles; she would turn her ankle some dark night and break her neck.

When they got to her door she asked Henry to come in, then

went up to her room for a sweater. When she came down, the fire was going again and Henry was leaning forward from one of the two chairs, stretching his hands out to thaw. Though full of sherry and wine, Eve took down the bottle of whiskey she had bought the day before and poured them each a small measure. They sipped it in silence for a while, staring into the flames, before Henry embarked on an incoherent apology for his behaviour of the day before.

'Horse's ass. Paranoid, actually,' he said, in the same tele-graphese with which Peter had apologised to her.

She turned in her chair to face him. 'What do you mean, paranoid?'

He continued to look straight ahead, into the fire. 'May I ask you something? Rather personal. None of my business, really.'

'What is it, Henry?' Eve was beginning to find his reticence nothing less than sensational. It made her want to take him by the hand and lead him upstairs, or climb into his lap.

'About your husband.'

'He's not my husband,' she reminded him gently. 'We're divorced. And he's married to someone else now.'

'Quite. Yes, yes, I know. You did say,' he said quickly. 'But what I wondered was if you . . .' He turned on her a pair of eyes so full of what could only be called anguish that she knew he had not been playing any games and was finding this attempt at intimacy excruciating. All his about-faces, it was clear, were the product of some inner tumult of his own; if anything, he was more full of self-doubt than she was.

'No,' she said finally. 'The answer to your question is no. The reason he phoned the other night was to ask me to –'

'No, no.' As if suddenly appalled at the idea of having pried, Henry put out a hand to stop her. 'No need to tell me.'

But Eve, wanting no more misunderstandings, soldiered on. 'To ask me to attend the trials of the two people accused of murdering my brother.' As if automatically triggered, tears pricked at her eyelids. She turned her head and sat back in her chair.

'Good Lord!' Henry too fell back in his chair. It was a minute or two before he asked, 'You'll go?'

'No,' she said, her voice thick in her throat.

Again they fell silent for a while before he put out his hand for hers.

'I'm so sorry,' he said. 'It must have been awful for you. And I thought –'

'I know what you thought, Henry,' she said quietly. 'But you were wrong.' And then: 'You don't really have to drive that hired car to the airport tomorrow, you know.'

'I know,' he said, and smiled, then set down his glass and got to his feet. 'I can't stay,' he said unhappily. 'But I'll come and say goodbye in the morning.'

A persistent rapping at the door woke her in the night. A blue light circled and swooped round the room like some great drunken bird. Outside, a patrol car, engine running, sat in front of her house. Two officers, one male, one female, stood on her steps. She thought for a wild moment that it was a ruse, that they only wanted a way into the house, but she was too frightened of them not to open the door.

'Mrs Oliver?'

'Yes.'

'Eve Oliver?'

'Yes.'

'Are you the sister of Evan Kenny?'

'Yes.'

'Mrs Oliver, may we come in?'

It was her own voice that actually woke her. *No. No. No.*

It was fully daylight; the rapping continued. That at least was real. Henry, she thought, leaping out of bed, afraid of missing him. He must have been rapping for some time to have produced that dream. She grabbed her dressing gown and ran down the stairs, hopped barefoot across the icy floor and pulled open the door. Her heart nearly stopped from shock.

'Martin!'

They sat at the table drinking the coffee Martin had asked her to make while he got a fire going.

Over her initial shock, Eve now felt nothing but dismay as he fleshed out the details of his mission, a last-ditch attempt by the prosecution to bring her to the courtroom. She explained as fully as she could her reasons for refusing, all of them sounding selfish, she knew: she didn't want to put herself through the horror of reliving her brother's murder; it wasn't closure she needed to achieve — Martin too had used the odious phrase — but distance and time; she believed grief had to be worked through at its own slow pace; and she did not believe there could be anything purging or cathartic about even the swiftest revenge, let alone two lengthy, back-to-back trials that would only prolong the nightmare.

'And if they can't get a conviction without me sitting there weeping in front of the jury, they might very well have arrested the wrong people. It does happen.'

He answered each of her points with a cursory nod, as if just waiting for her to finish speaking so he could say all he had planned to say. He knew how much she was dreading the ordeal, knew that she was afraid, but he would be with her; all she had to do was throw some clothes in a bag and get into the car and come with him. There were two business-class seats booked on the noon flight from Shannon to Chicago — she could rest on the plane, sleep stretched out flat if she wanted — and two more first-class seats on the flight from Chicago to Dallas, where there was a suite booked for her at a hotel.

'I wouldn't go if you'd brought me a subpoena instead of a first-class ticket,' she snapped, angered by the implication.

'If they'd issued a subpoena,' he said, just as testily, 'I wouldn't be the one delivering it, believe me. They can't force you to go. I agreed to come because I really think you should be there. I really think it's important. And I really think that if you don't do this for Evan, you'll regret it for as long as —'

'How dare you!' She shoved back her chair, but he reached across the table and caught her hand, holding her by the wrist.

'He was my brother, too, Eve. He was my closest friend. I want justice for him, I want vengeance, and I can't believe that you don't. *I'm* going to be there. Every day.'

She couldn't help herself. 'What about Susan?'

'She understands,' he said, letting go of her wrist. 'More or less.'

He looked exhausted, she saw now. The dark smudges beneath his eyes were darker, baggier. He was unshaven and rumpled from the overnight flight. And he *had* loved her brother. It was too easy for her to lose sight of that.

'I'm sorry,' she said, her voice choked with held-back tears. 'I'm sorry you had a wasted trip.'

'So am I,' he said wearily, digging at his eyes with his fingertips. His large hands, neither sensitive nor sensual or even practical, were his least attractive feature; she had forgotten this. The hands themselves were quite broad and the fingers, by comparison, short and square, his nails flat and — this was new to her — bitten to the quick. 'You really should be there. They need you.'

'I do appreciate what you're doing,' she said evenly. 'But I'm not going to Dallas no matter what you say. So we might as well stop all this.'

He sighed, a long exhalation through puffed lips, like a balloon deflating, and she saw just how sure he had been of his ability to persuade her.

'And I know exactly what you mean about wanting vengeance,' she said. 'It wasn't that long ago I wanted *you* to die in torment and go to hell.'

He looked up at her quickly, taken aback, then saw her expression and gave her a rueful smile.

'And now?'

'Now,' she said, as if considering the matter for the first time, 'I almost wish you well.'

This was said lightly, but what she was actually feeling, sitting at the table with him drinking coffee together, as they had done nearly every morning for more than twenty years, was the strong tug of her old life, like the pull of gravity. How effortless it would be to be drawn back into it.

'There's another reason I agreed to come,' he said, when they had finished their coffee in silence. 'I wanted to see you. When the girls told me where you were, I was worried about you.' He leaned back in his chair, pushing it onto two legs in that adolescent way he had never lost, looked around and gestured with both hands raised. 'Eve. *What* are you doing here?'

Momentarily at a loss, she was silent, then, her eye alighting upon her new purchases, she said, 'I want to start painting again.'

'Good.' He nodded, but in a way that told her he had not known that she had stopped. 'But why here?'

Again, she hesitated before telling him about coming across the photograph, and again he nodded.

'I see.'

But it was clear that he did not see. She knew it must seem like madness to him, her coming back alone to this place where they had been happiest together. Compressed into a sentence, what she had said sounded mad even to herself. She had acted, she saw now, purely on instinct. She had followed a whisper in the dark, a light in a mist, and there was no way she could put this into words.

'What *I* don't see,' she said tentatively, 'is how *you* could have come here.'

He brought his chair back squarely onto the floor and spread his hands. 'You wouldn't talk to me on the phone.'

'Or how you could have phoned the Hope-Rosses' house, for that matter.'

'You said that the other night.' He tilted his head to the side. 'They can't still be miffed about the book?'

She was surprised by this. 'So, you knew they'd be – miffed?'

'Not exactly, but they did strike me as the kind of people who might be less than delighted to discover an illustrious lesbian in their closet. And'– he shrugged elaborately – 'when they didn't have the courtesy even to send a note, I figured I must have been right. I don't suppose they thanked *you* for the copy I sent them?'

Not knowing what to think, she just looked at him.

'What?' He seemed genuinely puzzled. 'What's the matter?'

'Martin.' She hesitated again. 'Can I ask you something about that book?'

'*Now?* I come all the way over here to –' He looked at her as if she were truly mad, then glanced at his watch and opened his hands in a gesture of mock expansiveness. 'Ask away.'

But she found that she couldn't ask. To challenge or accuse him in any way seemed such a poor return for his errand. And having him right in front of her again made her realise that the bond between him and her brother was not the only aspect of him she had begun to lose sight of. Listening to Dolores had put him even deeper into shadow. Now, actually talking to him face to face, she saw that he was the same man she knew so well, and knew to be honest. He could be hasty and careless, overly enthusiastic. She could imagine him pouncing on those phrases in the diaries like so many nuggets of gold, counting them, stacking them up, even perhaps rearranging the heap so as to make the most of them. But only because he believed his premise to be correct. He had his faults, his limitations, but dishonesty was not one of them. It was so inimical to him that when he tried his hand at it, he'd turned grey, lost weight; his hair had started falling out. After only three months, he'd had to marry Susan to make an honest man of himself again.

'Never mind,' she said. 'It's not important.' Then, as he

glanced at his watch again, she pushed her chair back. 'More coffee before you go? Breakfast? It's a long drive to Shannon.'

'What I'd really like before another twelve hours on the plane' – he stroked his chin with a thoughtful hand – 'is a shave. And maybe a quick shower?'

'There isn't any shower. You could have had a bath if I'd turned the hot-water heater on an hour ago.' She got to her feet. 'I'll put the kettle on. You can shave with that.'

As she filled the kettle, she said, for she found it must be said, 'I should tell you that there's going to be another book. Dolores Depriest is doing it. Do you remember her? You met her that year we were here.' She turned to see him standing beside the table, kneading the back of his neck with a hand and regarding her speculatively.

'This may come as a surprise to you, Eve, but I haven't given Evelyn Hope-Ross a thought in years. I've done four other books since then. Well' – he shrugged modestly – 'three and a third. I'm working on Conrad right now.'

'She's going to prove,' Eve went on, 'that you were wrong, that Evelyn Hope-Ross wasn't gay.'

He gave a theatrical snort. 'Good luck to her. All the evidence –'

'They found a new journal last year,' she pushed ahead nervously. 'Down in that cottage. It makes it pretty clear.'

'Ah,' he said neutrally.

'You don't care?' she asked, her eyes on his. 'You really don't mind that there's going to be another book?'

'Why should I?' Again he shrugged. 'New evidence, new book. It happens all the time. Do you know how many books there are on Conrad?' He looked around for the canvas book-satchel she had given him many Christmases ago and slung it over his shoulder. The electric kettle switched off just then and she went to disconnect it. Martin addressed her back. 'Frankly, I don't see what difference it makes to you. What are you so riled up about? '

She handed him the kettle. 'The bathroom is at the top of the stairs. Through there.' He took it from her and headed for the door, then turned in surprise when she said abruptly, 'Dolores has asked me to help her with the book.'

'*You?*'

He gave her a look of sardonic amusement that was a much unkinder cut than any of the things he had said to her in the process of dismantling their marriage. Turning away to gather up the used cups and saucers, she was almost grateful for it.

Yet not half an hour later, as she stood at the open door, shifting from one still bare foot to the other, seeing him off, she found that the moment he touched her – putting a hand on her shoulder and bending to kiss her cheek – tears came rushing up of their own accord. She stood perfectly still, knowing that the slightest movement would send them spilling down her face. Martin looked at her closely, then the hand on her shoulder slid round behind her neck and he drew her head to him quickly, so that her face was pressed against the worn corduroy of the jacket she had also given him some years ago. His after-shave was a new one, she noticed, one she didn't recognise. Then he released her; it was over in a second.

'Take care of yourself,' he said, his voice catching on the words. 'I'll let you know how it goes.'

He opened the passenger door of his hired car, tossed in the satchel, then walked round to the driver's side.

As he was getting in, she called out. 'Martin. Thank you.'

He nodded and raised a hand in farewell.

As the car swung round to face out of the yard, Eve saw Henry wavering liquidly just inside the entrance, his eyes trained on hers with the intensity of lasers. But before she could do or say anything, he turned and disappeared through the gates, walking so quickly over the treacherous cobblestones he appeared to be limping.

28 July 1882
Derrymore

I have been driven mad these past days since the untimely arrival of Julia and Arthur Thornton. Arthur has, for years, inflicted himself upon us for a week each summer but has hitherto been put up at Duneske House, Uncle Charles being his godfather and his sights being set upon Charlotte. This year, however, he came to us and, worse, is accompanied by his mother.

Julia Thornton may be first cousin to Mama, to Uncle Charles, and to Madeleine, yet she is nothing whatever like any of them. She has none of their wit or humour, and her features, I believe, were set at birth in an expression of unmitigated censure. When one says anything the least bit amusing to her, she replies, in the most quelling manner, '*Indeed*?' The portly, pompous, and elderly Arthur (for he has reached the far side of forty), though intent upon pleasing, seems to have sprung fully formed from that same dull head. They have been with us five days now, which is to say five hundred. I see their plan, and it is as humiliating to me as it is odious. How could I possibly have the least interest in marrying a man of so little intelligence and so shallow a nature, a man completely devoid of any spark of brightness or fun? I would feel the same were he the only man on earth to have looked upon me with favour, but suffering his attentions after enjoying those of quite another sort of person is nothing less than a cross, and one not to be borne.

However, as Arthur stands to inherit many hundreds of acres of this island, Mama acts a most unworthy part, seating him next me at breakfast, lunch, and dinner so that I may listen to him talk exclusively of himself. Thus have I learned that he is unable to walk in the vicinity of Buckingham Palace, as he so resembles the Prince of Wales that the guards rush out and present arms. As if this were not irritation enough, he insists upon following me about from morning to night, attached to me like a perpetually wagging tail.

I tell him and tell him that the evening is the most I can give up to amusement, that I must at least have my mornings to myself. But he refuses to believe I can have anything serious to do and every morning I am dragged off to play tennis. I always win, which sends Mama into despair. But he won't take the trouble to play well, and chatters all the time, to the extreme detriment of his backhand.

Yesterday I refused to play at all, pleading a baddish sun-headache. But I had no sooner escaped Arthur when Mama dug me out of my foxhole and forced me back into the field. Let it not be said that any child of hers was allowed to desert the show when there were guests to be amused. Arthur had arranged two lawn chairs in the shade of the old oak and insisted I rest there, that I lay back and close my eyes. I thought I might at least be allowed to *think* and perhaps conceive the skeleton outline of another story. But no, Arthur must talk and talk, embarking on all kinds of huge flatteries, to which I was constantly forced to make suitable objections, and he would not stop. Exasperated to the point of insanity, I threw down the cloth he had put over my eyes. 'Really, Arthur,' I exclaimed. 'What is one to do with such stupid complimenting?' But try as I may, I can do no wrong. It seems he *likes* to be spoken to roughly.

'Oh, Evelyn, I do think you are the most ripping girl.'

Girl indeed!

How I long for tomorrow's return of Anne and Francis and Dominick and Gerald, all of whom went off in the company of

Madeleine to Creagh Castle for some spectacular tennis function and dance. I was to have gone, as was Mama, but she forced me to stay at home with her and my youngest brothers because the Thorntons changed their plans and came to us a week beforehand. Mama had been looking forward to the long weekend at Creagh and had bought a new tall bonnet with nodding plumes that suits her rather well and, as she has sacrificed her present pleasure in order to secure my future misery, she expects from me not only the most thoroughgoing kind of compliance but gratitude as well. And as I am able to offer only a poor semblance of the former and not a shred of the latter, I am constantly falling afoul of her.

29 July

This morning there was devised a really ingenious plan for ensuring that I have no time to myself. I am now to take over the house flowers, which honour I owe to the meddling of Cousin Julia, who remarked at breakfast that she was surprised to find Mama still doing them when she has a grown daughter at home. I ought to have the practice, she said, and Mama ought not to have the trouble. Indeed, it was a shocking thing in a marriageable girl not to have a great facility with flowers. No matter that Mama has always enjoyed doing the flowers and giving over the pleasure will dig a hole in her morning she will find rather difficult to fill, she agreed with her cousin that I ought to have the practice and passed the baton to me then and there.

Desirous of getting the chore over and done with as soon as possible, I left the table the moment Papa put down his napkin, slapped Mama's sunhat on my head, took up a basket, and set off at a trot for the garden, followed by Arthur, huffing and puffing and crashing into the laurels trying to wrest the quite empty basket from me, as if my fragile frame must find its weight too much to bear.

Mama had specified the mauve sweetpeas, as they are always good for a second day, and suggested that five small silver vases of them at intervals down the centre of the dining-room table would look very well for tomorrow's tea and raspberries for the hordes. However, a devil possessed me and I made straight for the new dahlias and, in my anger, not even bothering to cut them but ripping them out of the ground. Arthur stood over me trembling, proffering his pocketknife and making noises: 'Oh, I say. I *say!*' I had dozens of them pulled up – yellows and oranges and scarlets and wine-coloured – before Garrity saw what I was doing and came running from the glasshouse, shouting 'Miss! Miss!' and waving his arms. As I refused to hear, he went straight to Mama and there ensued yet another monumental row.

My misery was such that I decided to throw myself on Papa's mercy, as I once did with such happy results when I was a child, and went into the library without waiting for permission to enter. I knelt beside his chair and begged him to send me to Paris. I assured him he would not be sorry, that I would work hard and well, that I would be careful and live as cheaply as possible and not cost him much at all, as a year's study in a Paris studio would not cost one-fourth the amount of any one of my brothers' school or university fees.

I said a great deal more, but Papa seemed to hear only the word 'fees'. It was as much as he could do, he said, to educate my brothers. If I was so keen on getting to Paris, I should marry and make my husband take me there on our wedding trip.

My husband again, how I begin to loathe the poor creature!

While I was dressing for dinner, Anne came to my room still in her red hat and grey travelling cloak. I was far too happy to see her and far too full of my own preoccupations to sense that her haste in coming straight to me might signify a wish to convey some news of her own. I laid down the earring I had been struggling with and immediately began telling her all, including my unhappy conversation with Papa. She listened with the utmost patience and sympathy.

'Poor dear,' she said, stroking my hand. 'We must get you to Paris somehow. We must see what we can do.'

When I had the decency to enquire about her stay at Creagh, which she pronounced a fine old house, if one with a plethora of overlarge furniture, she did not immediately arrive at her point but took a more circuitous route.

'Perhaps because I am not grand enough to have a lady's maid of my own,' she said, with a wry smile, 'I was sent a rather fierce young girl who laced me up tight enough to break my ribs, fixed my hair with a hammer, and nearly choked me to death with my pearls. And when I escaped and went down in my white summer dress only to see that nearly every other woman was in black – black silk, black satin, black lace – I was feeling horribly out of fashion. Then Francis presented me with the most beautiful dark violets, which were striking against the white, and that quite restored my confidence.'

My admirable brother, I thought.

However, to my surprise she described how Francis at the very outset of the dance took her card and wrote his initials next to every number from one through eighteen, including supper. Naturally she could not give him so many dances, even were they engaged to be married, but he did manage to claim a third of them, and half of *them* he insisted they sit out in the darkened conservatory, where paired chairs shielded by potted palms had been strategically placed for that very purpose. It was there that he told her he loved her.

I got up and folded her in my arms and said how happy I would be to have her for a sister, how I could wish for nothing more. But, to my further amazement, she seemed thoroughly dejected.

'Oh, Evelyn, I was so sure of your sympathy. Did I not sympathise with you just now when you told me about Arthur's pestering?'

'Pestering? Francis?' I was offended and more than a little hurt for my brother. In addition, there is no one I would rather him marry than Anne and, once I'd been made a present of the idea, even for a moment, I was reluctant to relinquish it.

'It is nothing against Francis,' she hastened to say. 'He is kind and generous, and I like him very much, although I am bound to say he is not half as intelligent or as interesting as you are. But I do not want to marry him. I do not want to marry anyone.'

The dinner gong was beaten so fiercely just then that I guessed it was far from the first call. Anne said to say that she was feeling quite unwell and would not come down. Everyone was most concerned. Mama ordered a tray to be sent up and an unseasonable fire lit in her room. Francis was silent but looked as if he could slay the bearer of such bad tidings. Cousin Julia stared at me until Mama, too, began to fix her eyes so pointedly at the left side of my head that I put up a hand. I had, of course, forgotten to attach the second earring.

30 July

Forty-two guests here and at Uncle Charles's for tennis today. We had both grounds going and an immense amount of traffic between the houses. The weather and the raspberries co-operated beautifully and everyone seemed quite pleased, but we were all kept so busy we were exhausted by seven o'clock when the last of the traps was waved cheerfully up the avenue, all but the Harmons and Bessboroughs, who stayed on to dinner.

I saw that Anne was right, that Francis was making rather a pest of himself and to that end seemed to have formed an unholy alliance with Arthur. They stuck to our heels all day, despite Mama's strict injunction that the resident men were to spread themselves as generously as possible among the female guests, of which there were, as usual, an overabundance.

At dinner Anne was put next to Cousin Julia, who irritated her as thoroughly as she had myself. My dahlias, still in prime condition and rather strikingly arranged, I must say, queened it over the table. These offending blooms Cousin Julia — no doubt her nose out of joint at having been displaced by Lady Bessborough and shifted down the table — fixed her eye upon. She did not care for big bright overblown flowers, she said; her own taste ran to the small and the exquisite. She said much more; she had the most amazing amount of intelligence to convey on the subject. Anne listened to it all in polite silence, until the insufferable woman was quite finished, then turned her own lively eyes on those very dull ones and said, in an extinguishing tone, '*Indeed*?'

I'm not sure which of the boys laughed first. Both Oliver and Ben, who had been listening to that word for nearly a week, erupted in an explosion of guffaws. Papa sent them straight away from the table, snorting as they went. However, he could hardly keep his own face and Mama rose the very second Lady Bessborough's fingers began to detach themselves from her pudding spoon and led the ladies straight out of doors with the observation that as it was a fine evening and only half past nine we might as well take the air and walk about in the shrubberies; those who wished could have their coffee on the steps.

Anne and I managed to slip away up the avenue, which had not yet been raked again after the day's heavy traffic, the gravel so churned and tossed from all the hooves and wheels that walking was difficult. We were, however, grateful to see that Garrity had already had his men out with their shovels to carry off all gifts left behind by the visiting horses, and more grateful still for the first opportunity of serious conversation.

Anne was first to broach the subject so briefly touched upon last evening. Marriage is something we have hitherto avoided discussing, as each of us knew her own view to be of a sort not likely to enlist sympathy. We had talked of everything else but left the question of marriage altogether out of our conversations. Now we find our views on the subject nearly identical, although arrived at somewhat differently.

Until being thrust into the company of Charlotte and Henry this summer, I have had little or no acquaintance with unfortunate marriages. My parents are well suited and devoted to each other, as are Uncle Charles and Aunt Emmeline, and my grandfather worshipped the very ground my grandmother walked upon; he was not able live on six months after her.

However, Anne has had an entirely different experience.

Following the death of her father thirteen years ago, her eldest brother, Hugh, who could neither live in the family home nor afford its maintenance, decided to let it to strangers, an

English family who have made themselves so unpopular in the neighbourhood, Anne says, she fears they will be murdered in their beds. Hugh of course invited his mother and unmarried sister to live with him, but as his wife possesses that quality peculiar to the English of not caring whether she is agreeable or not, Anne has spent the past thirteen years moving with her mother from the house of one married sibling to another's. Not only has she been exiled from Ireland all this time, but she has been obliged to observe a number of marriages rather close at hand and has thereby witnessed a great deal of unhappiness. What's more, she has sadly lost all three sisters to childbirth.

Her eldest sister, Diana, was already gone from home when Anne was still an infant, but her drawings and paintings, everywhere about, were most promising creations and the old servants and Anne's mother and father and other siblings were full of stories of Diana's talent and courage. It was therefore difficult for Anne to reconcile this wondrous being with the actual sister with whom she gradually became acquainted on her infrequent visits to the north of England: a mother of eleven children, a grim and disappointed woman who rarely smiled and who had not so much as held a pencil or a brush in years. Worse, between Diana and her husband there passed, as far as Anne could see, not a single kind look or gentle word. Yet her sister must die giving birth to a twelfth child, while her brother-in-law proceeded to marry again within the year.

'Why?' Anne stopped to face me. 'This question has haunted me for years but has only led to a host of other questions. What was the purpose of Diana's life? What is the purpose of *my* life? What am I for? Have I none but a childbearing role to perform on this earth? What a repugnant idea!'

As she has seen very little in the marriages of her siblings to reconcile her to the acceptance of such a role, she has resolutely rejected it. She is, however, more fortunate than I, in that her mother does not try to force her hand in this regard. Madeleine has no wish to lose the sole companion of her life; nor, having lost three daughters to childbirth, is she eager to risk losing her fourth and last. And so she does nothing whatever to try to find a husband for Anne, whose future is left to fate and to her own devices.

She has had several opportunities to test her resolve, Francis providing only the most recent of them, but none has tempted her to capitulate. This, I am sure, is due to the tremendous strength of her character, which I have noted on many occasions. There is a spiritual dimension to her, and by spiritual I do not mean that she is excessively religious, for she is not. But there is a deep seriousness that protects her like a suit of mail; she knows her own mind, she has her own motives and hopes, her own abilities, and these will suffice.

She assured me again that she holds Francis in the highest regard, yet voiced indignation at the general assumption that any woman expressing amiability or cordiality to a man must be actively seeking him as a husband. She finds it frustrating and disappointing that she cannot be as great a friend to my brother as she is to me, that as soon as she converses sincerely and earnestly with him, as soon as she smiles, laughs, or amuses him, as soon as she adopts in his presence an aspect the least bit softer than stone, he must pounce and demand that she marry him.

6 August

Have received two cheques! One for our shocker, of which Anne refuses to take a farthing, claiming she has been well enough paid in interest and enjoyment for her contribution to it and insisting instead that it be added to my Paris fund. I thought a year must pass before I could earn half as much again, but that evening's post brought a cheque for twice the amount (and of this Anne did consent to accept her half) from the French publisher for our even more shocking photographs of each other. We were highly amused at this irrefutable evidence that our bodies are valued at twice the worth of our brains, but jubilant nonetheless at our success.

I am now in the possession of forty-five pounds, which must be enough for me to begin in Paris. If I advance such a sum myself, Papa cannot decline to contribute a very little. He would surely pay my board, as he feeds me willingly enough when I am at home. And I will continue to write and to earn what I can. Anne, who goes from Derrymore to her brother Hugh in London, promises to canvass all the publishers to find work for me. She has already written to the editor of the *Illustrator* to ask if he would not like a first-hand account of the life of a female student in a Paris atelier, and she is at this very moment closeted with her mother for the purpose of enlisting Madeleine's aid in persuading Mama and Papa to let me go.

'Surely, Evelyn,' she said, pacing my studio this morning, 'in all of Paris there must be some one person to whom your parents would not object?'

There is such a person, though it is I myself who objects to her: the last-but-one governess employed for Charlotte and myself, the bustling, brown-eyed Mlle Bourges, who un-expectedly inherited an old house in Paris and left us to become the *propriétaire* of a *pension*. Although Charlotte and I loathed her, Mama found her clean and respectable, if uncommonly inquisitive. When I think of all the tricks I played on her, I cringe at the prospect of writing to beg her to take me in. But write her I must.

8 August

The weather holding fine, it was suggested at breakfast that Francis and I should show Lough Annagh to Arthur and Anne. Dominick and Gerald wanted to come with us and, though Francis remained uncharacteristically silent on the subject, Anne and I pleaded their cause, but Papa, no doubt forewarned by Mama, insisted that he could not possibly mount more than four riders today, as that horse was needed for this and that was wrong with the other.

Ordinarily, I would ask for nothing more than an excursion to Lough Annagh on a fine day, but the transparent scheming of my mother and Arthur's heightened my blood. The sight of Arthur bouncing in his saddle like a pea on a drum did nothing to improve my temper, and once we had skirted Clonmere and were in open country, I fell back next to Anne, whose lovely eyes widened in delight at even the prospect of mischief. 'You keep close to me,' I said. 'We'll play them a trick.'

Moments later I turned my horse quickly and jumped the wall on our left. Anne cleared it a second later, Daphne taking it all in her stride, as I knew she would. I knew as well that we could not be followed, not directly, as Francis had the nerve but not the horse, while of Arthur the opposite was true. The next jump was a low wall we cleared easily, but I knew what was coming. The field is a combination of miseries, thoroughly churned and treacherously softened by burrowing rabbits, and it is bordered on the far side by a high stone bank with a wide ditch beyond it. The slightest mistake would land us up to our necks in muck, and I prayed Anne had as light a hand and as firm a seat as she looked.

With a most satisfying contraction and spring of her hindquarters, Sorceress sailed over the bank and ditch with room to spare, and even before I could look back, there came a triumphant 'Over!' from behind as Anne and Daphne landed solidly on safe ground.

Going to the lake was now out of the question, but I thought of another place, a ring of grey standing stones, believed to be a site of ancient Druidic sacrifice, that lies on the crest of a hill not two Irish miles (a good two miles, or a bad three) from where we were. The riding was easy as we passed at a stolid, bovine pace from field to field among the amazed cows, but the climb was difficult, the hill being steep, rocky and thickly clotted with gorse. We had to dismount and lead our horses, not only broiled by the blazing sun but hindered at every step by our riding habits, which we cursed to the fullest extent of our limited vocabularies.

A female rider, I have long believed, requires a great deal more courage in the saddle than does a male, who need never face a dangerous jump with the added risk of being dragged and killed by his own skirts. And I would like to see any gentleman of my acquaintance attempt a gallop perched upon a woman's side-saddle. This instrument of torture, designed to ensure our modesty, not only endangers our lives but deforms our limbs. I have known more than one elderly lady who came to resemble a heron more than a human, her one leg perpetually drawn up shorter than the other, as if trying to return to whence it came, and frozen in that position by long habit of daily exercise and by the stiffness of age.

We complained of these and other things as we picked our way up the hill. But once the crest was reached, a blessed sea breeze instantly bathed and refreshed us. The place, a wide ring of quite tall stones, has an impressive presence with which my cousin silently acquainted herself. Then, begging forgiveness of the gods, we perched on the single recumbent stone, long and flat as an altar, and speculated as to what manner of gruesome ceremonies it might once have lent itself. Anne is well up on ancient Ireland and finds particularly interesting the contrast between the position of women in Ireland more than a thousand years ago, when there were powerful queens, druidesses, poetesses, women physicians and sages, and our present position of semi-bondage. Women, or perhaps only ladies, she pointed out, are now held to be good and virtuous, but are virtually powerless, whereas in ancient Ireland women were powerful, but thought to be evil and the cause of man's downfall.

We discussed the merits and drawbacks of these very different positions in a lazy, desultory manner while savouring the briskness of the breeze and the sweet scents of heather and honeysuckle seasoned with turf smoke it carried to us as if upon a silver tray, and enjoying the distant view of a yellow field of maize, a green one darkened by the forms of grazing black bullocks, two stark white cottages that hailed each other across a distance of stone-edged fields, and the blue line of mountains back of it all.

'Which would you prefer, Evelyn?' my cousin asked. 'To be virtuous and powerless, or powerful and evil?' Then with startling energy she scrambled to her feet and, standing with outstretched arms upon the altar stone, cried out, 'I am Eve, great Adam's wife,' and proceeded to recite the ancient Irish poem, 'Eve's Lament', a performance as impressive as it was surprising, speaking out without hesitation every single stanza, of which I have only one by heart.

> *There would be no ice in any place,*
> *There would be no glistening windy winter,*
> *There would be no hell, there would be no sorrow,*
> *There would be no fear, were it not for me!*

Reluctant to leave, we lingered in that sacred sphere so far removed from time as to render all present manners and mores if not ridiculous at least of no importance. When hunger at last began to call us away, we each placed a hand upon the altar stone and made a solemn pledge to support each other in any way possible or necessary for the rest of our lives, for better or worse, for richer or poorer, in sickness and in health.

Sickness seemed the more immediate threat as the quickening breeze increased its pace to a full gallop, pushing in from the sea mountains of clouds as black as gunpowder and that proved, before we had descended the hill, to be full of buckshot. Pelted, bedraggled, nearly drowned as well as starved, it was several hours before we at last walked our horses up the avenue, and more than two of us had our tails between our legs.

Anne and I are both in Deep Disgrace.

22 August

This past fortnight, since Madeleine took Anne away from me, I have been working like a demon on another story, one for which I pray to God I shall be paid before my own departure.

Yes, I leave! Papa has just barely granted his permission for me to go and live in Mlle Bourges's house for as long as I can afford to remain, not only because he is finally out of patience with my constant hounding him, or, as he so gallantly phrased it, my 'screeching and howling', and not only because Mama is sick to death of the sight of me after my humiliation and subsequent routing of Arthur, but because both he and Mama, to name only two such souls, are scandalised by the appearance of the first instalment of my shocker (as Anne's name is not connected with it, I did not incriminate her) in the *Pictorial*, particularly by my use of poor old Driscoll's mysterious bludgeoning to death, so thinly disguised as to be transparent. But it is so difficult to plot a murder! Why should one not use the details of one that has actually happened? Papa says, however, that in implying a connection between this murder and an eviction, I have made his position among the tenants untenable. I pointed out that none of his tenants is likely to subscribe to the *Graphic and Pictorial*, but refrained from adding that they cannot fail to hear all about it if he continues his own screeching and howling.

He allows me to go to Paris but refuses to contribute a single penny and forbids anyone else in the family to offer assistance. He says that the sooner I begin to starve, the sooner I will be brought to my senses, and when that day comes he will be pleased to pay my fare home and give me a decent dinner.

'You should read this.' Dolores reached across the library table to offer a faded green file-folder she had taken from one of the elongated table's two locked drawers. 'You could always read it in the *Collected Letters*, of course, but I think it's so much more satisfying to hold the actual paper she wrote on.'

Reluctantly, Eve looked up from another century, from 'actual paper she wrote on'. On wet afternoons she liked nothing more than to sit in this room, reading the journal while the other woman worked: typing or searching for something on her computer, going through the books on the shelves, scratching handwritten notes on record cards.

'You won't have another chance.' Dolores waved the folder under Eve's nose. 'Henry's finally talked sense into Peter. He *hates* to let anything go out of the house. But Henry said, what if the house burned down or was broken into? And this will fix the roof at the very least, Henry says. He's handling the terms.'

Eve took the folder absently into her lap. Henry. Henry. Henry. Dolores seemed to take every opportunity to mention his name. And the sound of water splashing from broken chutes onto the flagstones outside the windows also brought him straight into the room, reminding her of how much she had come to enjoy those long days of enforced isolation with him.

She had been making such an effort not to think about him. He'd sent no message, no letter, no word, though it was obvious now that he had been in touch with Peter, and with Dolores, and she could not conceal, even from herself, how much that hurt. Twice, she'd begun a letter to him, but didn't finish either of them. Why should she have to explain herself to him? His behaviour did not bode well for any kind of reasonable relationship.

She'd found it difficult enough to understand the night he'd gone up to bed without saying a word; that he'd gone back to England without saying goodbye was beyond her comprehension. She'd thought, as he disappeared through the gates, that he didn't, for any number of reasons, want to run into Martin, to come face to face with him in the narrow yard; that he didn't want to intrude; that he saw she was upset and wanted to give her time to compose herself, or even to get dressed. But when she had dressed and he had not come back, she'd swallowed her pride and gone over to the house, only to see that the Hope-Rosses' car was gone.

As the weeks passed with no word, she tried to put him into perspective: a man she had known for three weeks, a stranger who had been extraordinarily kind to her. And he had helped her, helped as surely as if she had lost all sense of direction in some dark sea at night and he had swum to her, held her up, turned her round and pointed her towards land. Even the way he had occupied her mind after leaving Derrymore had helped her. Though she carried each absence with her, each in its own way, in brooding about Henry, she'd found herself going whole days without actively thinking about Evan, about Martin, about her father. If she never saw Henry Cole again, she should be grateful to him for that.

Inside the folder was a letter dated 1 May 1934 and written on both sides of a sheet of notepaper from the Eccles Hotel in Glengarriff, its ink faded to a brown the colour of rust, or dried blood. The hand was small and cramped, difficult to decipher, much more difficult than Evelyn Hope-Ross's hand. And in 1934 Evelyn Hope-Ross would have been at least seventy, a jump that Eve, who was still getting to know her in her twenties, wasn't yet prepared to make. She passed a desultory eye over the opening paragraph, in which the writer praised the beauties of Glengarriff.

Seductive … romantic … too beautiful here to move … a mixture of Italy, Greece, and Cornwall.

That's why Dolores wanted her to read this letter; the coincidence.

They had been to the Eccles Hotel in Glengarriff just two days before, taking a long Sunday drive, over the Healy Pass in the Slieve Miskish mountains, where at the highest elevation they had pulled the car into a lay-by and picked their way over perilous rocks and then sat on the cliffside for some time in silence, stunned equally by the ferocity of the cold wind funnelling through the pass, nearly taking the hair from their heads, and by the view: the green-giant mounds of mountains across the valley and the long silver lake far below. Later, they had stopped at the Eccles, a sprawling continental-looking hotel in a deep cove off Bantry Bay, an enormous cruise ship anchored at its mouth, the blue Gulf Stream water flecked with white sails, and bright foliage clinging to the steep cliffs that sheltered the cove.

'This could be Italy,' Eve had said. 'Or Greece.'

In the hotel's quiet bar they sat at a table in a window and ordered coffee and a plate of scones just as two coaches came to a stop outside, parking end to end by the sea wall, squarely blocking the view of the bay. Tourists swarmed in every direction, most making for the several souvenir shops up the road.

If this were on the Mediterranean or even upon an English shore, visitors would flock to it by the thousands. Yet, with the exception of an invalid lady and a German judge, we find ourselves quite alone here.

The bar began to fill up, its quiet shattered by shouting and laughter. The familiar accents made Eve squirm. 'I want a chicken-salad sandwich,' a white-haired woman three tables away enunciated, as if addressing a classroom. 'Now, let me tell you what I mean by a chicken-salad sandwich.' At other tables, plastic carrier bags were opened and goods displayed; sweaters, shawls, coffee mugs and towels splotched with violently green shamrocks and leprechauns.

Leonard told the landlady that we should like to have a house here, but she said that there are no houses and that if we had one we should not like it.

All the gentry have fled, and everything is deserted. I thought of you, saying how unnecessary it all had been, all the bloodshed and the suffering, when the one sure, simple solution had never been tried: giving Ireland what she asked for.

Leonard, Cornwall, of course. Eve turned the letter over. It was signed simply 'VW'.

You made me so welcome yesterday and were so kind. It strikes me that I never thanked you. I came away full of lunch and tea and hours of stimulating talk. Friendships with women is a subject that interests me deeply. I so wanted to see you for myself. Ethyl speaks of you even now, your humiliating rejection she finds unaccountable still, something of a tragic failing on your part.

Eve looked up and saw that Dolores stood now at the window. The wind had risen; spiked branches of a chestnut tree swung blackly against the grey sky.

'Who's Ethyl?'

Her eyes bright with interest, Dolores swung round, as if she had been just waiting, and not that patiently, for Eve to speak.

'Ethyl Smyth? Dame Ethyl?'

She came to stand near Eve, leaning against the polished mahogany table.

'Brilliant composer, ardent feminist, great friend of Virginia Woolf's. She was an ardent lesbian as well, but Evelyn Hope-Ross didn't know that when they met. She hadn't heard about all the flamboyant love affairs; she didn't move at all in the same circles. But Ethyl really admired several of Evelyn's paintings she'd come across, mostly in the houses of friends, and she arranged for an exhibition in London, at Goupil's.'

Eve reached for the black hard-backed exercise book she had bought for the purpose, and made a note of the gallery.

'G-o-u-p-i-l,' Dolores volunteered. 'Naturally, EH-R was extremely gratified by the famous composer's interest in her work. *And* by her constant avowals of affection. This was all fifteen, twenty years before this letter was written, by the way. Anne had died just two years before and Evelyn missed her terribly, missed her daily companionship and her conversation. She hoped Ethyl Smyth might be another such friend – interesting, independent, intelligent, quick-witted, *fun* – and was delighted when she invited her to be her guest on a trip to Venice. But when Ethyl tried to seduce her, she was nothing less than astonished. Worse, she was amused. She started to laugh, and couldn't stop. 'Laughed to exhaustion' was how she put it, and one quality Dame Ethyl did *not* share with Anne Morgan was her sense of humour, or sense of the absurd. She wasn't in the habit of going off into paroxysms of laughter, and certainly wasn't used to being the butt of someone else's laughter. It was the end of the friendship, as you might imagine.'

You must know what her ego is. And these Sapphists simply cannot comprehend a life without sensual fulfilment, or conceive of an intimacy such as that between you and your cousin, an intimacy that wishes to bypass sexuality, that wants only love and quiet and time for talk. It's difficult for me to say, since you asked, if you were right or wrong or were less than courageous. One feels oneself that if one adventures, adventure wholly. Yet if, as you say, the inner sanction is lacking ...

'This is the letter you were talking about,' Eve stated, rather than asked. 'The one Martin misquoted from. What exactly –'

'He doesn't actually quote from it.'

'Ah.'

'Hang on. He does worse. He just refers to the existence of it, as if it bolstered his argument; an intimate discussion about sexuality with Virginia Woolf, a reference to her having been to bed with Dame Ethyl.' Dolores shook her head. 'Why don't you read the book again and see for yourself? What are you so afraid of? That you're going to find out that he was less than candid with you? Naturally, he would have been defensive. Naturally.'

'He wasn't at all defensive. He was –' She broke off, unable to come up with a word for his reaction.

'Evasive?' Dolores supplied.

Eve fell silent, reading to the end of the letter, then reading it again. It seemed impossible that it could be misunderstood, except wilfully, and this made her feel inexpressibly sad. She'd been so sure that she knew him; now she was not.

'Thanks for letting me see this.' She closed the folder and handed it to Dolores, who tucked it carefully into a side pocket of her briefcase. Eve got to her feet and pulled on her waxed coat.

'I've got to run if I'm going to get my car in before the garage closes. It's developed a nasty cough already. I'll leave this here, or I'll be too tempted and not do anything else.'

Dolores took the journal from her and put it on one of the shelves behind her, the glass doors of which had been standing open. She shut the doors and took up her coat from the old leather chair favoured by Penelope, a once dark green leather that had mellowed over many years to a soft black.

'Wait for me. I'll follow you in and give you a lift back here.'

'Thanks,' Eve said, sliding back the bolts at the top and bottom of the French windows closest to the lane. 'I'll walk. I like to walk, and the rain's stopped.'

'I'll be delivering this in person, the day after tomorrow.' Dolores patted her briefcase with the flat of her hand. 'Want to come along?' And when Eve shook her head and then stepped outside, she called after her, 'Any messages?'

She went from the garage to Keneally's, where she picked up her paper six days a week and bought a lottery ticket every Saturday. When she'd gone in to collect the free ticket she'd won in that batch of instant-winners, he said there was nothing in those games, she ought to play the twice-weekly lottery instead. He told her that he and his wife bought two tickets each twice a week and that they had been doing it for ten years. When Eve, doing a quick calculation in her head, just looked him, he smiled. 'I know what you're thinking. It'd be a tidy sum put by. But you never would put it by, would you?' And while he and his wife had never won any ten million punts or euros, they had between them come up with enough match-threes and match-fours over the years to keep hope alive, which was the most you could ask from any day of your life.

Now Eve always bought a ticket on Saturday and on Monday she and Mr Keneally would compare numbers to see who had come closer. It was a kind of ritual.

Since Eve got no Sunday paper and had no television, Adele – who was going to have the pot-holed front drive resurfaced as soon as *they* won the lottery – took to jotting down the numbers drawn every Saturday evening, and on Sunday mornings Eve would find stuck in her letter-box or lying on her doormat a scrap of paper bearing six numbers exquisitely drawn in indian ink. Another ritual.

From Keneally's she went to the bank to cash a cheque and then on impulse headed for the shop across the way. Wednesday was Clonmere's traditional early closing day, but not all shops observed it and she was relieved to find the door unlocked, though the shop was permeated by the acrid stench of size, something she'd never noticed before, and there was no sign of the young assistant. Gareth, he was called, she'd discovered on her last visit to the shop.

She went straight to the easel she had resisted the first three times she'd come in, seized it like an unwilling dance partner and carried it in an awkward embrace to the front of the shop, where she leaned it carefully against the counter. Then, deciding it was time to stop buying ready-made canvases – *if one adventures, adventure wholly* – she selected some unbleached linen as well as cotton duck, gathered various lengths of wood for stretching, a hammer and nails, a staple gun, pliers. As she was going over the process in her head to see what else she would need, the assistant came up behind her and plunked a container of casein glue down on the counter.

'You'll be wanting this,' he said. 'And this.' He set down some gilder's whiting beside it.

Startled, Eve turned to him. 'Yes, I was just –'

'Have you one of these?' He lifted a broad bristle brush from a nearby rack.

'Thanks.' Eve nodded. He seemed so out of sorts, she wondered if the shop was meant to be shut after all and she had interrupted some work of his own. 'I hope you're not – the door was open; I mean, it wasn't locked.'

'That door is open Monday through Saturdays, nine till six.' As he glanced up at her she saw that the rims of his eyes were red and sore-looking, as if he'd been weeping.

'You know a lot about this,' she tried, indicating the items laid out on the counter as he went round the other side to tally them up. 'Do you paint?'

He gave something of a snort. 'I do not. Only the stretching and the sizing.'

'Did you stretch all those canvases I bought?'

He shook his head. 'Those ones came as they were. This batch is for herself. Six canvases this day. They have my eyes streaming.'

'I can see that.' She could also see what he'd meant that first time about being the Dutch woman's current slave. 'Six canvases is a lot of work.'

'It is, and God forbid there should be the ghost of a wrinkle. Then it's the boiling water treatment.'

'Boiling water!'

'Soak the reverse side and it dries flat.'

'That's good to know.'

'That's the plan, at any rate.' He thawed at last, flashing her a winning grin. 'Doesn't work.' He took her money, counted out the change and came round to hoist the easel under his arm. 'I'll take this out to your car.'

'Oh.' She let her head fall forward, covered her eyes with her hand. 'How stupid. My car's in the garage. I just left it there an hour ago. I can't believe I forgot. I'll have to pick all this up tomorrow, or the day after. As soon as my car's ready.'

'Will I help you carry it?' He brightened at the prospect of getting out of the shop.

She laughed. 'Thanks. But it's nearly three miles. I'm living out at Derrymore.'

'Ah. In with the gentry.'

'I live in the yard, the stable yard.'

'My great-grandda lived there. He was gardener.'

'Really? When?'

'About a hundred years ago.' He shrugged, as if the topic was of no interest to him. 'We'll stick these in the corner then.' He carried the easel away as he spoke. 'I'll write you up a receipt.'

She walked in the road for twenty minutes before being driven into the fields by speeding cars, vans, lorries, and farm vehicles with deadly appendages attached. Whenever two vehicles passed each other, she had to do everything short of leaping over the stone walls that bordered the fields. No one slowed. It seemed to be a point of honour for drivers to pass each other at breakneck speed without either vehicle giving an inch or showing a flicker of hesitation, like some crack cavalry unit let loose on the roads. When a small blue car came hurtling round the bend, she stepped out of its path but didn't see the cart it was pulling – the cart a good deal broader than the car itself – until it knocked the newspaper out of her hand. It could just as easily have cut her legs off at the knee if she'd taken a step to the right.

Shaken, she let herself over the wall and cut across the wet fields without benefit of gumboots. But away from the noise and the diesel fumes, she could at least breathe again, and could think.

She'd been trying to hold on to the idea for a painting that had begun taking shape driving into town, but now that she could hear herself think, it was Dolores she found herself thinking about. Since that first day when she'd come out into the rain to ask Eve what she was doing, she'd been nothing but good for her. It was she who had paved Eve's way back into the Hope-Rosses' good graces, simply by explaining her situation to them with a frankness Eve herself could never have attempted; she had done the same again after Martin's sudden visit. And it was Dolores who had brought her together with the O'Gormans and the Kilpatricks and those other local people she had come to know; and Dolores who had urged her to become better acquainted with Evelyn Hope-Ross, whose company she enjoyed almost as much as that of Dolores.

Friendships with women is a subject that interests me deeply.

The subject had never interested Eve. She had always been so close to Evan she never needed another intimate friend. As soon as they could speak, she and her twin had developed their own language, which not even their mother could fully comprehend. Neither of them had felt the need to make themselves known to outsiders. It was too much trouble, took too much effort, and 'friends', they noticed, often said ugly things about each other; alliances shifted and changed constantly. After each occasional foray into the emotional jungle inhabited by schoolchildren, she and Evan would fall back on their own untroubled insularity.

He had been her only confidant during her years with Martin, as she had been his during his several courtships and a brief, unhappy marriage. Her adult world had consisted almost entirely of husband, brother and father.

Are you all right? Do you mind my asking?

Martin had told her that the woman was too aggressive, that she talked too much; he had refused her invitation to lunch without even consulting Eve. And all these years later she had still taken him at his word, and had fled the introduction. But Dolores, though anything but friendless herself, had persisted.

They had been having a spate of wet spring weather, but there was a sudden snowfall in the night and the temperatures stayed cold enough in the two cloudless days that followed for the snow to remain on the ground, working its magic on the landscape. There was an hour late in the day, at dusk, when all the light in the sky seemed to drain into the snow, leaving the sky a deep midnight blue and the snow luminescent. Eve, who always walked at that hour, would stand at the edge of a lawn or field and watch, full of vague feelings of anticipation, as if she too were about to receive illumination, when all the while she knew she would instead be engulfed in complete darkness, that she would switch on her torch and pick her careful way back to an empty house and a solitary meal.

Yet loneliness was being edged out by something very like contentment. Just as the blank pages of her sketchbook slowly filled with ivy and moss, winter berries, alder catkins, tiny red stars of hazel blossoms, white snowdrops, and with rocks, shells, limpets, amputated crab claws, her life, which had been turned on its end and shaken nearly empty, was gradually filling again, new things going in one by one, each one now selected by her own hand.

She had twice volunteered to help in the garden, to no avail. The third time, she asked it as a favour to herself – after painting she needed the air, needed the exercise – and now most days she worked a couple of hours with Adele, mostly seeding at the moment, in the glasshouse. And she spent time with Dolores in the library, reading the journal and making notes of anything Evelyn Hope-Ross said about painting. Evenings, she walked, worked, and wrote longer and longer entries in the journal she had begun to keep again.

Mornings, she rose with the light to paint for several hours and on her early evening walks she kept an eye out for things flung up from the sea or down from the trees, or new things growing. She'd always resisted representing scenery in her painting, which came more from within than without, but here there was the most extraordinary light, constantly changing, and changing everything it touched, including her painting – she'd done two separate series of three so far, all changing light and colour – and her way of looking at the world. It was as if she was just now learning how to see.

One evening a fox crossed her path, not ten paces in front of her, a plump auburn-haired fox moving slowly and with a certain sulky confidence across the bright space between one dark thicket of bracken and another. She had heard much of the maraudings of 'the fox' from Adele, but this was a first sighting for her and she watched, fascinated, enchanted by the thick brush of tail and pointed-snout profile, hoping for a glimpse of its face. As if he sensed what she was thinking, he turned and looked straight over his shoulder at her, a glance of sly, almost human malevolence, before disappearing again into the shadows. Intent on capturing the face, she walked carefully home, holding the image as she would a fragile piece of porcelain: the perked-up ears, the narrowed, crafty eyes – straight out of Aesop – the long nose tapering to a moist black point and the surprising flow of white hair down its front.

Her head full of fox, she stepped out of her boots inside the door. Just then two brilliant arcs of light swept the face of the coach house across the way as a small van swung into the yard and came to a stop outside her windows; a figure stepped out on the far side and went round to the rear to open the van's doors. A tall, slim figure extracted a far slimmer one. Gareth, with her new easel.

'Thought I might as well drop this down,' he said, a little shyly, standing the easel against the doorjamb. 'I'll get the rest.'

'This is really very kind of you,' Eve said, as he returned with a bulging plastic carrier bag in one hand and bundle of wood lengths under the other arm. 'Could you bring that through?'

Lifting the easel, she led the way into the sitting room, from which she had removed most of the furniture and, the light being no good for work, used now only for storage. But Gareth, having set down his burdens and taking a look around, seemed to find the long room with its tiled fireplace far from charmless.

'Nice, this,' he said, with a nod of approval.

'I haven't been by the shop because my car still isn't ready,' Eve said, as they went back into the kitchen. 'They had to send away for a part. I don't know when I'll get it back. Sorry you had to come all the way out here.'

'No problems.' Gareth's eyes moved quickly round the kitchen, then back. 'To be honest, I was glad of the excuse. Mam's grandda –'

'Your great-grandfather – I forgot,' Eve cut in eagerly. 'Was his name Garrity by any chance?'

'It was. Eoin Garrity.'

'I came across his name recently,' she said, inordinately pleased. 'In a journal from 1882.' She told him the story of Evelyn Hope-Ross ripping out the dahlias. 'So, does that makes you Gareth Garrity?'

He shook his head. 'My name's Driscoll. He was –'

'Your mother's grandfather. Of course.' She tapped a finger to her forehead. 'Look, I was just going to put the kettle on. Will you –?'

He shook his head again. 'I haven't had my tea yet. I'm away so.'

'I wish it was still light out so you could have seen something.' She went over to join him at the open door. 'Why don't you come again in the daytime? I could ask Mrs Hope-Ross to show you the garden where your great-grandfather worked, if you'd like.'

'She'd not mind?' The idea obviously appealed to him. 'It'd have to be a Sunday, though. Unless it's when herself's gone on her holidays,' he added, a little sheepishly. 'She's off in a fortnight for a month in the south of France.'

'How nice for her. How nice for you! I'll ask Mrs Hope-Ross and let you know. But I'm sure she'd be happy to show you the garden.' On second thought, she wasn't so sure. The place seemed magical to her, but Adele was embarrassed by its semi-wild state. 'I'm so ashamed,' she'd said, finally allowing Eve in to help.

'Well, I'll certainly ask her. Come back in the daylight anyway and have a proper look at the yard.'

'Will I bring Clare? She's my fiancée.'

'You're getting married? Congratulations. When?'

'As soon as ever we find a place to live.'

'Clare is a lovely name.'

'It is. Clare Logan.'

'From Logan's teashop?' Eve knew right away it would be the girl with the black hair and delphinium-blue eyes.

'Where I should be these past thirty minutes. She's holding my tea.'

'I've been thinking about that Virginia Woolf letter.' Eve appeared to be addressing the contents of her wineglass.

Dolores gave her a wry look. 'Is that what you've been thinking about?' The details of her meeting with Henry had been met with silence, and more silence. Eve ignored the implication.

'She said something that helped me understand. What she said about – about Sapphists –'

'Sappho, Greek lyric poet – poetess – of Lesbos. In other words, lesbians.'

'I do know that,' Eve said a little crossly.

At the low table next to theirs in the crowded pub three middle-aged couples sat drinking and talking in low voices, the women with their glasses at the far end and the men with their pints at the end near Eve and Dolores. The man closest to Dolores sat on a low stool with his back to her, but at the word 'lesbians', he turned and glanced quickly at her over his shoulder.

'What I was going to say,' Eve kept her own voice low, 'was that what she said about Sapphists, about Ethyl Smyth, really, might apply equally to Martin. Maybe he really did believe Evelyn Hope-Ross was a lesbian because he simply couldn't – can't – conceive of a human being without sexual urges, or someone who would not indulge them. He has never not indulged his own; he's always been a kind of flesh-first person, if you know what I mean. I'm beginning to see that now, from this distance.' She spread her hands wide, as if they would speak for her. When the other woman simply waited, she went on.

'What I want to say is that I think I understand how he might have concluded – since she and Anne loved each other so much and lived together for more than ten years and never married, either of them, though they both certainly could have married – that they *must* have been lovers. He does tend to think all feminists are lesbians. In fact, most of the militant feminists we knew in college *were* gay. And she was a militant feminist, wasn't she? You once mentioned that she was a suffragette.'

'A suffragist, not a suffragette,' Dolores corrected, 'and she didn't have a militant bone in her body. Why are you always defending him?' She shook her head. 'I don't understand it. I asked Henry the same question.'

Eve looked up at her quickly.

'Rhetorically, it seems. He was not to be drawn on the subject. But I wish you'd tell me.'

Eve swirled the wine in her glass. 'It was just a thought.'

'Look, it's not simply a matter of his postulating that she was a lesbian. That in itself is of very little interest to me, or, quite frankly, to anyone else. If we were talking about a contemporary artist or writer, it would be of absolutely no interest whatsoever, no matter how much it put Peter Hope-Ross's nose out of joint. It's the fact that he *uses* it – whether he meant to or not – to explain everything she did in her life. This is a woman who made extraordinary sacrifices *not* to have her life ruled by her reproductive system, and here she is being *defined* by it.'

The man at the next table who had glanced at her earlier leaned in close to the man sitting next to him. A moment later, the whole table erupted in helpless laughter. Dolores, to Eve's extreme discomfort, appeared not to notice.

'After Evelyn's parents died, one right after the other, there was an exchange of letters between her and Anne discussing the pitfalls of living alone, without parents or husband. Evelyn's chief fear was of becoming like her father's sister, the maiden aunt her mother was always using as a cautionary tale: if you don't find a husband, you'll end up like Aunt Netty; selfish, lonely, a hypochondriac, a financial burden on your brothers, unloved, unwanted. Anne's fear was of becoming like any one of several sisters-in-law, women who never married because they were never asked, who had no choice but to live in a brother's or married sister's house, where, if they were lucky, their status was that of an upper servant. They discussed these things in several letters and renewed the pledge they had made to support each other in any way possible as long as they both should live. *That's* why, when Madeleine died, Anne moved in with Evelyn instead of with one of her brothers. But you know what *he* makes of their pledge. He says they exchanged solemn vows of eternal fidelity in a kind of marriage ceremony and seized the first chance they got to move in together. Don't you see?' She shook her head again, as if in sympathy. 'Don't you see how it trivialises and cheapens their relationship by reducing it to sexual terms?'

Eve nodded, wanting an end to the discussion. But Dolores was just warming up.

'Homosexuality is as old as time – look at the ancient Greeks – but these women were a hundred years ahead of their time, vowing to help and support each other till death did them part, despite the fact that there was no sexual relationship between them. There was a piece in the *New York Times* a couple of days ago – I'll show it to you – about how all over the United States older women, not couples, not gay, just friends, are beginning to team up and pool their resources and live together as a way of staying out of those miserable holes we call nursing homes. Some of the women have been divorced for years, others have been widowed – women live so much longer than men – and these days the kids don't take you in.'

Eve felt a sharp stab of guilt at this. It had never occurred to her to ask her father to come and live with her. He had been a widower since she was twelve; he had lived alone since she and Evan went off to college. Being alone had seemed his natural state.

'Two of the women interviewed had known each other since

they were children. Now they're now in their fifties; one lost her husband to divorce, one to cancer. They sold both their houses and bought a new one to share and, instead of being financially strapped, they'll have a nice little nest egg to live on, to travel with. And it's not just about sharing housing or expenses or avoiding loneliness; these friends are signing on to take care of each other to the end, no matter what, and no matter who first. The way Evelyn nursed Anne all those months before she died, planned the funeral, buried her. Anne would have done the same for her.'

She paused to take a long drink from the pint of Murphy's she had been nursing for an hour while Eve went through two quarter bottles of wine.

'It was this comradeship and support of each other that allowed them to pursue their careers. It simply wasn't possible to marry – not even a like-minded man, another artist, say – and plan on living a childless, productive life together. Not only because it wasn't done or because it was believed to be wrong – in the United States the morality of deliberately childless marriages was still a hotly debated topic well into the 1950s – but because no information about birth control was available. They would not even have *heard* of birth control, Evelyn and Anne. They would have thought God automatically started shipping the babies some time after the wedding trip, as soon as he got the address.'

She sat back from the table and threw up her hands.

'Oh, and listen to this! There was an article in the 1870s in the *Lancet* about withdrawal. This is the most highly respected British medical journal, and the article is warning doctors that husbands who practise preventative copulation will almost certainly suffer irreversible physical damage to guess what, and that their wives will gradually go nuts from being used as prostitutes, *if* they don't die first from cancer of the uterus, which they escape only by sheer chance. And *only* if no orgasm is achieved. That's a nice touch, isn't it?'

As if at a signal, all three men at the next table got up and moved to stand at the bar.

'Naturally, married women who didn't want to be baby-making machines took refuge in insanity or imaginary illnesses. But how much fun is that? Most of them went on having children year after year, like Charlotte.'

'How many children did Charlotte have?' Eve asked miserably. A crowded pub was obviously not the place to have a discussion of this kind with Dolores.

'Twelve, but only seven lived past infancy or early childhood.'

'And one of them was Henry Cole's grandmother?'

'Grandfather, actually. Ah. I see your point. If Charlotte had shut off the baby-making machine, there would be no Henry Cole.'

'I wasn't making a point. I was asking a question.' Discomfort had made her irritable. Why could she not not care what people thought of her? What a gift that must be. Desperate to change the subject, she asked, 'What's the difference between a suffragist and a suffragette?'

'A suffragist was anyone, male or female, who wanted women to have the vote. Some wrote or spoke in favour of it, but they didn't man the barricades. Suffragettes were women who demonstrated, marched, threw stones, broke windows, went to prison, went on hunger strikes, were force-fed. Anne and Evelyn were both suffragists. Anne published a number of essays on the subject and EH-R was a great draw on the speakers' circuit. Her standard stump speech consisted of a list of reasons why women should have the vote. At the top of her list was that it would be good for men.'

'Why for men?'

'Good for their characters, make them better human beings. She really liked men. The only thing wrong with them, in her view, was their superior attitude towards women, and even that she didn't particularly blame them for; they had inherited the attitude, just as women had inherited accepting their inferior position in society. If that attitude could be changed, men would be just fine. She was always very funny, unlike most speakers on the subject. Men used to turn out in droves to hear her. They loved her.'

Eve finished her wine and set down her glass. 'I love her.'

Adele had an ailing sweet-bay tree she had nursed back to health in the glasshouse over the winter and had just carried out into the garden. While Eve crawled nearby, sowing broad beans and peas, Adele trimmed the dark, glossy foliage.

'Gareth's mother told me that her grandfather used to bury the family's shoes in the garden.'

'Shoes?' Eve looked up to face her. 'Isn't that carrying devotion a little too far?'

Adele laughed as she always laughed. Her whole upper body shook, but she made not a sound and it was over in an instant. 'Those boots people wore then were made entirely of leather, even the soles, and leather is quite nourishing to the soil. After all, it is animal skin. And the salts from human sweat, I've read somewhere, are not without their uses.'

'I hope you didn't mind my sending them over. I had no idea he was bringing his mother.' Knowing how self-conscious Adele was about the state of the garden, Eve had been dismayed that previous Sunday afternoon when Clare, Gareth and his mother, all in church clothes, had turned up at her door.

'Not in the least,' Adele said. 'They all took such a keen interest in everything, and were so *appreciative*, I rather enjoyed showing them around. We gave them tea afterwards and Gareth's mother was just full of anecdotes, things she remembered her grandfather telling her about Derrymore. When they left, I wrote them all down. And I was delighted to have the mystery of the eyelets solved. When Peter first inherited, I used to find myself digging up little heaps of rusted eyelets. Nothing else, just the odd little heap of eyelets. Now I know why.'

They worked in silence for a while, each pursuing her own line of thought, then Eve told Adele that Lily and Rose were coming for their spring break and would stay for two weeks.

They were given one week's holiday and were taking a second so they could be with Eve for their birthday. Adele, calling cheerily over her shoulder, made all the appropriate noises: how nice for Eve; she and Peter so looked forward to meeting her daughters. She asked a few questions about them, what were they reading at university, what were their interests. Then, after a silence, she spoke in an entirely different tone.

'Some days I think we must be mad doing this. Some days it all seems a bit pointless.'

Eve sat back on her heels and looked up, then immediately resumed dropping a seed into each little hole she had bored in the richly composted soil. She knew from experience that as long as they were occupied, conversation would flow: questions, answers, observations, reminiscences, even confidences. But the moment activity ceased, Adele's natural reserve would seize her.

'We *have* been feeling that it's all becoming a bit much for us. And if one of us should suddenly drop off the twig, what *is* the other to do? We've never considered this to be *ours*. It was handed down to us to hand down to others. But now our son is gone . . .'

Eve glanced at her again, seeing her in a new light, seeing an entirely different person: a mother who had lost her children. She had known that both Hope-Ross children had died; she'd had the information for months, but had somehow never considered what this must mean, daily, hourly, to Adele and Peter. How did people get over such unnatural losses? She imagined losing Lily and Rose and knew that losing her husband, brother and father was nothing to what that would be. Realising that she was staring at the other woman, she stretched back further and looked up at the high arch of the sky, clear and blue for the moment, like a domed roof over the garden, the late afternoon sun warming its walls. She inhaled the smell of the moist black earth, more calming than Valium.

'Yes,' Adele said, as if Eve had spoken. 'What would I do without this? Cutting down, tying up, weeding out, dead-heading, planting, sowing, reaping. It's got me through the worst moments of my life. Peter as well. The work is constant. It keeps him occupied every waking moment.'

She left another silence, and then went on, 'When we're on holiday at Henry's flat, everything is so easy and comfortable, so *warm*. But one has too much time to *think*, and then one *longs* to start digging in the earth again.' Another pause, and then: 'I spend my nights in the garden as well as my days.'

This time Eve did sit back and openly stare, but Adele began to snip more sharply and rapidly, a signal for Eve to go back to work.

'You see, I find nearly as much solace in gardening books as in gardening itself. I go through other books as well, turning the pages, on the lookout for references to gardens and gardening. You'd be surprised how many there are. I write them down. I've filled a fat notebook.'

'I'd like to see it sometime,' Eve said, for something to say.

'Do you know how I started? I was sitting one evening not reading, just turning pages, in such turmoil, so *angry*, and my eye was caught by some lines of verse. "Be still, my soul. Consider the flowers and the stars." It goes on. There's more. But that evening I read only those two lines, repeating them like a mantra. Be still, my soul. Consider the flowers and the stars. It's from a poem by Gerald Bullet called "In the Garden at Night". That's what I call my collection of excerpts.'

'I really would like to see it,' Eve said, meaning it this time. She was thinking of mentioning her own book, full of berries, flowers, leaves, birds – each sketched with its date of first appearance noted – when, mentally turning back through its pages, she came upon the series she had done of Henry's head during those stormy days with him in the house. Dropping another seed into a deep hole, she absently smoothed the earth over it, then was startled to find Adele standing over her.

'You'll have to seed much more generously than that if you expect anything to come up,' she scolded. 'You know the rhyme: "One for the rook, one for the crow, one to die, and one to grow".'

She pulled weeds, cleared new plots, turned soil, dug beds, trimmed and pruned fruit trees. Her back and shoulders ached, then grew strong. Blisters, then callouses, formed at the base of her fingers. Her figure slimmed and tightened. Her skin drank in the moist fresh air.

Wild garlic appeared at the feet of moss-furred oaks and along the walled lane; crocuses bloomed then gave way to daffodils, and the crabapple trees started to bud. Watercress blanketed the banks of streams. She bought a wildflower book and learned to tell the difference between celandine and primrose, then a tree book and a bird book. She liked being able to name things: ash, holly, hazel, yew, chestnut, chaffinch, thrush, blackbird, magpie, jackdaw. She never got tired of looking, never lost the sense that it all was only on loan to her.

She was often lonely, but at the same time was beginning to discover the compensations of living alone. As a child, student, wife, mother, she had never for a single day of her life lived alone, and had been so afraid of the prospect she had doubted at first that she could in fact do it. Now she found there was deep satisfaction and real pleasure to be found in privacy, in having a bed to herself, in being able to sleep.

For nearly twenty years she'd been waking once or twice an hour, until exhaustion finally drove her to taking the occasional sleeping pill, then one every other night, then one every night. Now she found she didn't need them and suspected that her sleeping disorder had never been the 'natural consequence of ageing' her doctor had diagnosed, but a natural consequence of her husband's restlessness, his tossing and turning, snoring, flopping over in his sleep, sending waves rippling through the mattress. With one good night's sleep after another, week after week, she felt more alert and alive and had more energy than she'd had a decade ago. She no longer felt drowsy or nodded off in the middle of the afternoon; the dark circles under her eyes began to fade.

She not only had a bed to herself and a room of her own, but four rooms. She could draw and paint or do research uninterrupted, without consulting anyone else's schedule, without being in anyone else's way, without having to stop to shop or cook or clean until she felt like it. It didn't matter if her bed was unmade, if her rooms were cluttered, if there was a stinking pot of size simmering on the cooker or a sink full of paint jars, glasses, brushes.

Almost by default, by having no television or telephone, few distractions and little company, she became more and more serious about her own work, and as she began to see the difference that long hours and dedication were making in what she was able to do, the biggest change of all came about: she gradually began to regret her past more than her present, began to wish she could have just a few of those years back, and make better use of them.

Sunday
15 October 1882
Paris

I can't think why I am beginning this entry at this hour. I feel
profoundly unlike it, and have not got the time. I have just
written home, and to Anne, and to Stephen Clarke, and am weak
from the effort of inventing big and bigger lies, yet feel compelled
to attempt a fourth accounting (this one strictly truthful) of my
first week as a full-fledged *élève* at the Académie Julian.

I cannot believe I have been in Paris only one week. It seems
at least a year, I feel I know the city so well, so intimately. Perhaps
I have lived a former life as a Frenchwoman. However, if that
were so, I should probably not know the city at all, as the only
women one sees about, aside from servants and rag-pickers, are
foreigners. The ordinary French female is so strictly closeted, so
severely chaperoned, as to cast grave doubts, one would think,
upon the nature of her character and inclinations. The very few
French among the upwards of sixty women in the atelier in
which I have found a place are delivered there each morning by
carriage and escorted up the stairs to the very door of the studio
by their mothers or their *bonnes*, who return precisely at noon to
collect and carry off their priceless treasures.

I, however, freeborn *Anglaise* that I am, have walked twice
through the Luxembourg, have tramped both sides of the

Champs Elysées, have passed beneath the great Arc de Triomphe and have been to the Cathedral of Notre Dame and to the Louvre. I have climbed the Tour St-Jacques and not only appreciated the incomparable view of Paris it offers, but have *recognised* it. Yes, I am certain I have been here in a previous existence, and I most fervently hope that my former circumstances were more comfortable than those in which I find myself at present.

This attic cell Mlle Bourges in her goodness has seen fit to grant me could scarcely be more grim, the only brightness being afforded by a single dormer window, which opens to the north and from which one can peer into the narrow street far below. The wooden floor is bare, innocent of the least scrap of covering, and my clothes hang from a series of nails driven into a wall. A bed as narrow as the grave, a washstand with cracked basin and ewer constitute the original furnishings. As there is no fireplace, I have found it necessary to purchase a small stove, rather like a large pot, that feeds upon a complicated recipe of charcoal, wood and *feu diabolique*. It is said to require no chimney, but that is not due to any superiority of design but to its very inefficiency and smallness of size, which qualities alone combine to prevent my suffocation.

I have had to purchase a lamp as well, the lighting of which requires some five minutes each morning and evening, and a small writing table I have managed, through a series of threats and entreaties, to wrench from Mlle's lumber room. Today, I created another small disturbance and think I shall presently be allowed some sort of cupboard in which to stow my clothes.

Although I did request in my letter that Mlle grant me her very cheapest room, I cannot help but conclude that the extreme paucity of furnishings as well as the frigid temperature of my small closet betoken a long-harboured resentment on her part. I would imagine that many a governess must dream of just such an opportunity for revenge upon a former charge. However, as I would never have been permitted to come to Paris were it not for her 'protection', and as my punishment is no doubt richly deserved, I shall take it like a man.

I was hard put tonight to describe these elegant quarters in my long-postponed letter home. The delicacy of my position is exquisite. It is their own close-fistedness that forces me to live in a state of near-destitution, yet, as their chief fear is that an inadequate diet will spoil what remains of my looks and my chances of ever getting a husband, I must lead my parents to believe that I am quite comfortable, that I am writing in a jolly room by a bright wood fire while digesting a good and nourishing dinner.

I was even more hard put to explain the disappearance of Grandmama's pearls. I had rationalised to myself that the pearls are, after all, mine. I have been told since the age of ten, and by Grandmama herself, that they were to be given to me upon my wedding day. Had I married five years ago, the pearls would have been already five years mine. As I shall never marry, I may as well have them now when I have the most need of them. But it was no good. I knew I had stolen them. There is no other word for it. Despite my guilt, however, I have already placed them in the hands of a jeweller, as I found that studio fees were to be paid in advance and, in addition to my lamp and stove, I had also to purchase all manner of costly artistic paraphernalia.

From the moment I first conceived the idea of taking the pearls, I fully intended to write home before I had slept one night under Mlle's roof and let my parents know that I had helped myself to my inheritance. But ever-mounting guilt caused me to put off writing from day to day and, as each succeeding day passed without my being struck dead, I began reasoning with myself all over again. If I did not marry, the pearls might never be looked for or missed for some years, and with my debts mounting faster than my guilt, I asked myself why I should borrow trouble as well.

But upon opening my eyes this morning, it occurred to me that the disappearance of the pearls may have been discovered immediately, and that Norah or one of the other servants might have been accused, might already have been dismissed for my crime without my ever hearing of it, as my parents would hardly suspect their own child of being a thief.

Therefore I have written my confession. I shall post it in the morning, and then can only listen for the impending rumble of distant thunder.

Sunday
22 October

I went this morning to the American church, which is nearer than the church I attended on Sunday last, and was pleased to recognise in the congregation the straight narrow back and dark golden hair of one of my fellow *élèves* from the studio, an American called Celia. Neither of us looking forward to the prospect of a lonely Sunday afternoon, we took a late breakfast together of chocolate, bread, and a dish of stewed prunes, after which, having discovered a mutual passion for music, we attended one of the *Concerts Populaires*, offered each Sunday afternoon in the Cirque d'Hiver where we heard a Mendelssohn symphony followed by the *Polonaise de Struensee* by Saint-Saëns. A very pleasant and altogether different sort of day than the usual.

As for the usual day, I rise at half past six to feed my little belching stove and set a pan of milk to heat while I make a hasty and all too unsatisfactory toilet, gulp down my breakfast of bread and warm milk, then wend my way through a tortuous maze of streets, a journey of some twenty minutes, to the Académie Julian in the Passage de Panoramas, where I hurry up the four wearying flights of stairs to the huge brick-floored atelier, a dirty and noisy place with a veritable forest of easels arranged in serried half-circles radiating outwards from a central raised platform upon which the model for the day, or the week, is arranged. After a good deal of scraping of easels and screeching of stools and calling for charcoal, bread or tacks, silence falls. From eight until noon, we draw the head, from one until the five, the body. The model is allowed a ten-minute break each hour, a much-needed relief for us as well.

After visiting a number of studios, I chose M. Julian's because of the high quality of the student works I saw displayed there and because of the distinction of its masters: Gustave-Rodolphe Boulanger, Jules-Joseph Lefebvre, Adolphe William Bougeureau, Tony Robert-Fleury. There was as well the additional incentive of the several one-hundred-franc prizes M. Julian awards each year.

He is a man of massive head and broad shoulders at odds with his quite short and crooked legs, but he has large brown eyes, watchful and observant, a sensual mouth, full dark beard, and a charming voice. He insists that he occupies the position of manager only, deferring in every other respect to the masters he employs to make weekly visits to criticise our work. Yet this is not quite the whole truth, as it is he himself who ranks us according to our progress.

This he does by means of a weekly composition on a theme – biblical, historical, or mythological – he reads out each Saturday at noon. The student whose rendering of it ranks highest in his estimation is rewarded with first choice of working space for the following week. Because the studio is so very large and crowded, positioning is a crucial consideration and being awarded first place is therefore a coveted honour, and as the sole source of heat is from a single stove placed close to the platform for the benefit of the model, good positioning carries with it the extra benefit of warmth. We outcasts of the outer fringes, who to begin with can barely see the model, must work with numbed fingers as well.

Therefore, the first hour of every Monday morning is devoted to the all-important work of assigning places for the week. The *massier* or student leader calls out our names one by one and gives to each her choice of place. With the exception of first place, the names are called according to an accepted law of rotation. I have learned to stay in bed an extra half-hour on Monday mornings, for as a *nouvelle*, my own name falls at the end of the list and I need only to drop quietly into whatever seat is left vacant after everyone else has chosen.

I had imagined I would be a lone Irish woman among the French. Instead, I find that the students are English, Scotch,

Americans, Canadians (who, for some reason, resent being called Americans), Poles, Danes, Swedes, Finlanders, Spaniards, Greeks, Russians, Prussians, Italians, and a few French. For the present, I am handmaiden to them all. Until my period of initiation is ended, that is until my place on the bottom rung of the ladder is taken by another *nouvelle*, I am bound by tradition into servitude to my fellow *élèves* and must assist the *bonne* in carrying out all manner of menial chores. I stoke the coal in the stove, chase after errant models, fetch bread and charcoal and perform a number of other services for the general good.

Sunday
29 October

Money is flying from my purse at such a rate that short of a miracle I will not last three months. It was a cruel enough blow to discover that the weekly sum mentioned by Mlle Bourges in her letter was not meant to include meals and that to be fed at her trough requires an additional thirty francs a week. I find I can feed myself at something like three francs a day, which means a 'saving' of nine francs per week. However, it also means that I am spending twenty-one francs more per week than I had planned. And now Mlle rants and raves that she cannot permit my cooking, that I will drive away her other boarders with the smoke and the smell, and that I will burn her house down. I rant and rave that it was her own deceit which makes the arrangement necessary, that she most certainly led me to believe that the sum she stated in her letter included room *and* board.

She is the worst kind of imbecile and will not understand my predicament. She thinks I am tremendously rich. I have overheard her explain to one of the other boarders that my father is an 'English' nobleman! She cannot believe he will not send money, nor will understand why I cannot ask for it. She knows from Mama's letter that I am here with my parents' knowledge and therefore their permission. She is certain they would not wish me to starve. But, of course, that is exactly what they wish.

Wednesday
1 November

I have had a letter. My heart stopped when I saw that it was written in Papa's hand rather than Mama's, as she usually writes for both. No one can dip his pen in gall as can Papa when he chooses, and I thought I was in for a coarse time of it. I raced through his letter, eager to get to the point, to the matter of the pearls, to get it over with, to know the worst, to hear what an unworthy slut he thinks me.

But there was no mention of the pearls. At first I thought they had perhaps not received my letter; but, no, there were references to details which I had mentioned therein and which he could not otherwise have known. I read his letter again, carefully, although it was rather like drinking yet a second cup of over-strong cold tea, and the aftertaste exactly what one might expect from such a brew.

It was chiefly a long account of the cub-hunting season, an account so impersonal it might with scarcely an alteration have been published in *Sporting and Dramatic*. Not a word about himself or anyone else, not a word from Mama. I could almost hear her voice: Write if you must, but you are *not* to send *my* love. Nor did he send his own, but signed himself, 'with all due regard, I remain, your Father'.

This letter puzzled me greatly at first. Why had Papa not mentioned the pearls? Why had he written at all, if neither to chide nor forgive? Why had he taken the trouble to send me a letter, if only to withhold his love at the end? That was it, of course, and it did not take me long to work out the rest.

Papa has always been enormously concerned with the outward appearance of things. It would not do for a young woman away from her family to receive no letters from them. It would appear as if she had been forsaken by them; her reputation, and theirs, would consequently suffer. That is why he thought it necessary to write me. Otherwise, Mlle Bourges would wonder.

Yet he was aware – no doubt apprised of her snooping habits by Mama – that Mlle would not only see but would sooner or

later *read* the letter. I have already twice noticed that the papers
on my writing table have been disturbed, which is why I always
take care to keep this volume locked in my steamer trunk.
Therefore, Papa said nothing in his letter that would give rise in
a third party to the slightest suspicion of estrangement between
us. His closing, strictly translated from English to French, would
not seem in any way inappropriate. Yet to me he managed to
communicate perfectly. In giving no news of home, he has shut
its door to me, and in neglecting to send his or Mama's love, he
has most eloquently expressed, for my ears alone, their extreme
disapprobation and anger. For only I can know how scant is the
share of their regard now 'due' me.

Sunday
5 November

The model this week was a dark middle-aged man I could
scarcely bear to look at. However, my position in the studio was
such that I could scarcely see him. It has been M. Bougeureau's
turn to criticise this quarter year and his weekly visit, which lasts
nearly three hours, is a solemn occasion, greatly enhanced by the
silence attending it, a silence that falls so instantaneously and so
absolutely upon the master's entrance that it is quite frightening.

Until yesterday M. Bougeureau had spoken not one word to
me, an inattention for which I inwardly went down on my knees
and gave thanks. Yesterday, however, he sat down at my stool,
which I hastened to vacate, and looked long at my drawing,
which I had done in my usual way of quickly dashing in the
form, then working laboriously at the effect and shading through
a system of cross-hatching I was taught at South Kensington.

M. Bougeureau uttered a sound like a soft curse when he saw
what I was doing. He is a big man and sat astride my little rush-
bottomed stool with legs spread wide, a hand on each knee. He
looked up to the model, then back to my drawing, then swivelled
round to face me, as if to see what manner of moron I might be.

'You have drawn a man, to be sure, Mademoiselle,' he said,
nodding his great head in the direction of the platform, 'but it is

not *that* man.'

He took up a piece of charcoal, not the carefully sharpened one I had been using, but another, and snapped it in two with such violence that had not paralysis rooted me to the spot I would have leapt, and holding it lightly within his extraordinary fingers, like little French sausages, and making a few sure, swift strokes, blew life into my drawing; then, as if unaware of having performed a miracle, moved quickly on to the next student.

Upon his departure, a huge communal sigh was heaved, as if a god had descended among us, in whose presence we scarcely dared breathe. M. Julian, who had been waiting respectfully in the wings, then read out the week's composition theme, The Judgment of Paris, which I botched so badly I did not even submit it. What was left of the afternoon I spent in the Louvre, then worked well into the night on the article about the life of a female student in a Paris atelier which I am hoping Anne will be able to sell for me in London.

This morning after church, Celia and I breakfasted together and went on to the *Populaires* concert, where we heard two Beethoven sonatas. Again, the evening was almost entirely devoted to writing.

19 March
Derrymore

Not yet ten o'clock, Lily and Rose are both in bed.

When making plans we failed to take jet lag into consideration as well as how much longer it takes to get here from California than from the east coast; they were more than twenty-four hours getting from door to door. Thought we'd go from the airport to the Burren for three days (Adele's idea) and then on to Dublin for four, then back here for their second week. I stayed in Limerick last night rather than have to get up at five and drive from here to meet their plane, so I was fresh and ready to go, but one look at the girls and I could see they were dead on their feet, not only from travelling but from the week of mid-terms they'd just finished.

There was a ten-second delay before I recognised them when the doors at Arrivals swung open and they pushed their trolleys through. Although perfectly aware that they are nineteen (twenty in two days), I always think of them first as children, as little girls dressed in blue and white, when they are now as tall as I am and have developed a similar penchant for dressing in black. Rose wore a short charcoal skirt with black tights and has cut her hair in an effort to differentiate herself from Lily in black jeans and long dark hair woven into a single braid. 'Lily! Rose!' I called out, as if surprised to see them, as if I'd run into them there by chance.

'What?' Lily hugged me first. 'Did you think we'd miss the plane?'

They were surprised by me as well, no doubt picturing the mother they'd last seen in January, a complete, utter wreck. We stood in a huddle, exclaiming over each other, turning some heads. We must have looked like a confab of black spiders, long black arms slithering over each other. We had breakfast in the airport cafeteria, as it was so early nothing on the road would be open for hours. They claimed to be still up for 'seeing stuff', but both were asleep before we drove out of the car park and it was pouring with rain, so I took it upon myself to change our plans and headed back here instead.

I woke them to see the most amazing rainbow. There are often rainbows here because of the constant cycle of sun and showers and sun again, but I've never seen such a perfect one, with the full spectrum of red, orange, yellow, green, blue, indigo and violet clearly defined, or one so bright, so huge, a vast arc across the road ahead that seemed to span miles and miles. Both girls opened their eyes, stared, and said at the same time, 'Oh, my God!'

As they were awake and it had stopped raining, we took a slight detour to see a medieval High Cross that Peter had said was not to be missed but that I didn't bother with yesterday, as it was raining buckets. Took several wrong turnings, despite his written directions, because road signs kept disappearing and we wandered in a maze of extremely narrow lanes until we simply stumbled upon the place by accident. The cross is in a field adjacent to the graveyard of a twelfth-century Romanesque church, which is itself something to behold, though the door was locked, and padlocked.

We stood in the porch for some minutes and just looked at the cross from a distance, which we later realised is the way it ought to be viewed. The field slopes up in the centre and the cross – massive, made of stone and a good ten or eleven feet tall – stands on high ground, dramatic against the grey sky and swiftly moving black clouds. I don't know why we thought we had to go right up to it. Maybe because Peter had said one had to climb a wall in order to get to it. The power of suggestion. At any rate, after standing and looking for some time, we treaded our soggy way among the tombstones to the graveyard wall.

We didn't exactly have to climb the wall, there's a stile, but its two steps are widely spaced and were so wet and slippery we did have to push and then haul each other up and over. On the other side was a huge cowpat – what dainty names, pats and pies, for those great piles of dung – that made the last step quite a leap. The field was, as EH-R had described a similar one, a combination of miseries, sodden and full of concealed holes dug into the rain-softened ground by the hooves of many cows and then grown over with grass, and it was mined with cowpats, some still steaming, though not a cow in sight. But then we had to watch our step so weren't really looking for them. And we couldn't spend more than thirty seconds at the cross itself because from there you naturally have to look straight up at it and the skies opened again just then and rain pelted straight into our faces. None of our coats have hoods and it was such a blinding rain we had to take them off and put them over our heads just to see where we were going. It would have been so easy for one of us to step into a hole and break an ankle.

When we reached the wall, there were, in addition to the cowpats, two cows squarely blocking the stile. Nothing seems larger to a city girl than a cow up close, except maybe two cows. Rose was for pushing them out of the way, but Lily thought they might bite, upon which Rose appealed to me. 'Cows don't bite, do they?' I had to admit that I had no idea, at which point we all started laughing, helplessly. Finally, we just squeezed past, Lily mooing softly and Rose saying, 'Here, kitty, nice kitty,' and all of us still laughing. Lily slipped and was covered in mud. Brushing against the rear of one of the cows, Rose and I both got smears of dung on our coats, which we cleaned off as best we could with leaves and rain. Naturally, it stopped raining the second we drove off. As good an introduction to Ireland as any.

We had to stop the car later while a herd of cows was moved from one field to another. At one point the herd parted round us, the cows pressing up against the car on both sides, their swollen udders looking quite painful. Cows look even bigger when you're sitting down in their midst with their tails swishing against your windows. But the amusing part was that when the last of them lumbered past we saw that it was a small boy, no more than ten, who was driving them with just the occasional twitch of a twig, which, thinking how silly we three grown women had been about those two cows, sent us off into gales of laughter again.

A small thing, I know, but how good it feels to laugh out loud. Especially with my children.

When we got back here, we passed Adele in the lane. She was on her bicycle, so turned round and came up to the car. She was surprised to see us at all and doubly so to see us looking like drowned rats and no doubt smelling worse, judging from the quick step back she took when I let down the window. It never rained here at all today. The girls had dozed off again but woke while I was talking to her about the change of plans and were confused when she invited us for dinner Saturday night. She said she was afraid it would be 'a dreadful bore', as all the others guests would be 'quite ancient'. I tried my best to refuse. Obviously, this dinner party was planned for while I was to be away, and now, just because we changed our plans at the last minute, she feels obligated to include all of us.

By way of an excuse, I told her that Saturday was the twins' birthday and we'd be doing something to celebrate, which made it worse. She absolutely insisted we come and celebrate with them.

When they'd drunk a couple of pots of tea and their hair had dried, we went for a long walk. They are so amazed by this place, by the beauty of it all, I realised the sheer folly of the sight-seeing plan. This is as new to them as anything else could be, and I found myself seeing it all through their eyes, and not only the obvious things like the spectacular long afternoon light and the sea and the cliffs, but rooks, for example. I've gotten used to the ruckus they make every day at sunset and used to the sight of them, the size of penguins (said Rose) and such a deep glossy black, and those long beaks, you forget how it is to see and hear them for the first time, how you keep thinking they'll attack, like Hitchcock's birds (Lily).

And then the grassy cliffs that get the most of the sunlight are blanketed with blue and yellow, wild daffodils and something as blue as a bluebell or a hyacinth called, according to my wildflower book, spring squill. And the dozen or so crabapple trees that are all that is left of the once flourishing orchard and serve now chiefly as a windbreak, are in full pink-white bloom. It was all fairly stunning under the cerulean sky and the huge white puffs of clouds sailing swiftly overhead and the seagulls with their wings spread wide and motionless, catching a lift on the breeze.

Not a sheep in sight, though. Rose speculated that they must have fallen over the edge 'as any normal person would do'.

When I took them to see the cottage, both were horrified at the thought of my having contemplated living down there in such an isolated place, without a telephone. They really love these stable-yard rooms – the whole complex of buildings – and like it that I'm so close to the house. Also, it must have been obvious to them that there was no room for them in the cottage and we would have had to be on the road the whole time, whereas here the large spare room has a twin bed and armoire on each side, the armoires separated by three casement windows looking out over trees and lawns in, as Lily said, a thousand and two shades of green. The dark green of the holly, the blue-green of the spruce, the almost black-green of the cypress, the yellow-green of the new beech leaves, the silvery grey-green of the limes, the jade green of the grass . . .

20 March

The fox got thirteen hens today. Adele, who found them, had gone to get Peter, and we met them on their way back and went along to help. The henhouse looked like the scene of a massacre, which it was, with dead bodies everywhere and the few left alive – including the rooster, or cock as the H–Rs say, which I can't quite manage – running frantically in circles. The fox actually only killed two and carried off a third, alive and fighting, judging from the trail of feathers and blood leading to Bluebell Wood. The rest were literally frightened to death and died of heart failure. Now I understand what the phrase 'chicken-hearted' means. We felt terrible for Adele and Peter, both looked so sad and defeated. But they were philosophical about it, as they are about most things, explaining that the fox is more industrious at this time of year because he has his young to feed. They are practical as well and have cancelled the beef order and will serve roast chicken tomorrow.

While we were at the chicken yard or henhouse or whatever they call it, we discovered where all the sheep have gone. They're shut up in a long, shed-like enclosure called the lambing house. I *thought* they'd been getting awfully fat. I feel such an ignoramus, but first-hand acquaintance with animals has been completely left out of my education. Or out of me, as Mr Keneally would say. *The painting was left out of me, and the music as well.*

21 March

Too tired to write more last night and now there is today and the dinner party. One may as well begin with 'the fox', which is what Adele always says, Peter too, so I thought there was only one, one resident fox at Derrymore anyway, and when the slaughter of the hens came up, I was telling the man on my right – a retired admiral whose name I forgot as soon as I heard it, as I always do when I meet six or seven new people at once – how I had seen the fox a few weeks ago and how it had glanced back at me over its shoulder with that crafty and calculating look. He didn't overtly correct my idea of a solitary fox, but told me about a recent hunt or pest-control manoeuvre in this neighbourhood that got a hundred and six of them in a matter of hours, using jeeps with bright lights to paralyse the animals, which were then shot with rifles.

Another man, who looked a little like a fox himself, un-naturally reddish hair and pointed features, small sharp eyes, said that the last time the local hunt had applied for permission to draw his place he had turned them down because of the damage the horses had done to his fields in the past and because last year the hounds killed a pet dog of his wife's that they'd shut up in the house but had managed to get out and have its throat torn open.

Peter said he had no choice but to let the local hunt through, as he had come from a long line of sports men and women and his great-aunt had been Master of Foxhounds for a number of years. 'If I were a good neighbour, I would invite them to meet on the gravel sweep, and serve them drinks. But, I fear, I am not a very good neighbour.'

'Just as well, just as well,' the foxy man grumbled. 'Butchers and bakers who ride out nowadays, they're either abstainers or drunkards.'

His wife, tall and thin with a long neck and wide, slightly bulging eyes, objected. '*I* thought they were very nicely turned out.' She turned her head first to one side and then to the other, exactly like an ostrich. 'Very nicely indeed.'

Lily and Rose fell in love with Peter, who, because it was their birthday, sat them on either side of him at dinner and devoted himself to them, Lily on his right and Rose on his left. Lily does happen to be two hours older than Rose. Does he somehow *know* these things? There were drinks in the drawing room first. When Adele went round with sherry, she didn't offer the girls any, thinking of them as underage. Then Peter brought round the Martini pitcher and gave them each one, and then a second. There was a lot of wine with dinner and I noticed him refilling their glasses several times, their eyes getting brighter and their cheeks getting rosier. There was soup, chicken poached in a cream sauce with mushrooms, a custard for dessert. Cheese and biscuits. No one ever mentioned the food, which was delicious. Apparently, it's not done. I did it anyway, quickly seconded by Lily and Rose. Adele smiled, but did not trouble to respond.

At one point when the men on either side of me were

talking to the women on the other side of them and the woman directly across the table from me was also at a loose end, she asked how I liked Ireland and, when I said I loved it, she asked what I 'loved' about it. I said, 'The light. The air. The rainbows.' At which she blinked twice. I thought I should add something more concrete and said I loved (yes) the fact that there was still so much countryside, that there were discrete towns and villages with open country between them, while in the United States, on the east and west coasts the cities and towns have all grown into each other, into one endless urban sprawl, and that in the middle of the country the majority of small towns had lost their centres, businesses being boarded up one after the other as people started doing all their shopping at suburban malls. She looked at me in silence for a moment, then caught her husband's eye and exclaimed, 'Godfrey, do you know that in America all the towns are *gone*!' At which Lily looked down the table at me and lifted her eyebrows, as if to say, How on earth did you manage to elicit *that*?

After a birthday toast at the end of dinner, Adele ushered the women from the room, leaving the men to their cigars and port. Rose, who was deep in conversation with Peter, didn't realise what was happening and had to be pried out of her chair. 'What?' She turned round when I stopped and put my hands on her shoulders. 'What? Are we leaving already?' Ushering her ahead of me, I was the last to file out and turned for another look at the table and the room, the only time I've seen it in use: fire lit, candles lit, flowers, china, crystal, mahogany and mirrors gleaming. The ageing men in their aged dinner jackets.

The last thing to catch my eye as the admiral waited to shut the door on my back was Evelyn Hope-Ross in her riding habit and tall hat, the only female portrait in that room. I remembered Peter telling Martin and me that she had hung the portrait there herself, that she had commissioned it shortly after becoming the first female MFH in Ireland or England and had removed a venerable ancestor from his seat of judgement above the fireplace to establish herself there. It was a cold eye she directed at the dining-room door and it was Peter's fancy that it was the departing women who were the object of her contempt and that she was thinking, Accept your banishment, you sheep. I'm staying right here.

He also told us a story circulated by a housemaid of the time – a story he 'rather thought might be true' but, as he had himself left early that morning to return to school, could not know for certain – about how the very next day after EH-R's funeral, his mother, now absolutely mistress of Derrymore, ordered his great-aunt's portrait removed from the dining room, as she did not want to face it at every meal. But not one of the servants would touch it. Furious, she mounted a stepladder herself and, in reaching out to grasp the sides of the portrait, lost her balance and fell to the floor, breaking an ankle.

Out in the hall, Adele directed some of the women upstairs and others to the downstairs loo, a mahogany and porcelain retreat with an anteroom crowded with fishing gear and hung with generations of hats of all descriptions and old wooden tennis rackets in their wooden presses. Then we reassembled in the drawing room, drank coffee and 'talked', after scrounging desperately for a topic, about the weather this year and the weather last year, and other years, remarks falling like widely isolated raindrops, or hail stones. I don't know why; everyone had been talkative enough at the table. That forced and artificial separation of the women from the men after dinner was definitely a custom that deserved its doom. Not that I knew it still existed.

And the smugness of the men when they finally joined us after close to an hour! They swaggered in, full of port and good cheer and cigars, bestowing their presence like a gift, which at that point it certainly was. Godfrey went straight to his wife, sat on the arm of her chair, picked up her hand which was lying there like a lost glove. '*How* have you been?' he asked, as if she'd spent the past hour standing out in the rain. She was silent for a long moment – which seems to be her way, and which gives more weight to her responses than they otherwise might merit –

and then said, to the extreme discomfort of Lily, who had been struggling valiantly to make conversation with her, 'Tired, Godfrey. Very, very tired.'

Tuesday

Lunch with Dolores. The girls loved her, loved her cottage, loved her cooking, loved the Kilpatricks. We stayed all day, well into the evening, and had supper there as well.

It's been raining torrents these last three days. Yesterday Rose bought a postcard to send to her father and gave it to me this morning to mail. I couldn't resist taking a look. It said simply, 'The scenery is great but the weather sucks. Love, R.'

Wednesday

When I came out of the bath this morning, Lily was in my room, standing in front of the dressing table. I have tucked family snapshots inside the mirror frame, all the way round. I have done this all my life, or all Lily's life, and she particularly, though Rose does too, has always spent time examining them, perhaps checking for additions or subtractions. But when I moved further into the room and her reflected face in the mirror came into view, I saw that she was looking not at the snapshots but at the two quotes I had copied on fortune-cookie-size slips of paper and tucked into the bottom rim of the mirror, where I would see them first thing every morning and last thing every night. One is Evelyn Hope-Ross's, from her twenty-third birthday resolution that *no one shall ever again hold in their hands the absolute power of my life.* The second I added just a couple of weeks ago, after talking with Adele. *Be still, my soul. Consider the flowers and the stars.*

She stood there for some time, and when she turned away, all she said was, 'Sorry, Mom. I guess you want to get dressed.'

Have I said how much the girls love it here? Have I said how impressed they are with, or maybe just surprised by, my new work? Of which I have, of course, done not a lick, not a stroke, since they arrived. Not that I expected to be able to work for these two weeks. I just didn't expect it to bother me so much.

Rose thinks I should publish my – my what? My sketch-book? My nature notes and scribbles? While I was skinning a chicken, she was sitting at the kitchen table looking at it, going through it backwards, the way I always go through a magazine, and suddenly said, 'Who's this?' and, 'My God, what a face! Here he is again. And again! Who *is* this?' I waited, feigning ignorance, until she brought it over and showed it to me. 'Oh,' I said. 'That's Mr Cole. You know, the man who was taking care of the house when I was stuck there with pneumonia.' What a fraud I am.

'He looks so *in*teresting,' she said, taking the book back to the table.

'He is,' I was able to say with equanimity. 'He's very interesting, he's brilliant, knows all kinds of things.'

Saturday

The girls went with me as usual to pick up the paper (Mr Keneally makes a huge fuss over them) and to do some food shopping. From the newsagent's we walked the length of Clonmere, the three main streets, as it wasn't raining and they wanted to look at everything and count all nineteen pubs. We were hungry after our walk and went into Logan's for lunch before going to Egan's for the groceries, a crowded free-for-all kind of activity that takes all your energy, as you have to zip through as fast as you can. If you stop to examine the ingredients listed on a label, you get rammed with shopping trolleys. But then, you get rammed anyway. Why is everyone in such a hurry? On the roads, on the pavement, in the shops. I can't figure it out. Why the rush?

We'd nearly finished our soup and sandwiches when Clare stopped by to say hello and ask the girls if they wanted to meet her and Gareth at 'the' pub tonight. She's been as friendly as can be since Gareth brought her out to Derrymore.

Sunday

Was writing the above while waiting for the girls to get home from the pub last night. There's only one key to this place, an ancient and rusted key I would imagine is impossible to copy. I didn't want to go up to bed and leave the door unlocked and couldn't give the key to the girls, as they would have had to lock me in from the outside, so I waited up for them and was at the kitchen table when they came in, reeking of smoke and drunk as skunks, having worked their way through four imperial pints, each of the four having bought a round.

'Lily got slapped,' Rose said, sitting at the table in the chair that has become hers over the past week. She ran the fingers of both hands through her hair, releasing yet more stale smoke into the room.

'He only slapped my hand.' Lily turned on the tap, let the water run cold, filled a glass, drank it down, and filled another. She sank into one of the easy chairs. 'How was *I* supposed to know?'

'Know what?' I said. 'What are you talking about? Who slapped you?'

'The bartender,' Rose answered for her. 'Or whatever he's called.'

'Well, when it was my round, he filled two of our glasses and put them up on that little shelf,' Lily said. 'I thought he was finished, so I picked them up, and he swung around with this paddle thing and whacked my hand.'

'He told her not to fuck with the process,' Rose said, and started laughing.

'He did,' Lily said gravely. 'That's exactly what he said.'

They seem so young to me, so awfully young, and when I think that I was not much older when I was married and on my way to becoming their mother, it makes me want to do something to save them from making the same mistake. I want them to have a clear idea of who they are before they marry, or at least an idea of who they want to be, an idea that won't be lost in a 'we'. I lay awake for a long while thinking about them.

Drifting off to sleep, a much more useful fairy tale than the one I was told came to mind, a tale in which it is the kiss of the Prince Charming that puts the princess to sleep, for years and years, until she gets a rude awakening and opens her eyes to find that she is someone else, and alone.

Of course, I know I can save them from nothing.

Tuesday

Rose invited me to take a walk with her and said again how good I look – 'You may have forgotten that you're Irish, but your skin remembers' – and said, again, how much she loves it here, 'and not only because of how good it is for you', which touched me to the heart, but because she herself feels so at home. Her exact words: 'How is it possible to feel you're coming home to a place where you've never been before?'

Wednesday

Dolores came for a 'farewell' spaghetti dinner and elicited the very useful information from the girls that they would really rather stay here than spend their last few days in Dublin, which was probably what Rose was leading up to yesterday but never got around to saying. They really want to see Dublin but don't want to leave here. So our plans for setting off tomorrow were abandoned. I really have to go to Dublin to track down several paintings and have them photographed, but I'll go on my own after taking the girls to the airport.

As usual with Dolores, the conversation worked its way round to Evelyn Hope-Ross. She must be a good teacher, the way she was able to sketch in some incredibly complicated Irish history while telling the girls about her and her life here after her brother was killed, surrendering with grace everything that was asked for: horses, guns, bicycles, silver, food. And how, after a brief spate of getting on her feet financially, by breeding horses and selling them in America through her friend Celia, there came wwii and the horses could no longer be shipped, and how the

London warehouse where her publishers stored her books was bombed and all copies were destroyed and nothing could be reprinted until after the war, by which time people had lost interest in her and her whole 'politically incorrect' world, and how, with no royalties coming in, she'd turned to gardening and selling the produce in the village, and how, when the war finally ended, Peter's parents arrived to dispossess her.

When she left, she exchanged addresses and phone numbers with the girls and promised to take them out to lunch or dinner next October, when she'll be in San Francisco for a conference. They seemed genuinely pleased. Not as pleased as I was when she took the journal out of her attaché case and said, 'Thought you might be missing this.'

Sunday
12 November 1882
Paris

It seems to have become my habit to write only on Sundays, my other days being so full. We work until five o'clock, although the light – which at best comes to us sifted through a smoky fog – goes soon after four. We pack our belongings into our *cartons*, wash our hands and faces by turn at a single zinc-lined trough, and throw off our dirty calico smocks. Then, for those of us who must find our own way, there is a mad dash through the darkened streets, where the gas lamps cast an eerie yellow glow on the wet and treacherous cobbles and shadowy figures glide silently past. Celia, who rushes away in the opposite direction, taught me the trick of throwing a shawl over my head for these dark homeward journeys. In this disguise of a true *paysanne*, I have yet to be molested.

I grab up an unidentifiable lump of meat from a butcher's stall along the way and burn it to a cinder on my stove, not a very nourishing or even tasty dinner, yet an oddly satisfying one, because I have bought it with my own earnings and cooked it myself on a fire of my own making. After nearly a quarter of a century of four strictly regulated meals each day, this hand-to-mouth sort of dining has the flavour of a perpetual picnic. I only hope I will feel the same when the time comes to choose between buying day-old bread to eat and fresh bread with which to clean my drawings.

As for employment, in addition to my journalism, to which I faithfully devote all my evenings and most of my nights, I have now found a Sunday job as organist at the American church, which was strangely silent last week due to the sudden and quite serious illness of the man who has occupied that post for some twenty years. Celia was nothing less than astonished when I accosted the vicar in the vestibule after the service and offered myself as a substitute. He seemed inordinately relieved and asked me to return the next morning to play for him, but as I said that I would not have a free moment until Saturday afternoon, he agreed to hear me then and there.

Rev. Peterson was enough satisfied with my performance to offer me the position at five francs per week, which is just one franc more than the studio model earns for three hours of posing. And I must practise, while she need not. However, I shall reserve that occupation for an even rainier day than this has been. It has, in fact, rained the entire week. Sixty-three dripping umbrellas have hung daily from the backs of sixty-three easels, treacherously puddling the dirty floor so that all our skirts are hemmed in mud.

I have commandeered for purposes of rehearsal the old piano M. Julian keeps at the back of the studio for the occasional fête held by his students. Each time work ceases for the ten minutes' rest allowed the model every hour, I fly to the piano and wrench a Sunday hymn from the battered keyboard. Celia says I am generally believed to have been seized by a sudden religious fervour.

This opinion was no doubt fortified yesterday by the speed with which I completed this week's composition. The subject read out was the Conversion of St Paul, which I did not have to struggle hour upon hour to bring forth by means of inward vision. I had only to close my eyes to see the same theme depicted in the side window of our church in Clonmere, the memorial window commissioned by Papa upon his own father's death, the very window at which I have spent hundreds of hours gazing while being bored to stone by the sermon. I closed my eyes and looked at it again for several minutes, then took up my charcoal and sketched for thirty. Thus it was not yet one o'clock when I found myself a free woman.

· Our 'free' time, we are told, should be spent in attending lectures on anatomy, perspective, or archaeology, in visiting the Louvre and Luxembourg galleries to study the Old Masters, or in library research that will assist us in producing our weekly compositions. I usually choose to visit the Louvre and today paid my fourth visit, not to study the Old Masters but to study the young artists at work copying the Old Masters, for this I think will be an excellent subject for the illustration to accompany the last instalment of my article on the life of female art students in Paris.

Coming upon an industrious-looking group of half a dozen young women at work before Titian's *Man with the Glove*, I stationed myself nearby, although slightly behind them so as not to attract their attention, and began to sketch the copyists as they copied. I worked for several hours, as diligently as they, making a series of sketches, at last catching one young woman stretching her arms and yawning at the ceiling. This was exactly what I was after, as I wish to convey the tedium of the copyists' hard work, as well as its difficulty.

When I had done all I could for the day, I too felt the necessity to stretch my numbed arms, and was quite unable to suppress a yawn. I was then taken aback to find myself the object of another's scrutiny. A man, nondescript and of uncertain age, sketching with a pencil in a large leather-bound notebook, had positioned himself just behind me. As I swung round and faced him down, he snapped his notebook shut and with the slightest of bows, a mere inclination of the head, took himself off.

Why should the observer mind so very much to find herself observed? Nevertheless, she did.

Monday
20 November

Arriving at the studio this morning, late as usual on Mondays, I was surprised to find that bedlam still reigned. Not a single student had yet chosen her place. My fellow *élèves* milled about in a riotous throng, gesticulating and talking. The moment I was seen a shout went up, my arms were seized and I was led, nearly dragged, to the front of the room to M. Julian, who held in his hands my composition of the Conversion of St Paul.

Not only did I win first choice of place for this week, but I was informed with great ceremony that my composition was to be *accrochée sur le mur,* an even greater honour, for only two or three drawings each year are chosen to be hung. Since my arrival not one had been added to those which helped persuade me to choose the Académie Julian when I was searching for a studio. So it was with the greatest confusion of pleasure and embarrassment and pride that I accepted the congratulations of M. Julian and my most generous rivals and quickly chose the place I have coveted throughout the past month.

How elated I am (and also cast down) by trifles! I was awarded a certain lowly rush-bottomed stool in a dirty, noisy, crowded room rank with pernicious air. Yet I was as gratified as any queen ascending her throne.

Upon returning to my room, I found two letters waiting. Aunt Emmeline writes quite sternly that Mama has not been at all well of late and that she and Uncle Charles urge me to plan on remaining at home after Christmas and to make my arrangements here accordingly.

As if I could afford, financially or otherwise, to go home for Christmas!

Stephen Clarke writes that he must come to Paris early in the new year for an article he is working up for the *Magazine of Art*, and that he particularly wishes to speak to me upon a matter of some importance.

Sunday
10 December

How cold and dark Paris is in the winter. How I long for a breath of fresh Irish air and a glimpse of the high, swiftly moving island sky. Here the winter sky is oppressively low and grey, and always the same, day after day, week after week.

Celia left on Friday to return to Philadelphia for Christmas and for her sister's wedding, cleverly scheduled for the 27th of this month in order to entice her home by means of a double lure. I nearly wept when I saw her off at the boat train. Not only because I shall miss her, although I certainly shall, but because it had just occurred to me that her ship will pass, is perhaps passing even as I write, close to my beloved Irish shore and that the trees and roofs of Derrymore will be well within her view.

The thought added much to the loneliness I felt at her departure. I was in fact suddenly quite dejected and, when her train had pulled away, I sought a bench upon which to collect myself and secure a few moments' rest before joining the throng at the taxi stand for the bone-rattling journey from the Gare du Nord back to this more habitable part of Paris. It was no easy work to find a place to sit and I was not seated two moments when a man came to a halt before me and demanded, rather gruffly, '*Que faites-vous ici, Mademoiselle?*'

I looked up, startled. Who could possibly presume the right to know what I was doing there? My surprise was great indeed to find myself looking up at none other than M. Bougeureau. Naturally, I got to my feet quickly enough and told him that I'd come to see my friend off on the boat train, which had just left, and was now awaiting the arrival of energy sufficient to the task of securing a taxi.

'You are unaccompanied, Mademoiselle?' He seemed nothing less than astounded.

Thinking my accent at fault – had I perhaps conveyed the impression that I had been abandoned? – I repeated more slowly that I had come with my friend, Celia, the American student whose work he so admired.

'And now, you are alone?' As this was clearly much more a condemnation than a question, I did not answer.

The master then ordered me to speak to no one until his return, a matter of several minutes, at which time he escorted me briskly through the crowded interior to the open door of a *fiacre* standing outside. As the carriage was already occupied by three women dressed in the black crepe of mourning, I drew back. But M. Bougeureau is not inclined to tolerate insubordination, so I complied. He handed me inside and demanded my address, which information he relayed to the driver, shutting the door, quite firmly, after me. Unable to allow a young woman to return alone to her *pension*, and deeming it highly improper to see her there himself, he had secured for me the company of three black widows. Never have I travelled in such dour company for such a duration of time. I looked out at the rain and the night the entire way, for the women addressed not one word to me, although they scrutinised my person most mercilessly and whispered and hissed among themselves. I understood very little of their strange dialect. One phrase, however, was clear. *Singulières femmes, ces Anglaises!*

On another day, in another mood, I might have found the experience amusing, however it only increased my feeling of isolation. I wish more than I can say that, like Celia, I could risk going home for Christmas, especially if Mama is truly unwell. But I dare not go, not only because I cannot spare the fare, but because I *know* that once home all things will conspire to keep me from returning to Paris. They may have gone so far as to find a husband for me, and it is all a ruse about Mama's illness. She *cannot* be very ill. I refuse to believe it. She has always had the constitution of a horse. However, I do believe her to be perfectly capable of deliberately *making* herself ill if she thinks that is the speediest way of accomplishing her own ends.

Sunday
17 December

Never has anyone felt a bigger fool than I do at this moment.

Yesterday I received another two letters, a second one from Stephen Clarke and one from Anne, but did not read either until this evening, not because I did not have time, although I have been much occupied, nor because I had no expectation of pleasure to be derived from them. Quite the contrary, I was so looking forward to the pleasure to be afforded by these two communications that I was moved to postpone opening them until today, when I would read and enjoy them at what otherwise promised to be a lonely Sunday lunch. Until then, mere possession of them, and anticipation of reading them, would suffice.

However, I did not read the letters at lunch because I had greedily ordered up another bit of solace for myself in the form of a shapely slice of veal pâté, into which had been inserted several generous slivers of black truffle, and also because I had still the pleasure of the concert ahead of me, while beyond that the hours of the evening stretched a barren wasteland. Therefore, I carried my letters still unopened to the concert, after which I walked along the Seine for some time, despite the fog and the bitter cold, appreciating the impressive length of the Louvre opposite and the majesty of Notre Dame rising out of the mists ahead.

It was only after consuming my simple supper of toast and hot chocolate that I gave myself up to the long-awaited pleasure of reading my letters. I opened Anne's first and found a cheque from the *Illustrator,* which, I quickly calculated will translate roughly into another three months in Paris. I was beside myself with joy until I read the letter and discovered that only half that amount is in payment for the last-but-one instalment of the article I am writing about the women's atelier. The second half represents advance payment for an illustrated article on the subject of what one must do in order to exhibit a picture in the Salon. This somewhat tempered my joy, for in order to produce such an article I must first produce a picture good enough to be accepted by the Salon jury. Only then will I be able to provide the details of Receiving Day and Varnishing Day and all the rest.

However, Anne says I must return the money only if I choose not to write the article. If I do manage to have a picture accepted and do write an honest account of the process, the editor agrees to forfeit the advance should he refuse my finished piece. Rare and noble girl! What efforts she has made on my behalf she barely hints at. She herself has contracted for a series of political articles for the *Illustrated London News* and, always on the lookout for opportunities for me, has suggested I might do something in the way of caricature for them. She writes that caricature is in vogue in London just now, and she has therefore shown the editor of the *Illustrated* some of the marginal illustrations in my letters to her. These have highly amused him, she says, particularly those of Rev. Peterson and the sanctimonious young woman with whom he is infatuated. My post as organist has afforded me a rare vantage point for viewing this entertaining courtship. If I could tell a little story on such a subject in, say, six frames, Anne assures me of receiving a most sympathetic consideration.

I next read Stephen Clarke's letter and was as horrified by it as I had been gratified by Anne's. It was a single sheet containing the brief message that he had found it necessary to come to Paris much sooner than he had expected in order to accommodate the schedule of the painter about whom he is writing his article for the *Magazine of Art* and that he would call upon me at two o'clock on Sunday, the 17th. Today.

I was so stunned by this information I did not move for some minutes. Then, suddenly galvanised, I flew down the stairs and hammered on Mlle Bourges's door, rousing her and nearly everyone else in the house. She was (quite rightly) angry and sulky and in no hurry to answer my questions. But, yes, an 'English' gentleman had indeed called for me. He had waited in the parlour for upwards of two hours, necessitating the offer of some refreshment, which offer, accepted by him, would result in a one-franc surcharge being added to the weekly charge for my room.

'Did he say nothing?' I demanded. 'Did he leave no message for me?'

She thereupon regarded me in silence for some moments, assessing my extreme agitation. 'And your parents?' she asked, in the most arch manner. 'They are acquainted with this gentleman? He calls upon you with their permission?' But she must have seen murder in my eye, for she soon capitulated.

'He asked if you had received a letter from London on Saturday. I answered that you had received two. At this the gentleman said that, should you desire to communicate with him, he might be found at the Hôtel de Mont Blanc.'

With that, Mlle retreated, shutting her door with a noise that shook the house. I crept miserably back to my attic. I had only myself to blame, my childish, if not indeed sybaritic, desire to prolong my own gratification. Never have I been so mortified, nor felt such an utter imbecile. Sleep, of course, is out of the question this night, as is any meaningful work. I am haunted by the image of my old friend waiting two hours in that odious parlour, while I traipsed about Paris carrying his unopened letter. What's worse, I must wait until the afternoon to find the Hôtel de Mont Blanc, as to be late at the studio tomorrow morning, now that I have risen so high in the ranks, would mean loss of a choice of place for the entire week to come. However, so as not to lose any more time, I shall be bold enough to call at the hotel myself rather than send a note.

Sunday
24 December

This has been the longest week of my life thus far, a trek through Purgatory and into the other place.

At the dinner break on Monday I hurried to the Hôtel de Mont Blanc, only to learn that Stephen Clarke had given up his room not an hour before. If my disappointment was great, my chagrin was greater still; for again I had only myself to blame. If

I had not been loath to lose my wretched place, I would have gone straight to the hotel before going to the studio. I could have left a message at the desk he would have found upon rising. Now I had missed him again.

But where can he have gone? Surely his stay in Paris was not dependent solely upon me? I returned to the desk and asked if he had not left word as to how his letters were to be directed. This enquiry met with a stare so insolent, a sneer so knowing, I believe that had I a weapon to hand I might have been forgiven its use. Instead, my cheeks flaming, I laid a few centimes upon the desk, which promptly produced the information that M. Clarke had requested all letters to be held for him.

I was a good deal cheered by this, as it seemed to indicate he planned to return within a day or two. Otherwise he would have directed his letters to be sent on to him. Another few coins produced paper, an envelope and pen, with which I scribbled a hasty explanation of last Sunday's misunderstanding and asked Mr Clarke to please contact me as soon as he returned.

As if I were destined to be punished to the full, my place for the week, purchased at such a price, proved as worthless as the week's model. She seemed to change her position fifteen times in an hour, so that I would just finish blocking in the figure only to have to begin again, and again. She shivered and shuddered. More and more coals were heaped upon the fire; my position near the platform and thus the stove became a torment; the charcoal turned to mud in my hand.

And then came a blow such as I had never received.

As I returned home on Tuesday evening, Mlle threw open the door of the red parlour and told me I had a visitor within who had been waiting for some time. Assuming that my visitor could be none other than Stephen Clarke, I removed the old shawl that had covered my head during the dark homeward journey from the studio, and hastened into the room, where I was struck dumb by the shock of finding Charlotte there, pacing impatiently, and not only Charlotte, but Henry was seated in a corner with his hat on his knee, his eyes closed as if he had been bored to the point of death.

Charlotte in turn was taken by surprise, so shocked by my appearance she emitted a small shriek. Mlle also seemed startled by the contrast, when we two, who were so alike as children, stood together before her again, one soft and plump and feathered in fine plumage, the other as thin and scraggy a bird as ever ventured from its nest: thin-faced, tired-looking, and badly in need of a good wash and a new suit of clothes. I am not as yet so devoid of feminine pride that I did not suffer from my cousin's shriek.

Henry leapt to his feet at the noise and seemed covered in confusion, no doubt recalling our last moments together and how I had run from him, sobbing, on that rainy night. Still, I could not but extend to him a welcoming hand, if one not altogether clean.

When Mlle had withdrawn, Charlotte, who had waited quite long enough and refused even to take a chair, immediately stated the reason for their visit. They have been these past six weeks at Duneske House, where their children remain for Christmas, Charlotte being given some weeks in Paris as a long-sought-after Christmas gift from her husband. Upon leaving, she had been instructed by her parents and mine to come directly to me and insist that I return home at once. When I began to say why I could not, she said that she and Henry would gladly pay my way, and when I still declined, she called me pig-headed and wrong-hearted and accused me of a most unnatural lack of family feeling.

'Charlotte,' Henry intervened. 'You go too far.'

'I'm quite finished, Henry,' she fairly snapped at him, withdrawing from her smart silk bag a flat parcel wrapped in brown paper. 'As you refuse to return home,' she said, putting the parcel into my hands, 'I am instructed by your father to give this to you.'

With that, they departed, not saying if they would see me again or even where I might find them. Already shaken by the encounter, I took the package to my attic room and opened it with trembling hands that were horrified to find themselves holding the satinwood casket which had once held Grandmama's pearls. Inside the otherwise empty box was a single folded sheet of paper with a note from Papa.

> *My Dear Evelyn,*
> *Please accept the enclosed as an emblem of the love your mother and I bear you and of the esteem in which we hold you and your artistic endeavour. You have all your life heard these pearls spoken of as Grandmama's, yet they had been in the family for many generations before passing into her care and belonged to her no more than they now belong to you. She understood, as I pray you will one day understand, that they had been given to her to hold in trust for future generations, just as Derrymore had passed through her husband's stewardship into mine and is now passing into the care of your brother Francis. To let them go out of the family would be the most grievous breach of that trust.*
> *Wishing you joy in this blessed Christmas season, I remain*
> *Your Papa*

Again, not a word that could not be read by any prying eyes. Their import could be translated only by myself and, far from bringing me joy, this Christmas package brought me grief such as I have never known. My father's disappointed and sober words moved me more than far sterner ones could have done. Bent under their sorrowful weight, I fell upon my bed and wept for hours, wept until I was quite empty, as empty as the little satinwood casket, and until I had made myself ill. For the remainder of that day, I kept to my bed, Marie-Claire, Mlle's poor, overworked *bonne*, performing for me the occasional errand of mercy.

25 December

I dragged myself to the American church to play for the two morning services. But I thought my heart would break.

Through the hymns I could see the drawing room at home and all the family gathered round the magnificent tree, the one

Papa and I chose and marked a twelve-month ago. He and Mama would have decorated it last evening behind closed doors and after church this morning, he would have lighted every one of the candles himself before admitting all the family and servants who had gathered in the hall. Oh, would that I could have been among them!

I came home from church this Christmas Day and, my cold being not much improved, returned to bed and brooded more about Christmas at home, and about tomorrow, St Stephen's Day, when people will come from all over to ride and the Wren Boys will later troop up the avenue disguised as old women, to dance and sing and taunt until paid with pennies and apples and cakes.

31 December

I began this morning thinking that this is a wrong way we have of marking time, that Christmas and birthdays and anniversaries of any kind are so many spikes driven straight through our lives, pinning us down, impeding our progress, forcing us to revolve round them, to move in cycles and circles. Monday, a day on which I am usually full of purpose and energy, this week nearly destroyed me, nearly caused me to raise the white flag and surrender. And why? Because this Monday was called Christmas, and because it was so very different from Christmases past.

The days should be not named but numbered. They should march in a straight line from the past into the future, with no circling back, no illusions of repeated opportunities. Instead of Last Christmas and This Christmas and Next Christmas, it should be Day 9,125 and Day 9,490 and Day 9,855, Day 10,220, Day 10,585. We might then have a clear notion of time steadily and relentlessly passing, we might see that no day that passes will ever come round again. Our days are numbered in fact, why should they not be numbered in name?

This rational and unsentimental frame of mind saw me through the morning services today, during which I kept a critical eye on Rev. Peterson and the veiled *jeune fille* with pursed lips and downcast eyes whose family occupies the first pew, and for whose ears alone the sermon was composed, written, revised, and delivered, and during which I managed to make a few swift side-long sketches for my set of caricatures. After church, I very nearly enjoyed my solitary lunch of cold leg of chicken. It was at the concert that I fell apart.

There was no orchestra, the holiday having lured away too great a number of musicians. Only the piano remained, one young man who played Chopin as I imagine Chopin himself must have played, evoking an entire universe from within the frame of a single keyboard, drawing from that instrument harmonies and rhythms that were nothing less than electrifying. Never has music seemed the pouring forth of such pure feeling expressed with all the eloquence of French poetry and all the melancholy of Slavic passion. I somehow withstood its hammering at my heart. It was during a rather academic Étude that I succumbed. Without warning, I began to cry and could not stop. The tears came of their own accord. The most I could do was try to keep them silent.

I was grateful that I had chosen a lonely seat. Those on either side as well as before and behind, indeed all round me, had been left vacant. I knew that I could not have endured a single curious glance. However, I had no sooner formed the thought when the seat immediately to my left was taken, and by a gentleman. I saw only a pair of grey knees and the tip of a black boot. That anyone, but particularly a gentleman, should have taken that seat when there were so many others available, struck me as so intrusive as to be more alarming than annoying. I would have fled had it not meant having to slide past my intruder, the exit to my right being blocked by some six or seven quite elderly Parisians at the far end of the row. But then there came a voice into my ear, a sardonic voice, unexpected and familiar, in the welcome language and tones of my own country.

'You are quite right to weep, Miss Hope-Ross. These extended broken chords have been the despair of many a pair of small hands.'

How Stephen Clarke had come to arrive near the end of the concert was explained over tea, which we took at a nearby hotel that honours the ceremony. He had returned within the hour from Barbizon, where he had accepted an invitation to spend Christmas with friends, and, finding my note at the hotel desk, had called for me at the *pension*. Not finding me in, he had come to the concert to look for me.

'But how did you know I would be there?' I asked, as I had made quite a point of never telling Mlle where I was going.

He waited a moment before responding, a smile playing about the corners of his mouth. 'I saw you there on Sunday last.'

'And you did not speak to me?' It seemed scarcely to be believed that a friend had been so near, that the wretched loneliness of the past endless week might have been staved off with a word, yet that word had been withheld.

'I did not want to intrude,' he said, 'as I was quite certain that you did not wish to see me.' He explained: he had come to this house at the time mentioned in his letter. After waiting above two hours, he began to hope that I had not received his letter, but an enquiry satisfied him that I had done. He took his leave, telling Mlle where he might be found. He went to the concert not because he hoped to find me there but because, when he was a student at the École des Beaux-Arts, he had thus beguiled the hours of many an empty Sunday afternoon. He saw that I was there alone, which meant I could not have pleaded a previous engagement, then followed me to the river and watched me saunter aimlessly for above an hour in the most inhospitable weather, which convinced him that I was avoiding the *pension* and the chance that he might be waiting there for me.

'Mr Clarke!' I exclaimed, nearly as angry as I was surprised. 'It is extremely unlike you to have followed me about without making your presence known.'

'Yes,' he replied in a quiet voice. 'It is most certainly unlike me.'

However, we were soon friends again and he asked if I would do him the favour of accompanying him on a visit tomorrow morning to his old friend, Edgar Degas, about whom he is writing his article for the *Magazine of Art*. He explained that since the days when they saw each other frequently, M. Degas has become something of a recluse, while he himself has become that vilest of creatures, a journalist, and he fears that M. Degas might not be quite as forthcoming. My own presence, he believes, will reassure the artist, and to that end I am requested to bring along my own sketchbooks and any other portable works upon which I might reasonably seek the opinion of a great painter.

'*Is* he a great painter?' I asked, and was astounded to hear Mr Clarke's no doubt mistaken opinion that the name Degas is certain to be revered long after those of Dagnan and even Bastien-Lepage have been forgotten. I find this impossible to believe.

There was a letter lying on the mat inside her door when Eve got back from Dublin, as well as a small strip of paper with Adele's script in indian ink. Buying lottery tickets had been the furthest thing from Eve's mind the past week in Dublin. She crumpled the paper and tossed it into the empty grate.

It had been a warm day, a long hot drive in the sun, and the chill, stone-entombed interior of Mrs Matt's was a welcome relief from the overheated room she'd occupied in a Haddington Road B & B, a Victorian redbrick house with radiators going full blast all night, windows all but sealed, and every centimetre of wall or fabric painted or dyed a uniform shade of peach. But the landlord, an old widower Eve assumed must have been colour-blind, was pleasant and interesting, the bed comfortable, the breakfast good, and the location convenient, just a brisk ten-minute walk from the city centre, and she was able to leave her car parked behind the house the entire time. She'd never wanted to get into it again. After driving across Ireland, thinking she was almost there, she'd spent an hour and a half crawling along the Naas Road from the outskirts of Dublin into its heart. Today, it had taken her nearly as long to get out of the city.

In the end, she was grateful the girls had decided to stay at Derrymore; three days in Dublin wouldn't have been nearly enough. Everything had taken longer than she'd expected; two days to locate the EH-R painting owned by Trinity College, where there was no record of where it had been hung. The

National Gallery knew exactly where theirs was: in storage, from which it took the better part of a day to be extracted, brought to light, and then photographed. The Municipal Gallery's painting, in storage as well, had been retrieved within minutes, but the photographer, who'd been late for both previous appointments, was even later for that one.

The O'Gormans had insisted she look up their daughter Deirdre, who suggested, when they met for lunch, that Eve ought to buy herself a decent camera and learn how to use it rather than continue to be dependent on the schedules of others. But she wasn't eager to take up photography at this point; there was so much more to it than looking through a lens and pressing a shutter button. She'd have to learn to develop film, set up a darkroom, acquire an enlarger, special lights, chemicals, pans and trays and papers, instruction, knowledge, technique; it was not the art she wanted to pursue. And that morning, when she picked up the prints, three stunning reproductions, she knew she'd been right to seek out a professional.

The letter was from Rose, she'd known the instant she saw the blue envelope lying on the mat. Lily used a blue stationery and Rose a bluer one. Since January these alternating shades had been arriving like clockwork in alternating weeks, the letters as different as the twins themselves, Lily's long and literate, Rose's brief and chatty, full of slang, misspellings, malapropisms. Now the cycle was beginning all over again, the girls back in California, their visit a thing of the past.

In many ways, those last clear, warm days had been the best part of their visit, another reason she was grateful they'd decided to save Dublin for another time. Their very last evening, alerted by Adele that Bluebell Wood had burst into bloom, Eve had taken them there, not only because she was eager to see it again herself, but because she wanted to see their reaction to it, and when they simultaneously gasped at their first sight of it – a vast waving carpet of unbelievable blue under a cathedral ceiling of beeches whose buds were just beginning to open, so that the branches seemed barely misted with the palest of greens, incandescent in the sun – she told them what had brought her back here: coming across a photograph of this same place taken at this same time, seven years ago. Both girls had put their arms around their mother, the three of them standing close together and in silence, and Eve thought that if she had ever wondered what all those years had been for, she had her answer now.

She opened the envelope right there at the door. It was more or less a thank-you note. Rose had had a good time in Ireland. She'd eaten like a pig, slept like a dog, gained five pounds.

She had always got things slightly wrong, such as sleeping like a dog instead of like a log, so that they'd frequently had her hearing tested. She heard Old Timers for Alzheimer's and mental pause for menopause. She confused marshmallows and mushrooms into mushmellows, and manoeuvre with manure; she was mortified to tears in kindergarten when told that her snowsuit was too small to manoeuvre in.

It was a short note, the work of a minute. But in the lower left corner she had drawn a small bunch of flowers in painstaking detail, each violet darkly purple, each buttercup a deep orange-tinged yellow, the bouquet tied with a fluttering ribbon of green. It was exactly like the bunches of flowers she used to present to Eve on Mother's Days or birthdays when she was very small, letting herself out of the kitchen door at first light, still in her nightgown or pyjamas, and picking whatever she could find growing behind the house, small things growing close to the ground, clover blossoms and tiny pinkish star-shaped flowers, violets, buttercups, arranged in miniature bouquets tied with a bit of coloured ribbon or a blade of grass. Clutching her tribute, she would jump onto Eve's side of the bed, her small rounded baby feet still damp with morning dew.

This fragrant baby Rose came rushing at Eve with such force that she had to reach out to the wall to steady herself. And Martin was suddenly there too, lying warm in her memory, hands behind his head, hair dark under his arms, dark eyes heavy with sleep. There was a bottle of baby oil they kept in the drawer of the night stand. He took it out one night and found two bright pink hearts, joined at the hip, drawn on its label. Rose, they knew, because she was always 'decorating' things. She couldn't possibly know what it was used for – they knew that too – but it made them nervous all the same.

Then they were gone, her family vanished as suddenly as they had appeared, leaving her alone in another house in another country, another world, Lily and Rose thousands of miles away again, Martin even further, in another life, and her brother and father further still. As she carried her bag across the kitchen and, too tired to eat, went heavily up the stairs, her new home, now that the girls had been and gone, seemed empty. It was the eternal conflict. While she had loved having her daughters with her, she'd been aware of her own work pushed to the back burner, going cold. Yet now they were gone and she could work twenty-four hours a day if she wanted, she missed them terribly.

She lifted her bag onto the bed and began unpacking what was mostly laundry now, which she tossed into a corner to deal with in the morning, or perhaps not, a slovenly new habit she must, she thought, subconsciously enjoy; it had been months now she'd been forgetting to buy a laundry basket. She flung a last pullover into the corner, zipped the overnight bag and slid it beneath her bed, where dust had begun to form itself into rolling clouds. She must remember to look for a dust mop as well, or whatever it might be called here; the broom was useless for this.

She gathered up her sponge bag, hairbrush and comb and carried them to the dressing table, where her eye was caught by a new slip of paper that had been tucked into the lower rim of the mirror, this one in Lily's hand.

No snowflake ever lands in the wrong place. (Zen)

Up at dawn next morning, she made a pot of coffee, drank it black, as the milk was spoilt, and, still in her pyjamas, worked for four hours before cleaning up and going over to the house to let the Hope-Rosses know she was back. With their custom of drawing the curtains at dusk, no matter what the weather, she couldn't know if they'd seen her lights the night before. Walking around to the kitchen door, she found Adele in her yellow gardening gloves and battered sunhat on her knees in one of the rose beds behind the house. Head tilted back, she regarded Eve from beneath the wide brim of her hat.

'Ah, there you are! We wondered where you'd got to. How did it go?' She had opened the soil at the base of a rose bush and was in the process of laying down a blackening banana skin she took from a plastic-lined basket.

'Very well. I got all three. I should have brought them. They're gorgeous.' She left a pause. 'What are you doing?'

'Awfully good for roses, banana skins. Full of calcium, phosphates, whatnot.'

'Potassium?'

'That's the one.' Adele leaned back further to glance up at the sky before bending back to her work. 'Brilliant day, isn't it?'

'It is. Yet another one.' As always from this spot, Eve's eyes were drawn out to sea, different at every hour of every day and now turned a shimmering silver by the glancing power of the sun. A solid bank of cloud was gathered on the horizon along which the slender black form of a ship moved by centimetres; next stop America.

'How *do* we manage to collect so many?' Adele extracted another blackening skin from her basket. 'One would think we kept a pair of gorillas.'

Eve smiled. 'Then you don't want me to save mine for you?'

'No, no, no, just keep putting yours into the compost. I've far more banana skins than roses.'

'A splash of dew and a bee or two. A drop of dew?' Eve said, after a silence, trying to recall the words she had written in Rose's baby book.

'What's that?'

'Emily Dickinson. It's how she described a rose. A splash – or a drop – of dew and a bee or two. She sketched in words. If she'd been a visual artist instead of a poet, she would have done line drawings.' She thought for a moment. 'It might even have been a flash of dew and a bee or two.'

'I *do* hope it's *splash*. A splash of dew and a bee or two.' Adele sat back for a second. 'That's lovely. I shall put it in my book.' She shifted her basket and moved on to the next plant.

'Roses much prefer dripping, but if I tried that here, the fox would instantly dig them up. The roses I help tend in Henry's scrap of garden are always fed on fat. They flower stunningly, well into December, he tells me. He's rather fond of roses,' she added after a moment.

Eve turned her eyes out to sea again, keeping them trained on the progress of the distant ship; she made no response. For a moment or two there was only the sound of soil being tamped with the back of a trowel. Then Adele surprised her, speaking all in a great rush.

'Forgive me, my dear, but I've known Henry all his life, he's like a son to me and I a mother to him, and I simply must say something.'

Eve swung round to face her, but Adele fished another banana skin from the basket and talked while she worked.

'I saw him when we left here in January and I saw him when we returned. And the morning he left, I saw him just before he went to wish you goodbye, and I saw him when he came immediately back.' She left another silence. 'He could say nothing. He simply folded himself into the back of the car and was silent. All the way to Cork. He was – there really is no other word for it – miserable.'

This image brought Eve such unexpected pleasure she had to turn away until she could bring her face under control. The trellis that framed two sides of the terrace onto which the kitchen door opened was blanketed with pink climbing roses just beginning to open, and she made a pretence of examining these. But what she saw was Henry in his dressing gown and slippers, hands plunged deep into his pockets. *Best put it out of its misery, no? Can't very well shoot it, can we? A bit small for that.*

'Henry has always been rather suspicious of – He's always

believed himself to be too much the – He has absolutely no confidence in – No idea how – '

She sounds exactly like him, Eve thought, willing the other woman to finish the sentence, any sentence. But Adele surprised her again by suddenly producing a string of completed sentences.

'Henry was married for many years to a simply dreadful woman. No, I suppose one shouldn't put it quite that way. He was married to a woman who led him a dreadful dance. *Affairs*, the lot. She left him not once but twice, before she actually – and rather humiliatingly – left him.' She broke off, and again Eve turned to face her. Adele, sitting back on her heels, said, 'He phoned here a day or two after he left. He asked to speak with you. He sounded simply awful, as if he'd caught cold. I was just on the point of going to call you to the telephone when he suddenly changed his mind.'

Again, Eve had to look away to hide her expression. How much that simple piece of information, that Henry had asked to speak to her, would have meant two months ago.

'I suppose I should have told you sooner, but he asked me not to. He was quite adamant that I should not mention it. At first, I assumed that you had – but when Professor Depriest told us that your former husband had been here that morning –' She held out a hand. 'I know, I know. She explained why he was here, and I must say that it is all to his credit. How*ever,* what I mean to say is that one can't help put two and two together, can one?'

'Can I ask,' Eve said, after a moment, 'why you're telling me this now?'

'When he phoned to tell us he wouldn't be coming for Easter –' Adele broke off again before blurting out, a little petulantly, 'Henry has *never* not come for Easter.'

'I see,' Eve said. 'I think. I'm sorry if –'

'As I said,' Adele pushed on, her cheeks, despite the floppy sunhat, a bright rose colour, 'I had assumed that you had sent him packing, so to speak. Then, while you were away I had tea with Professor Depriest.'

'I think I do see,' Eve said, with an embarrassed smile. She would have liked to have heard that conversation. *You've got to be kidding me! She's been eating her heart out.*

'*Do* you see? A simple note would do. You might say you'd like him to see those extraordinary reproductions you've brought back.' She pulled off her gardening gloves and tossed them into the basket along with the trowel, and passed the back of her hand across her forehead. She looked exhausted, but got to her feet with surprising agility, scooped up her basket and headed for the house.

'I don't have his address,' Eve called after her.

'I pushed it through your letterbox a day or two ago. You must not have seen.' She put her shoulder to the door, then turned. 'Come to lunch? I've something to show you.'

'I'd love to.' She was ravenous now and there was nothing in her fridge that wasn't black, green, or pink with mould.

'Tomorrow. One fifteen. We're off to Cork this afternoon.'

Her mind full of Henry, Eve turned back to the sea. The ship, which had seemed hardly to be moving at all, had already vanished from view, and without that clear line of demarcation, it was difficult to tell where the sea ended and the sky began.

Instantly, like the fox digging up buried riches, her mind dug up Lily reading at her grandfather's funeral, from Rimbaud she thought, but couldn't be sure. At the time it had meant nothing to her. Lily's assuming responsibility for putting something together in such a hurry – Eve imagined her desperately turning the pages of her course books on the plane, looking for something, anything, that might be remotely appropriate for the cremation of a secular humanist in a family of secular humanists – had certainly meant something to her; it had meant everything to her. But the words themselves had been just words, a few more of the thousands of words of empty consolation people uttered or read or wrote at such times.

Now, as if for the first time, she saw Lily standing like a poised young priestess, her clear, precise voice offering a poet's description of eternity.

It is the sea gone with the sun.

She stood and looked, all thoughts of Henry Cole pushed over the curve of the earth and her mind rapidly filling with the need to paint this vision of eternity, this beckoning, bright, shining, endless absence.

She was on her knees on the kitchen floor, crouched over a canvas to which she was applying a thick layer of white with a short stubby brush, when there came the quick double rap at the door she had come to recognise as Peter's and looked up just as he was drawing his face back from the glass pane in the door. She instinctively glanced at her wrist, though it had been months since she'd worn a watch, and struggled to her feet. Her back ached from the bending and stretching; her knees felt as if nails had been driven into them from several angles. Her left foot had gone numb. She hobbled to the door and opened it.

'Peter! Am I late? What time is it?'

'Not at all. Not at all. I'm so sorry to disturb you.' His complexion darkened with embarrassment. 'We've got ahead of ourselves and wondered if we might push lunch up a bit. But I can see –'

'I was just finishing. I'll wash up and be over in five minutes.' Glancing down at her paint-stained shirt and jeans, she laughed. 'Well, ten.'

'I must say, Eve, that looks a damned uncomfortable way to go about the thing.' He indicated with his chin the canvas lying on the slate floor. 'You should have an easel.'

'I do have one, but it's got something on it, something else I'm working on.' She waved a hand in the direction of the sitting room. 'I often work on two things at once. I get started on one and then something else just takes over.'

'I dare say there's an easel or two gathering dust in the old studio. We'll have a look after lunch. Shall we?'

'I'd love to see her studio.'

'I use the term loosely,' he cautioned. 'The place has been a tip as long as I can remember.'

'A tip?' Eve examined the backs of her hands; paint had caked in the grooves of her knuckles and beneath her nails; she might have been finger-painting.

'What you Americans call a rubbish dump, I believe.'

'Garbage. I'm afraid we say garbage dump. Garbage can, garbage day, garbage night.'

'Garbage night? What on earth is that?'

'It's the night before garbage day. It's when you put out your garbage cans.'

'I see,' he said doubtfully.

'I'd really appreciate the loan of an easel.' She stepped back to pick up a rag and container of turpentine from the floor. 'I tried to buy one yesterday, but the art supply place was shut.' Aware that Peter's amiable expression had become suddenly grave, she asked, 'What? What is it?'

'You *have* been away,' he said. 'The woman who owned the shop has had the most dreadful accident.'

His use of the past tense was not lost on her. 'You mean she's — she died?'

'Sadly, yes. A horrendous car accident in France. But I won't detain you any longer.' He was already backing away from the door. 'Come to the kitchen. I'm afraid we'll have to dispense with the sherry, if you don't mind, and go straight to the trough.'

'Good! I've had nothing but coffee today.' And if there was any worse drink than sherry, she thought, shutting the door, she couldn't imagine what it might be.

Famished, she scrubbed quickly at her hands and nails, changed out of her painting clothes and hurried over to the house.

The mould-mottled cover read simply, *Receipts*.

'It was at the back of a cupboard in the butler's pantry,' Adele said, 'on a shelf of cookery books, all modern, but out of date, from the first half of this century — or I suppose one must now say the past century — most of them. But this one, I believe, is rather special.'

Eve turned its brittle pages with care. There was a recipe for bread, then one for cement. 'Stuffed Pheasants for Twenty' was followed by 'Herbal Mixture for Chilblains', oxtail soup, and rat poison. The book was written entirely by hand, seemingly the same hand.

'I should like to have known that cook,' Peter said.

'*I* should have been terrified of her,' Adele said. 'She might have put the ingredients for cement into the bread.'

'And rat poison in the soup,' Eve added.

'I think it's eighteenth-century,' Adele said hopefully. 'Look at the way the S's are formed. And the F's. What do you think?'

Eve said her only point of comparison was the 1882 journal, and this book did look much, much older than that.

'I do hope it's eighteenth-century.' Adele took it back from Eve and set it on the flat surface of one of the dressers.

'I hope it's before the Famine, at any rate,' Peter put in. 'It wouldn't do, would it, transcribing recipes for stuffed pheasants for twenty?'

'Oh, Lord! I never thought of that, only of how pleased Henry would be.'

'Why don't you bring it to the National Library?' Eve suggested. 'Someone there would be sure to know.'

'Henry will know.' Adele laid the topic to rest.

'If we could delay coffee a bit,' Peter said, pushing back his chair, 'I'll take Eve to the studio to choose an easel.'

'Oh, do take one. There are dozens of them rotting away.'

'Hardly *dozens*, my dear.'

'I'd better skip the coffee,' Eve said, as she got up from the table. 'I drank an entire pot this morning.' It had taken that much to wake up after spending half the night trying to compose a note to Henry. Easier to paint eternity, she thought, than to write five lines to Henry Cole. In the end, she had simply taken Adele's advice and said she hoped he would be coming to Derrymore soon, as she was eager to show him the photographs she'd had done for the book.

'I do worry about your coffee consumption.' Adele stood and

began gathering plates. Eve had learned not to offer to help but, used to guests pitching in, it still bothered her to just walk away from the table. 'There've been such *heaps* of coffee grounds in the compost, we'll have the broad beans dancing.'

'I'll be doing the lawn later.' Peter held the swing door open for Eve. 'You'll have heaps of grass cuttings to put a damper on things.'

There were no lamps or overhead lights, but there were a number of windows and two murky skylights, one at each end of the forty-foot room. Under one skylight an odd collection of galvanised buckets and old paint tins held varying amounts of rank rainwater. As promised, the long room held the refuse of decades.

'It's all at that far end. Mind your step now,' Peter cautioned. 'I'll just empty some of these buckets.' This was said cheerfully, Eve knew, because the roofers would be coming soon. She'd heard this at lunch, and deduced from it that Henry had completed the sale of the letter.

'Blast!' he muttered, as Penelope shot in ahead of them. 'Damned cat!'

'I'll make sure she comes out with me,' Eve offered, eager to explore the room.

She picked her way through a forest of easels of all heights and sizes, all well used and spattered with paint in every imaginable hue. There were four rush-bottomed camp stools and two sketching umbrellas with torn black panels and missing gores. Perching warily on the fragile weave of an opened camp stool, Eve traced a finger along the umbrella's shredded silk and saw Evelyn Hope-Ross and Henry Brooke hauling this same paraphernalia through the orchard and out into the brilliant light of the sheep meadow.

There were jars and bottles and tins, brushes whose bristles had been eaten by moths or mice, and stacks of shallow dishes splotched with colour blackened by time and dust, open boxes full of mouldering clothes, no doubt costumes for Evelyn's models. There were piles of old hats, a large carton full of empty palette cups, several pairs of riding boots, their black leather crumbling to reddish dust, an ivory-handled crop, parts of an etching machine, a single roller, a press-bed, a crank. When Eve's eye fell on the ancient black stove that stood in the fireplace against the far wall, she could see Evelyn and Anne in their long skirts and striped shirts lying back in front of it, their feet up, smoking unfiltered cigarettes, filled with satisfaction with the studio they had created.

Against the nearest wall was a stack of brass-cornered suitcases and several wooden sketch boxes, one of them engraved with a scripted *EH-R*. This she carried back to the camp stool, where she lifted out the wooden palette and handled the broken pieces of charcoal, the palette knife, the little jar that once held linseed oil, the flattened and crinkled tubes of paint, the half-dozen brushes. A perfectly preserved splash of vermilion on the palette she recognised as having been used in a travelling cloak in the picture that hung at the very top of the stairs.

She sat with the open box on her knees. The room hadn't been used as a studio in more than half a century; it had ended its life the way it had begun, as a storeroom, no doubt returned to its original use by Peter's jealous mother. Yet it still smelled of turpentine and paint, as if its spirit struggled to live on. She thought of the two friends hauling out all Evelyn's early efforts and hanging them on these walls and wondered which they'd been, where they were now, what had happened to them. She thought of all the paintings in the gallery and the bedroom, the ones in storage in Dublin, and the ones – perhaps in storage as well – in Belfast and London, Philadelphia and in the houses of the descendants of all the individuals who had bought one. They deserved to be seen; all of them.

The sudden clatter of an empty tin rolling on its side reminded her of Penelope's presence. She called to the cat and was gratified to see her promptly emerge from behind the stove.

She held out her hand to the animal, then jumped to her feet so quickly the camp stool fell over on its side as Penelope, confident of the merit of her offering, proudly laid the slain mouse at Eve's feet.

5 January 1883
Paris

A shocking day, bitterly cold with sharp winds, snow on the ground, the river full of huge blocks of ice that go rushing past along with barrels, boxes, and all manner of debris.

Mr Clarke hired a carriage to make the quite short journey to M. Degas' studio. When I saw it waiting in the street, I said he needn't have gone to such trouble and expense, as I am well used to walking great distances in all weathers. He replied, in the driest of tones, 'That is most considerate of you, Miss Hope-Ross. I, however, am not at all used to it.'

We called first at a gallery in the Rue Lafitte, the owner of which (M. Paul Durand-Ruel), Mr Clarke informed me, acts the part of spiritual and material godfather to the group of painters who call themselves Impressionists, of whom I have of course heard rumours, but who are held in such very low esteem by the Académie that I had made no effort to see their paintings. Even had I known where to look for them, when would I have had the time? Mr Clarke, however, was of the opinion that it was indeed time for me to become acquainted with their work.

I was amazed. I was dazzled. I was nearly blinded by what I saw hanging on the red walls of that gallery. Such works I have never seen before. Such colour. Such *freedom*.

Yes, the overwhelming impression I received was one of utter freedom. Freedom of method, of colour, of form. Freedom of choice of subject. Freedom from plumb lines and measurements. Freedom from the studio model. A world of light and colour and movement, of the outdoors, of the streets and the fields. I hardly knew what to think. I could do little more than wander about in a daze, and that shock was soon succeeded by another when we were ushered into M. Durand-Ruel's private office, the walls of which are crowded with smaller oils, watercolours and photographs.

Once the formalities were dispensed with and the art dealer deep in conversation with the art critic, I allowed my eyes to wander over the photographs. What I saw among them is not to be believed. I cannot believe it still: to the left of M. Durand-Ruel's head hung the photographic studies Anne and I made of each other on the strand last summer. It was only at that moment that I realised why the name Durand-Ruel had struck a dull chord when first I heard it mentioned by Mr Clarke: it was the name of the 'publisher' on the cheque Anne received at the end of the summer, the cheque which caused such merriment and glee, the cheque which was in part responsible for my occupation of that very chair at that very moment.

At first I did not know myself, unacquainted as I am with my unadorned back view. I had never seen the photographs because it had been necessary, in order to avoid the risk of discovery, for Anne to send the undeveloped plates to France. It was the strand I recognised and the large flat stone I have from infancy known as Table Rock. It was but the work of a moment to realise that the harlots cavorting on my strand were my cousin and myself. And then I could feel the blood ebbing away from my heart, as if a knife had been suddenly plunged into it. If ever I have come near to falling into a swoon, it was at that moment. M. Durand-Ruel turned to see what had caused my too obvious dismay.

'They are striking photographs. No, Mademoiselle?' he said. 'Particularly this one.' He indicated the one in which I, naked as the newborn day, am looking out to sea, stretching towards it, with one hand shielding my eyes and, thank God, the better part of my face. 'A very fine composition, and the model is of such exquisite articulations.'

He said a great deal more in praise of my unparalleled beauty, but I did not attend, for the blood that had drained away so suddenly came rushing back with equal force. My face was on fire, my head throbbed until I thought it would explode. When Mr Clarke looked from me to the photograph and back to me, I could endure it no longer and jumped to my feet, making the excuse of feeling overwarm and in need of air, and rushed from the office without taking leave of the highly amused M. Durand-Ruel.

I know not how we arrived at M. Degas' studio. I could think of nothing but the photographs and was visited by scene after scene in which some member of my family – Francis or Dominick or, worse and most likely, Henry – called in at the gallery to purchase a painting for a birthday or a Christmas gift and saw the photographs, recognised Table Rock and Derrymore's strand and went on to draw the inevitable conclusion.

And as for M. Degas, when we arrived, I found him a disappointingly ordinary-looking man in a pepper-and-salt suit with a blue tie knotted about his neck. Yet I had the distinct impression that I had seen him before. He was clearly delighted to see Mr Clarke again and was, consequently, charming to me as well. While at first glance he looks nothing if not bourgeois, he is a man absolutely transformed by the act of conversation, for he has the most arresting voice as well as a warm and riveting and wholly attentive gaze. All Gaul is divided between his two eyes, each a burning coal.

His studio is large and gloomy, lit only at one end and full of greasy lithographic machinery, stacks of stretched canvas, and queer pieces of sculpture, wax dancing-girls wearing skirts of real muslin. I would have liked to wander and to look, but he seized the sketchbooks Mr Clarke had requested I bring with me as an excuse for the visit, and perused them quickly and in silence, pausing at the first sketch of the copyists at the Louvre.

'I see, Mademoiselle,' he said, glancing up at me at last, as if relieved to have found *something* he might comment upon without causing pain, 'that you think as I do, that you aim to take a subject that has never before received artistic treatment and bring it within the sacred sphere.' Returning my books to me, he added, 'You and I, we find all we want in what the Académie painters leave behind.'

Here in two simple statements I was given more instruction than I had received in four months at M. Julian's, and three years in South Kensington, instruction that could not be more opposed to that which I have been slaving in order to receive. For I have been told and told again to think of the studio model and nothing but the studio model, to capture as accurately as possible her character and action, to take for life's most fundamental truth the line that drops through her ear and breast and heel.

The astonishing work I had seen at M. Durand-Ruel's gallery had already begun to fill me with self-doubt. Now I felt something like despair. I saw, all in a crushing instant, just how little the narrow world of the art student impinges upon the great world of Art. I had worked so hard and caused so much trouble to get to Paris for the privilege of entering a life class. Now I was overwhelmed by the suspicion that I would have been better off staying at home, that I was merely plodding stupidly along a well-beaten track, while the real artists had struck off on their own.

'You believe, then, Monsieur, that I have been wasting my time at the Académie Julian?' I fairly wailed, for I had not been deceived by his kind inclusion of me as a practitioner of his artistic theory and method.

'Non, non, non, non, non,' he chided. 'Learning is never wasted, Mademoiselle. Never. Especially if what we learn is to put in long hours of hard work each day. It is excellent training. And, of course,' he added, 'in order to violate the principles of art, one must have those principles firmly in hand. N'est-il pas vrai?'

He excused himself and walked, with a peculiar round-shouldered gait, to the other end of the studio, while I looked round me with new eyes at the hard-working dancing-girls at their practice, a perspiring laundress bent over her ironing, and a nude, not a pale nymph exhibiting classical proportions, but a lumpy, middle-aged woman bending to wash her red and swollen feet.

'His genius,' said Mr Clarke, who had remained at my elbow, 'lies not only in his choice of subject matter – he is far too modest on the subject of his own work – but in his ways of disposing his figures upon the canvas, and in the startling and unexpected angles of vision they afford.' He indicated a circus woman suspended in the top-left corner of a canvas that was otherwise all empty space and light. 'And here, you see how the figure and face of this shop assistant are cut in two by the looking-glass in which the well-dressed customer examines herself, oblivious even of the presence of the poor, featureless assistant.'

I'm afraid that what I saw most of all was that Mr Clarke had already written his article about M. Degas, and that he was overfond of quoting himself.

'*Pour vous, Mademoiselle*,' said M. Degas, who had noiselessly rejoined us. As he spoke he tore a page from a large leather-covered notebook he had gone to fetch from his table, and handed it to me with a flourish. It was a drawing of myself. But a more ill-favoured likeness I have never seen, and, for the second time that morning, I did not immediately recognise myself in the slovenly creature looming out of the lower left corner, head thrown back, mouth stretched in an ugly yawn, arms akimbo, hands curled and seeming quite capable of administering a consoling scratch to an arm or a leg. Yet she was myself, for next to her was my pelisse and in front of her my drawing of the copyists at the Louvre, round the edges of which could be seen slices of the copyists themselves, and in the top-right corner hung Titian's *Man with the Glove*.

M. Degas walked away again, leaving Mr Clarke to rhapsodise upon the harmoniousness of the composition.

'A perfect example of his technique. You see how the eye glides across the diagonals of paper and easels, from the lowest of the low in the bottom left corner to the high art hanging in the top right. Yet, there is no communication between them; the intermediary easels serve as barricades rather than as links, and the hopelessness of the art student's position is all too apparent –'

He broke off, for only then did he realise that the lowly art student, the lowest of the low, was my lowly self. For my part, I would happily have ripped the drawing into shreds, despite his exhortations to me to handle it with the greatest of care. My displeasure must have been quite obvious, for he gently relieved me of the paper, carefully rolled it and took care not to return it to my possession.

His own discomfort soon supplanted mine, however, for during lunch, which we ate at M. Degas' apartments – a pleasant place in the nearby Rue Pigalle overlooking a courtyard full of snow-laden chestnut trees – our host launched an attack upon the 'meddling parasites' who earn their living writing about art, thus revealing that he had guessed all along the real purpose of Mr Clarke's visit.

'Critics do art nothing but harm. You do nothing to improve public taste, which has never before been in a worse state, despite the unprecedented amount of words churned out on the subject. You destroy the confidence of highly sensitive artists, and you encourage an equally destructive taste for celebrity in highly susceptible ones who, the moment they attract the attention of the crowd, begin to clamour for medals and to conduct themselves as if they have no talent at all. Look at Whistler. One can no longer speak to him; he is always rushing off to be photographed.'

It was a turbulent meal with many arguments raging. The female artist Berthe Morisot, and her husband, Eugène Manet, were trying to discuss plans for an eighth Impressionist exhibition to be held this coming May.

As far as I could gather from the torrents of French that went rushing past with the speed of the ice floes in the Seine, M. Degas insists upon the exclusion of anyone who also exhibits in the official Salon. He himself did not exhibit in the seventh event because the artists Pissarro and Gauguin refused to include several young painters whom Degas had recruited for the sixth exhibition to replace Pissarro and Gauguin, who had refused to participate in that exhibition because of something that had occurred in the fifth. Monet and Renoir are refusing to exhibit in the eighth. To take their place, Berthe Morisot urged the inclusion of Georges Seurat and Paul Signac, against whom Degas argued savagely, as they are associates of 'Piss–arro'.

Berthe Morisot, alone, reasoned calmly and without rancour and I found my eyes resting on hers with increasing frequency. She is perhaps forty years of age and, although she might certainly be called beautiful still, her features, with the exception of her wide, clear, all-seeing dark eyes, are rather haggard. I had seen several of her extraordinary oils and pastels that morning, and M. Degas had spoken highly of her work as we walked round the corner from his studio.

I was as intrigued by her as I was wearied by the bickering of the others and, for perhaps the first time in my life, grateful when the housekeeper announced that the ladies' coffee would be served in the drawing room, and we two rose and left the men to their wine and cigars and animosities.

'As usual,' she sighed, the moment we were left alone, 'Degas' perversity makes the project almost impossible.'

I must have seemed startled by this quite frank comment about our host, for she smiled. 'Do not misunderstand, Mademoiselle. I have only the greatest respect for him, as he does for me.' She told me that it was Degas who first encouraged her, more than eleven years ago, to join the society of artists who were planning the first exhibition independent of the official Salon, and that the other artists had been at the start more interested in her as a model, although a fully clothed one, than as a confederate.

'But with Degas' support I became a founder member of the group, although propriety forbade me, as a single woman, from attending any of our meetings.' At this she smiled wearily. 'That did not, of course, prevent the press from denouncing me as a whore. For our loose brushwork and unfinished daubs, the others were called lunatics or monkeys with paintbrushes. I was called a whore.'

Angry with myself for blushing at the coarse word and having no idea what to say to it, I took it upon myself to pour our coffee. She accepted her miniature cup and saucer wordlessly, and drank it down, without benefit of either cream or sugar, before speaking again.

'I will tell you a little story, Mademoiselle,' she said, setting down her cup and saucer and leaning back comfortably in her chair, both hands upon the arm rests.

'When my sister Edma and I were still quite young girls, the artist who was hired to teach us to draw and to paint, as others were employed to teach us music and dance, English and Italian, went to our mother one day in great distress. He warned her that my sister and I were achieving more than the pretty drawing-room talents he had been hired to give us, that we had ability and had shown application as well as ambition, that, in short, her daughters were in grave danger of becoming painters, artists! He was well aware that in my family's high bourgeois social milieu, this would be considered nothing less than revolutionary and that she would one day curse the art, and the artist, she had allowed into her respectable and peaceful household. Was she quite certain that she wanted him to continue our lessons?' She smiled at the recollection.

'I may assume, Madame, that the lessons continued?'

'Oh, yes, the lessons continued. But we were wisely given a new teacher, one who had himself been a student of Ingres.' Again, she smiled. 'Within two years we both exhibited at the Salon.'

When I asked if her sister was also a member of the Impressionists' group, she replied with regret, 'Alas, Edma was by that time married and a mother. She had ceased to paint.' She refilled our coffee cups before adding, 'A great pity, for she was exceptionally talented. Our teachers never failed to find her the more biddable pupil. Salon juries never refused her, not once. Critics always singled her out for a word of praise from among thousands of entries. And I believe, although she adores her husband and children, she has suffered a good deal from regret. It is not easy to break with a life of work.'

'But was it necessary for her to stop altogether?' I asked. I could, of course, see that marriage and motherhood would make it impossible for one to devote oneself to painting. But surely one might find an hour or two each day.

She regarded me in silence for a moment, as if considering whether I were worth the trouble of a response, if I were old enough or wise enough.

'Few men, Mademoiselle, can tolerate hearing their wives vilified in public. Or praised, for that matter. And my sister could not have failed to achieve notoriety of one sort or the other.' There fell another silence, which I, sensing that she had more to say on the subject, did not try to fill. Soon, she set down her coffee cup and fixed me once again with her frank, direct gaze.

'Edma was far too serious about her art to dabble in it to the extent concordant with her position of the wife of a naval officer. She did not take to her new home so much as a pencil or brush. She gave to me what she thought might be of use, and destroyed the rest.'

'But why on earth,' I could not help asking, 'did she marry a naval officer, if she knew she would never be allowed to paint again?'

Amused at my naïveté, she spread her beautiful hands. 'She married him because she fell in love with him, and she fell in love with him because she met him, and she met him because Manet brought him to our home, and Manet brought him to our home because they had served as cadets together in 1848, and they served as cadets together in 1848 because France was at war with –' She broke off with a most Gallic *c'est la vie* shrug.

'But you, Madame,' I said, 'are also married. Yet you did not find it necessary to stop painting.'

'My situation is entirely different,' she said. 'I was much older when I married. I had already achieved notoriety, had already been called a whore by the press, so there was no possibility of my husband being shocked and injured by it. I married a man who had no career of his own and who was prepared, indeed quite eager, to devote himself to mine. He himself paints a little. He understands. His brother Édouard is a very gifted – I would even say great – painter who has been constantly and viciously attacked by the press.'

Indicating that I should follow, she rose and crossed the room to a portrait M. Degas had done of the elder Manet, in which he had thrown himself upon a white sofa in an attitude that defies description. There is passion, intensity, yet also lassitude, even something like despair.

'This is my husband's brother, who is gravely ill. Those who know him well can scarcely look upon this likeness without pain. The expression, the pose, the disposition of the limbs were all once habitual to him. But now he suffers terribly. He is quite changed.'

Clearly experiencing a great deal of pain herself, she continued to gaze at the likeness for some minutes, in silence, completely absorbed by her own thoughts, as if she had forgotten my presence, even my existence. But suddenly she turned to me.

'Do you know why I have spoken to you of these things, Mademoiselle? Can you guess why I have been so frank?'

I did not mistake her meaning, and to pretend to do so would have been a poor return for her candour.

'If you refer to Mr Clarke, Madame,' I said, blushing furiously again, 'no one could be more disinclined to marry than he – or I, for that matter. Indeed, our very friendship was founded upon this common indisposition.'

At this, she laughed quite merrily. 'Forgive me, Mademoiselle. But, you see, my sister Edma was famously understood to be disinterested in marriage. It is the one quality above all others that men find irresistible.'

The men entered, full of wine and looking quite satisfied with themselves, though I doubt their conversation could have been half so interesting as ours. Their coffee was served and drunk, and within half an hour the group began to break up. On quitting M. Degas' apartment, I thanked Mr Clarke for a most interesting day but insisted upon finding my own way back to the *pension*, saying that I was far too full of lunch not to want the walk. In truth, I wanted to be alone with my thoughts and review all that I had seen and heard and learned. I expected some objection, some little protest, but he too seemed preoccupied, no doubt mentally polishing his article for the *Magazine of Art*, and accepted my suggestion without demur, and indeed without the least indication of the likelihood of a future engagement.

I meant to devote the whole evening to my caricatures, but I have used it all in recording the events of this most memorable day.

Tuesday
6 January

I rose from a restless and unrefreshing sleep too discomposed to go to the studio, and too aware of the futility in doing so, having through yesterday's truancy secured no good place for the week. Instead I made my way through the snow back to the Rue Lafitte, drawn to the gallery almost against my will by an overpowering desire to look more closely at the paintings of Berthe Morisot.

M. Durand-Ruel, I was pleased to learn from his young assistant, was not yet about the premises. I wished to be left alone, to walk and look and think, but the young man, who suspected a sale, would not leave my side, and *would* not keep quiet, although I ought to have been grateful, as he was full of otherwise unobtainable information. I learned, for example, that Mme Pontillon, the subject of so many of Morisot's paintings, is none other than her sister Edma. We were standing then before a lovely oil in which she sits by a cradle gazing in wonder at her firstborn. But indeed there were so many other portraits of this mother and her child, and her subsequent children, that I could not but be struck by the fact that, as the one sister gave up painting for motherhood, the other had given up motherhood for painting and seems as painfully aware of her own sacrifice as she is of her sister's.

I was then struck by the eloquence of another light-filled oil, a double portrait of the artist's sister and mother. The young married Edma, dressed all in white, and with a subdued expression and downcast eyes, sits on a sofa, her hands resting idly in her lap. Her mother, dressed all in black and occupying twice the space as the slim young woman, sits in a chair placed diagonally to her daughter's. She is reading, but her daughter is merely waiting, and one suspects, from the resemblances in their features and from the way the eye progresses naturally from the central figure in white to the one in black that fills the right half of the canvas, that she is waiting for nothing more than to grow to become her own mother.

'You can see Manet's hand here,' volunteered my attendant. 'Here, and here, and here.' He pointed to the hem of the mother's dress, to her bust, her head, then went on to tell a story that evidently amused him very much about how Mlle Morisot, prior to sending the painting to the Salon admissions jury in 1870, allowed her mentor, friend and future brother-in-law to criticise it.

'Manet pronounced the double portrait very good, but soon added a few brush strokes to the hem of the black dress, and then got completely carried away trying to improve the painting. Making jokes and laughing like a madman, he worked through the afternoon adding accents here and there as Mlle Morisot watched with mounting horror and despair. The carter was waiting to take the painting to the submissions jury and Manet himself handed it into the cart, the paint not yet dry. When both Manet and the picture were gone, Mlle Morisot became hysterical, claiming she would rather die than have such a caricature appear under her name. Her mother naturally assumed she would be doing her daughter a great service by having the picture withdrawn, and went to some trouble to have it returned. Upon its return, however, Mlle Morisot became even more hysterical, claiming that she would rather die than offend Manet, whereupon Mme Morisot had to go to even greater trouble to have the picture resubmitted to the jury.'

My informant jabbered on at great speed: the picture was unanimously accepted by the jury, only to be uniformly ignored by the critics, etc. etc. etc.

But I had stopped listening, so entranced was I by the contrast between the portrait he had drawn of the hysterical young woman of fifteen years ago, weeping that she would rather die than offend Manet, and the impression I myself had formed yesterday of the tranquil older woman communing with the portrait of her dying friend. In the union of these two images, something very like the two halves of a torn photograph, I saw that she loved him.

And, as I looked at nearly a dozen portraits of her painted in every mood and manner of dress by Manet, this notion grew into the conviction that he had once loved her as well. In one particularly intriguing picture she sits sideways on a straight-backed chair, one hand holding up to her face a spread fan, through the openings in which she peeks at the viewer. Her legs are crossed at the knee, raising her satin gown to reveal slim ankles and small white feet in fashionable slippers. It is an informal, even whimsical portrait and, charmed, I stood before it for some time.

'This is graceful, is it not?' asked my guide. 'It was Manet's last, and I believe best, portrait of Morisot. He did it in 1874, just before her marriage to his brother. You see,' he added, pointing to her raised hand, 'he has already painted a gold ring on her finger.' A ring, I could not help but notice, a bit larger than the actual ring she wore yesterday, thus making the ring the detail to which the eye is drawn first, and last.

When the assistant went away to attend to another arrival, I was free to wander on my own. Leaving the works of the other painters for another time, I looked only at those of Manet and Morisot and was further intrigued to find in them a continuing conversation. Morisot, for example, has done a portrait of a respectable woman lying on a day bed, taking an afternoon rest, dressed in a white muslin gown and yellow slippers, which clearly pays homage to Manet's portrait of a prostitute who lies on a similar day bed wearing the same yellow slippers and nothing else. The two women have adopted the same pose and even meet the viewer's eye with the same frank gaze. In another of Morisot's oils a young woman in her petticoats stands before her cheval glass in the privacy of her own room, an empty sofa in the background. An oil of Manet's, painted the very next year, shows another young woman in petticoats standing before a glass; but the sofa in the background is occupied by a gentleman in evening clothes and top hat.

Both Manet and Morisot have painted women in evening dresses, their backs to the viewer, each again examining herself in her mirror. Each has done an oil of two figures in a boat, from a very close range, as if the artist were inside the boat with the boaters. And Morisot painted two decorative half-length female figures in seasonal dress, entitled *Summer* and *Winter*. The following year Manet painted his reprise, two half-length female figures called *Spring* and *Autumn*.

The act of turning from Manet to Morisot, from Morisot to Manet, produced a strange and haunting music that filled my head as I went away, humbled by what I had seen, deeply moved, and profoundly inspired.

Again I have done no work, but coming fresh from the presence of such a divine sublimation, I could hardly fashion with any success the caricatures of such a vulgar flirtation as that between the Rev. Peterson and his *jeune fille*.

Saturday
10 January

It is small wonder that Parisians so often commit suicide. The streets are black with mud and filthy snow. It is dark at four. One cannot even look forward to the comfort of an open fire, as the French have only their wretched stoves. Not a word from Mr Clarke. But I have finished the imbecile caricatures and have shipped them off to Anne.

And I have had a life-saving letter from Celia, written at sea, which made the return voyage across the ocean in the pocket of a ship's steward. It seems that on her first day out, she made the acquaintance of a young man named Anderson, who has been studying at the École des Beaux-Arts these past three years and who has convinced her of the necessity of adequate studio space in order to paint anything, let alone to prepare a Salon entry. He recommended to her in the strongest possible terms the premises that he and a fellow-student, a Russian, have just vacated in the Rue Notre Dame des Champs, and in which remain a number of articles of furniture which the two young men have left behind.

As Celia suggested, I rushed to the address as soon as I had read her letter, and found both the studio and sleeping quarters, as well as the furnishings, more than adequate. My share will cost no more than my present arrangements. I hadn't thought it would be necessary to decide immediately and was exercising my brains trying to think how best to put the proposition to my parents. But as I was coming out of the apartment, two young men were coming up the steps to have a look. I therefore went straight back inside and paid the first month's rent on the spot. I have already written to Celia and to my parents and have given notice to Mlle Bourges, who, as I expected, created a scene.

Now that an avenue of escape has been miraculously opened before me, I find that I can scarcely bear to remain another hour under this roof. Although Celia cannot possibly join me before the end of the month, I see no reason why I should not remove myself to our new quarters as soon as possible.

Sunday
11 January

I cannot believe that only twenty-four hours have passed since my last entry, perhaps because I have in that time seen the remainder of my life pass before my eyes. But I will begin at the beginning.

Having slept well and soundly and being therefore late for church, I flew down the stairs this morning and was horrified to find Stephen Clarke waiting to accompany me there. I had made only the hastiest of toilettes and, with my bustle slipping astern at every step, was hardly decently dressed, while he, frock-coated and top-hatted, was impeccably groomed. There was little time, however, to indulge my mortification, and as we went at a full gallop the entire way and were both quite blown with the effort, conversation was out of the question.

It never occurred to me that he did not know of my position as organist, but he did not, and my pious haste must therefore have greatly puzzled him. He seemed thoroughly amazed when I bounded through the side door of the church and fairly leapt onto the organist's bench, leaving him to sink into one of the rows of seats allotted to the schoolchildren who, along with their schoolmistress, form the choir. All the congregation had witnessed our breathless entrance, and the curious glances my companion's presence attracted must surely be adequate punishment for my own most uncharitable observations. Nevertheless I strove to repel them, pulling out half the stops and making an awful noise. The swell creaked, and the boy who blows the bellows kept casting fearful looks at me, sure that the swell box must burst. But he did not dare relax his labours for an instant.

I believe I knew even then what was coming and that it was *that* and not the curiosity of the congregation I strove to fend off with such bravado. At lunch I saw it coming as certainly as one sees a storm rolling in from the sea and, although I tried my best, was equally powerless to change its course. I talked and talked; I talked without cessation. Afraid even to ask a question that might be turned against me, I kept up a steady stream of the most egotistic chatter – about the atelier, about Anne, about Celia, our new studio, my ideas for a Salon painting, other ideas I was developing for two works of fiction, one about two painters who speak to each other through their paintings, another about two sisters, one who has sacrificed painting to motherhood and the other who has sacrificed motherhood to painting.

I went on and on, but Mr Clarke did not seem to think me any kind of babbling idiot. To the contrary, he received my every word with such rapt attention I might have been Homer, reciting from a work in progress.

Yet when I came to a halt – for I was far too hungry not, at length, to devour every morsel of my *galantine* – he spoke as if he had heard nothing of my plans and objectives. He himself had not touched the excellent lunch he had ordered, and unconsciously propping his elbows upon his edge of the table and folding his hands beneath his chin, he regarded me in the most woeful way.

'Miss Hope-Ross,' he began, in a voice as pitiful as his expression. 'Evelyn. I may call you Evelyn, mayn't I?'

How I longed for a familiar sardonic smile or ironic word. How I longed to say that, if the Stephen Clarke I knew and liked so well would only return and send away this poor diminished creature who had taken his place, he might call me however he pleased.

'I cannot bear to see you thus,' he went on. 'Working in the studio all day, then writing and drawing all the evening, rushing off to play the organ on Sunday, so terrified of losing your post that you would kill yourself getting there on time. You don't eat properly. You –'

'Mr Clarke,' I protested. 'I do no more than you. You refuse no honest work. Nor do I.'

'– you must let me help you,' he said, as if there had been no interruption. 'And you must help me. I know that you think me cold and dispassionate –'

I protested that I did not think any ill of him at all, that, to the contrary, I have always seen him as the embodiment of those qualities which I have been endeavouring to acquire for myself: intelligence, industry, independence. 'And the greatest of these is independence,' I added, trying to leaven the overweighted atmosphere with a bit of biblical humour.

I had chosen my words carefully and believed their meaning could not be mistaken. But again he spoke as if I had not.

'– but I do keep a heart about me somewhere, and I believe that only you know where to find it. Miss Hope-Ross – Evelyn – will you do me the honour of – will you be my wife?'

This was followed by some truly awful moments, as the

waiter appeared just then to change our plates.

'Tell me I am not mistaken,' he said, when we had been left alone again. 'You do – you do like me a little?' His proud lips trembled, as if playing the role of suppliant only against their will.

'I like you much more than a little,' I hastened to assure him. 'I like you immensely. But I do not want to marry you. I want to *be* you. And, failing that, as indeed I must, I want to be your friend and supporter.' But I saw from his smile that he *would* not understand.

'Is that not what you would be, as my life's companion: my friend and supporter? Our separate lives would henceforth be one life, our separate endeavours one endeavour, our joys one joy, our sorrows one sorrow.'

I objected that he was describing not friendship but marriage, that friendship was richer than marriage precisely because there were *two* of everything, two separate lives, two separate worlds.

'And what of life's sorrows?' He smiled again, rather complacently, I thought. 'Our troubles would consequently be reduced by half.'

'Would that it were so! But trouble is the one thing that is not reduced by marriage. It is soon doubled, then trebled, and then –' I broke off. Not wishing to pursue that line of argument, I took another. 'Mr Clarke, I am not fit to live with. I seek my paintbrush sooner than my toothbrush. I work all day. I write far into the night –'

'But that would no longer be necessary,' he cut in. 'I should never have asked you to be my wife were I unable to offer you a good measure of material comfort.'

'But I *want* to work,' I protested.

'Of course,' he said, with a maddening little gesture of the back of a hand, as if he were brushing away an irritating fly, 'you should of course be allowed to do whatever you choose.'

Allowed! How the odious word rankled. However, finding inspiration in his own impeccable dove-grey, I returned to my former argument. 'You are an orderly person. You would want your meals on time. You would want to entertain your friends with lunches and dinners. You would at least want your wife to be neat and presentable. You would come to hate me. I know you would. Look! My hands are not even clean.'

Like an infant, I held them out for inspection, but he would not look. He kept his eyes on mine and did not speak for a moment.

'Am I to understand that you refuse me? I am not to hope?'

'I am not meant to marry,' I said after a silence, my voice full of misery. 'I see that fully now. My mind was not formed for marriage. Even as a girl I had only contempt for other girls who thought all time wasted that was not spent in talking to a gentleman, and for those who believed that the most interesting piece of information a girl could ever possibly have to convey was whom she was going to marry.'

'If you were not so discerning a young lady, I should not be asking you to be my wife!' he exclaimed with some heat. 'Oh, Miss Hope-Ross, do not say that you are not formed for marriage. You are full of passion, intensity, seriousness, humour, intelligence. That it should all be wasted is surely a sin against nature.'

Wasted? I thought. Because it is not put at your disposal?

He must have seen from my expression that further conversation on the subject was useless, for a silence fell between us like a curtain at the end of the play. We left the restaurant and, still in miserable silence, walked back to this house where, at the door, he withdrew a large envelope from inside his coat and placed it in my hands.

'I secured these when I saw that it pained you to see them displayed.' With that he bowed coldly and walked quickly away, while I was filled with an unreasoning anger. For I knew at once what the envelope contained, even before I opened it, upon gaining the privacy of this room, and withdrew the photographs of myself and Anne that had hung on the wall of M. Durand-Ruel's office. I knew instinctively that he had returned them to me not to lessen the embarrassment I had suffered at seeing them displayed while in his presence, but to embarrass me to the full extent of his power. He who just moments before had professed to love me, who had begged me to be his life's, his soul's, companion, had all the while carried on his person the instrument of his revenge should I refuse him!

I sat at my table to begin this entry but, full of conflicting emotions and nervous energy, had not got far when I knew that I must have air. I rushed down the stairs and went out again, merely nodding to Mlle and ignoring the barrage of enquiries that pursued me into the street.

I longed for the comfort of music but dared not go to the concert and simply walked until fatigue, as well as the cold and the coming darkness, drove me indoors. Upon regaining my room, my nose caught a trace of the scent habitually and too liberally used by Mlle and I saw immediately that my things had been interfered with, that my trunk had been opened and examined. I flew to my table and caught up this journal, which, in my haste to be out of doors, I had left lying out in the open. If my relief was great at finding the envelope still tucked between its pages, how much greater was my horror when I saw that the photographs had been removed.

I paced this little cell, backwards and forwards, backwards and forwards, trying to decide what best to do. Twice I went part way down the stairs, only to turn and climb them again, for I realised that short of murdering Mlle there is nothing to be done. The less fuss I made about them, the better. She most certainly will not recognise me as one of the models, never having seen me thus; and Anne she has never even met. If I say nothing about them, she will think them of no consequence and perhaps destroy them.

This, however, is the last night I shall pass under her roof. Save what is needed for the morrow, my packing is done. I shall go early to the studio in order to secure the best possible place for the week, and at noon will send a carter to remove my trunk to the Rue Notre Dame des Champs.

Au revoir, Mademoiselle!

'I want more.' Eve ran a hand across the back of the leather-bound journal. 'Are you sure there aren't any more of these hidden away somewhere?'

There had been three consecutive days of fog and a steady heavy drizzle, too wet for gardening or walking, followed by this fourth day straight from what Evelyn Hope-Ross called 'that witches' cauldron back o' the hills'. Eve had been only too glad to spend the dark afternoons tucked up in the library, cheered by the fire – an unusual luxury in May – to which Peter insisted on adding more and more seasoned oak. Reflected flames danced in the glass, in the cabinet doors and the French windows, so that the two women seemed surrounded by a troupe of whirling dervishes generously laid on for their private entertainment. Dolores, working her way through stacks of letters, looked up.

'You *can't* be finished?'

Eve smiled. Her greater ease in reading EH-R's hand had become something of a thorn in the side of the trained textual scholar. 'I wonder why she didn't keep it up.'

'I've no idea.' Dolores went back to the letter she'd been trying to decipher, then sighed, resigning herself to conversation. 'Yes, I have; several.' She took off her glasses and massaged the bridge of her nose, then held up a thumb. 'A: she got too busy. As soon as she moved into that studio-flat she started working on her Salon entries, and never looked back.' A forefinger subsequently shot up. 'And B: she started turning it all into fiction. It was the end of the "shilling shockers" she'd been serialising in magazines. The one major thing she learned from the Impressionists was to take her themes from everyday life, not only for her painting but for her writing. *The Governess's Revenge* and all that. She wouldn't have had the time to write everything twice, and there was always her daily diary with the necessary details: names, dates, places, etc.' She was silent a moment, then shrugged.

'In my humble opinion, this is why her fiction isn't as good as it might have been. No time for any of that "emotion recollected in tranquillity" business. This was *business*. She needed the money, and everything was immediately grist for the mill.' With a grunt of a laugh, she swept the back of a hand above the neat columns of letters spread across the table. 'What am I talking about, write everything twice? It was more like four or five or six times. I can't tell you how many versions of the same event, vignette, anecdote, thought, idea or opinion I've read. Look at all this. And this is only a fraction of her letters. They're great letters, by the way, if you'd like to have a look. In fact, I'm thinking of editing a volume of them.'

'And you'd like help transcribing them?'

'Am I so obvious?' Dolores smiled sheepishly.

'Have you got any to Stephen Clarke there?' Eve asked hopefully.

'You mean after –' Dolores gave a nod to the journal. 'You've got to be kidding. They became mortal enemies, those two. Just a few minutes ago, I'm reading a letter she wrote to Anne in which she describes him as a half-dead wasp; she never knows when he's going to get up and sting her again.'

'Why? What did he do?'

'He never stopped punishing her for refusing him. It must have been a terrible blow to his pride. A man who's vowed never to marry, he finally finds someone he's willing to break his vow for, and she refuses him, she won't have him. He must have been mortified.'

'What do you mean, he punished her?'

'He stole from her. Not only that Degas sketch of her, which he never returned, and probably sold in New York for a fortune, but ideas, what we now call intellectual theft. That is, when it wasn't out and out plagiarism.' Again, the thumb went up. '*Conversation in Oil*? The one she based on Manet and Morisot? He published a novel the very next year about two writers whose every work was a comment or reprise on the other's.' Then the forefinger. 'And *Two Sisters*? The one about the one sister sacrificing her painting in order to become a mother and the other sacrificing motherhood to become a painter of mothers and children? He did the same thing again, again using writing instead of painting. It went on and on, everything she published. And, unfortunately, he was a better writer.'

'So it was art imitating life imitating art imitating life.' Eve smiled. 'It sounds very like Manet and Morisot. I like that. They had their own *Conversation in Oil*, a conversation in print.'

'Oh, and his *French Leave* was about her. I mean, everything: their conversations in which he first encouraged her to go to Paris, her difficulties getting there, even her very words in rejecting him. She was furious. She felt he'd stolen not just her ideas but her life.' Dolores shook her head. 'No. This was no delicate minuet danced by two artists paying respectful homage to each other. In fact, in a letter to Ethyl Smyth, she likened it to the duels the new students in the men's ateliers in Paris were forced to perform. They had to strip naked and do battle with paintbrushes, seeing who could smear the other with the most paint. And speaking of naked, let's not forget how he deliberately embarrassed her with those photographs. She was mortified to the full extent of her well-bred Victorian capacity for it.'

'I wanted to ask you about those photographs,' Eve said. 'Are the originals here? I'd love to see them again. I just vaguely remember them in Martin's book and thinking how lovely they were. But I didn't pay much attention.'

'Henry has the originals.' Dolores leaned both elbows into

the name. 'Mademoiselle Bourges was on the point of sending them to Evelyn's parents along with the news that she'd flown the coop. Then Charlotte came by looking for Evelyn to tell her that her mother was actually on the point of death, and Ms Bourges lost her nerve and gave them to her. Most of Charlotte's stuff came down to Henry. Peter borrowed the photographs when he was getting everything together for your husband. I just happen to have a copy of that book.' She raised an eyebrow. 'Sure you wouldn't like to read it again?'

Eve shook her head. 'I'll wait for yours.'

'Ours,' Dolores corrected. 'What about one of her novels, or have you read them all?'

Eve shook her head again. 'I've only read the first two. I've been reading this.' She ran her hand across the time-softened cover of the journal.

Dolores opened the drawer of the table and took out a set of keys, then got up with her customary creaking of stiffened joints and went to one of the cabinets to take a book from the shelf. Coming round to Eve's side of the table, she handed it to her, its dark olive cover embossed with gold lettering.

'*An American Cousin*,' Eve read aloud.

'It's based on Celia, on her coming to Ireland, and on her falling in love with Francis.'

'She fell in love with Francis? Did he reciprocate?' Then, remembering Francis's fate, Eve said, 'I hope not, for her sake.'

'I won't spoil the ending,' Dolores said. 'But in real life, no. Francis was in love with Anne. He died still in love with her.'

'How sad,' Eve said absently, turning to the first mould-mottled page of the book.

'Do you really think so?' Her arms folded, Dolores looked down at her. 'Marriage is so often the end of a strong attraction rather than the beginning of something more. They had some great years together, those three, Francis, Evelyn, Anne, each of them free to come and go as they chose, unfettered by marital bonds and demands. Celia came and went too, as did all their friends. They led a happy and relatively bohemian life here.

Ironically enough, the sort of life Stephen Clarke initially wanted for his debutante heroine.'

'Hmmm.' Eve, only half listening, had begun reading the first page of the novel, which opened on a ship steaming in from New York:

'I suppose that is Ireland?' she said, pointing to the land. This new phase of life that had once seemed impossible seemed now inevitable. Her future was, perhaps, hidden among those blue Irish hills.

'And this is exactly what *I* want. Thanks.' Eve closed the book but held on to it. 'You know, I really want to do something for her.'

'You are, believe me,' Dolores said, as she walked round to her side of the library table.

'No, I mean something specific.' Eve held the book close to her chest, as if reluctant to let go of her idea. 'I've been thinking about it ever since Dublin. Wouldn't it be great to have an exhibition of her paintings? As many as we can beg, borrow, or steal? Or even buy. Here, I mean, in her own house, in her own studio. It's certainly big enough, and it wouldn't take much to restore it to what it was like when she painted there.'

Dolores took less than two minutes to reflect. 'We could even have an opening that would coincide with the publication of the book. A kind of exhibition-cum-book-launch party. Cheap white wine and all.'

Eve, her eyes shut now, could see it: the walls and ceiling a freshly painted cream, that great length of floor sanded and finished, the old fireplace and stove cleaned up, two easy chairs, Evelyn's and Anne's, positioned on that worn carpet she'd seen rolled up against a wall. At the other end, Evelyn's easels set up, a rush-bottomed stool, a table for her paints and palette. And both long side walls hung with her many paintings, crammed with them, the way the Louvre walls were hung for Salon exhibitions. And, yes, a table holding copies of the new critical biography.

'Have you heard a word?' Dolores was saying. 'Or are you asleep?'

'A word about what?' Eve said, her eyes still shut.

'I was saying that it wouldn't necessarily have to be a one-off thing. It could be a permanent exhibition, open to the public. There is that separate entrance to the yard; people wouldn't have to tromp through the house. There could be an admission charge to cover expenses. Maybe even a grant. Who knows?' After a brief silence, she added, 'There'd be all kinds of tax advantages for the Hope-Rosses if they opened even part of this place to the public. Inheritance taxes, for example, or estate taxes or whatever they call them.'

'What a marvellous idea!' Adele set down the teapot and, with a silver tongs, transferred two small scones to a plate, then handed the plate up to Peter along with a cup of tea. 'Don't you agree, darling?'

'I couldn't agree more.' The cup rattling in its saucer, he crossed the terrace to where Eve sat with her back to the sea so as not to be distracted by its motion. It always drew her eye, even against her will, like a constantly flickering television screen in the corner of a pub. And then, she'd done only two of her planned three sea-gone-with-the-sun paintings and was reluctant to look at the real thing until the series was finished.

She smiled to herself, remembering how Dolores had told her, when she had asked, that Evelyn Hope-Ross, although she'd gone back to see Degas at his studio several times to seek his artistic advice, had never again sought out Berthe Morisot, despite their promising beginning. 'She was already turning her into fiction; she would hardly want to be reminded that the flesh-and-blood person actually existed.'

'No, thank you,' she said, as Peter came back to her with both cream and sugar, as he never failed to do, though she had yet to use either. She balanced the plate of scones on her knees and kept a firm hold on her cup and saucer, a blue and gold Russian porcelain so thin it seemed translucent. She was afraid the cup's slender handle would snap between the pressure of her finger and thumb.

'We know dozens of people who own at least one of her things, and some of them own dozens. I'll start phoning them up tomorrow.' Adele transferred two scones to another plate for Peter, who accepted them with an affectionately reproving shake of the head. Eve already knew what he would say. It had become something of a refrain.

'Hardly *dozens*, my dear.' He carried his plate and his tea to a chair placed squarely facing the sea and set them down on a small nearby table, then returned to where Adele sat behind the tea tray, to collect knives and napkins. 'I've been meaning to get round to that eyesore for years. This will put my feet to the fire.'

'I wanted to talk to you about that,' Eve said tentatively, not wanting to tread on any toes. 'I wouldn't want this to be any extra work for you. It was always part of the plan to –'

'Have no fear. I won't pitch a thing of hers, or anything remotely to do with her. The rest will go up to the attics.'

'Surely that *has* to be a step in the wrong direction.' Adele handed him a small dish and spoon.

'Very well, very well. It shall all go to the basement.' Again, he crossed the geometrically patterned bricks to hand a knife and napkin to Eve, then proffered a dish with a mischievous smile. '*Do* try some of Adele's quince.'

'He'll simply be overseeing it,' Adele called to her. 'Young Gareth will do the heavy work.'

'To be honest,' Peter grimaced down at Eve, as she attempted to transfer a spoonful of quivering amber preserves to her plate from the dish he held just a little too high, 'I've already spoken to him about it. It's near the top of our list.'

'Gareth?' Eve set her cup and saucer on the ground to deal with the scones and preserves. When she'd asked Clare, last week in Logan's, what Gareth was doing now, she'd said glumly, 'At the minute, he's out in the kitchen doing the washing up.'

'Yes!' Adele beamed. 'We've found our couple.' With the ease of a girl of eighteen, she rose from behind the table and carried her cup and saucer and plate to a chair near Eve's. 'He came to the door one day to ask if we might have work, in the garden or anywhere. We had him in and had quite a talk with him, didn't we, darling?' But Peter had lost himself to the setting sun. Untroubled, Adele chatted on.

'We were rather reluctant to spell out exactly what we'd had in mind. As you know, we'd been thinking of a couple in their fifties, who'd retired from their jobs, perhaps.' She paused briefly. 'Perhaps an English couple who wouldn't −' She broke off for a long drink of tea. 'As you know, Gareth's great-grandfather lived and worked at Derrymore. One doesn't like to cause offence, which one often seems to do by merely existing.' Again she fortified herself with a swallow of tea.

'However, it seems that he and his fiancée are desperate to find a place of their own so they can be married, and his fiancée is equally desperate to get out of the teashop where she works. She's paid nothing because it's her family's shop. She lives at home and works in exchange for being fed and housed.'

'I didn't think you could do that now, even to family,' Eve said, realising that Clare's initial taciturnity, which she'd always taken for personal, or even national, animosity, had never had anything to do with her.

'Naturally, her parents are very much opposed. Gareth told me that Clare's mother had positively wailed at him, "You're taking my best one!" But his parents are quite keen. He brought them both here to tea a day or two ago. I believe they'd been afraid he would have to leave Clonmere to find work. And I know how that is. Our son had to go to Sydney.' She paused for another sip or two. 'Gareth's mother was particularly delighted. She said something rather charming. What was it she said, darling?' When Peter smiled and nodded but made no response, she thought for a moment. 'Oh, yes, I remember. She said, "God never shuts one door that He doesn't open another." I suppose she was referring to his former employer,' she added, her voice lowered. 'You do know about her accident in France?'

'Yes, Peter told me,' Eve said, then changed the subject. 'Clare is a hard worker. I can vouch for that. I've seen her in action. And so is Gareth.' She managed to say this with enthusiasm, though her heart was sinking. Now that they'd found their couple, she would have to vacate what she had come to think of as her home. She would be very sorry to give up Mrs Matt's. It was so perfect for her.

'They'll live down in the cottage while the rooms next to yours are being done up. I'm afraid there will be rather a racket while it's going on, but Peter has come up with the most brilliant plan. A place for you to work in the meanwhile. He thought of it the moment we decided to have the roofers in.'

'Thought we'd knock down the divider between the two loose boxes at the far end of the stables,' Peter explained. 'If that would suit. Plenty of room, more than you've got now, and plenty of light, even when the doors are shut. And on fine days they can be thrown open and you'd have a view down the farm road to the orchard and the sea. For inspiration.' He gave Eve one of his more ironic smiles. 'Should inspiration be required.'

Eve was moved to the point of having to fight back tears. 'But I know you'll want Mrs Matt's for them. It's what you planned from the start. You did tell me this was only a temporary arrangement. I'll go back to the cottage. It's much better for one person than for two.'

'You'll do no such thing,' Peter said. 'You'll stay just where you are, just as long as you like.'

'It's all arranged, my dear,' Adele said. 'Gareth and Clare were enchanted by the cottage and Clare has already been through the attics with me selecting some temporary furnishings. When they're ready to move up to the yard, we'll let the cottage again. And then Gareth will begin work on the front gate lodge, and we'll let that out as well. It was his idea. A little holiday business. We can do it now we'll have some help.'

Peter added, 'O'Gorman's been suggesting it for years. There's of shortage of holiday places in this area, you know.'

'But is the cottage –?' Eve began, remembering her last sight of it.

'It's thoroughly dried out,' Adele assured her, 'and Peter's been at the floors again. The awful thing is, those great scars in the gable-end wall are rather ugly, where those wretched windows have been bricked in and cemented over.'

'Two precisely window-shaped scars,' Peter put in, but refrained from assigning blame.

'Not one of my better ideas, I must say.' Adele shook her head sadly. 'Peter was against it all along, but I insisted. That wall simply cried out to me for windows. It still does. Clare suggested hanging curtains over them.'

'*Not* such a bad idea.' Peter got to his feet and went to the table for the teapot.

'If you'd like,' Eve said after a moment, 'I could paint two windows in those spaces, with a sea view in each.'

'Now that *is* brilliant,' Peter said, as Adele exclaimed, 'What a kind idea!'

As they talked and joked about what the view might be, morning or evening, calm or stormy, the same in each 'window' or different, birds or sailboats or rising dolphins, Peter refilled all their cups and brought round the sugar and the cream, then the plate of scones, the quince preserves, and settled in his chair again.

'It's all worked out so nicely.' Adele took a sip of her tea. 'The timing couldn't have been more fortuitous. We'd only just heard from Mrs Roche.' She couldn't stop beaming. Her blue eyes, brighter, seemed also bluer. Even her lovely smoke-grey hair, recently trimmed, seemed stronger. 'She was our daily. Three times a week, for nearly twenty-five years.'

'Nineteen years and five months,' said Peter, 'to be exact.'

Adele ignored this. 'At Christmas, while she was visiting her daughter, she fell over in Cork and broke a hip.' She swallowed a bite of scone before continuing. 'We've been loath to replace her after all these years, and we couldn't bring ourselves to stop her pay. We simply waited, not knowing *what* to do. We've visited her, of course. But as you must have seen, things have been getting a bit out of hand.'

Her own mouth full now, Eve silently shook her head, denying all knowledge of any household chaos.

'When we went to visit her the other day, she told us she wouldn't be coming back. Her daughter insists she stay on with her.' Adele raised her cup to lips, then put it down suddenly without drinking. 'Oh dear, I *shall* miss her.'

Saturday morning, not having slept much, she got out of bed soon after it was light, drank her two mugs of coffee, and went out, bringing along the novel she'd nearly finished before finally falling asleep with it lying open across her nose and mouth; she could almost taste it, the mould and the dust and the hundred years of wood smoke baked into its brown-edged pages. Cutting across the sheep meadow, she filled her lungs with the fresh sweet scent of dew-soaked grass cut by the sharper salt smell of the sea. Normally, this was her best time to work, but yesterday she'd finished the third and last of her sea-gone-with-the-sun series and was too depleted to immediately begin work on the cottage. She at any rate needed to give some thought to it first, although she did know that the westwardmost 'window' would have the long slender black form of a ship on its horizon.

At the far side of the meadow, at the edge of the cliff, she found a flat, dry, sun-warmed shelf of rock, relatively free of sheep pellets, and sat there. Laying the book beside her for the moment, she drew up her knees and rested her chin on them. Seagulls swooped and swirled, ducking in and out of their nests in the cliff face below. Before her, the open sea stretched a broken green glitter of sunlit waves, a mirror image of a description she'd read just hours ago.

At least part of the book might actually have been written here, she thought, imagining Evelyn and Anne, or Evelyn alone, sitting on this same shelf of rock contemplating the ships plying backwards and forwards between Southampton and New York, many of them stopping at what was Queenstown, and all of them passing close to this shore.

Yesterday, she'd worked straight through the day until she knew that one more stroke of brush or swipe of cloth would be one too many. Exhausted, she'd gone to bed early and fallen almost immediately to sleep, but was awakened just before twelve by the sound of footsteps in the yard. She'd left her bedroom windows open to the unusually warm spring night and, in the utter stillness that fell upon Derrymore once the rooks had gone noisily to bed, had distinctly heard footsteps crossing the cobblestones, stopping briefly in the vicinity of her door, then crossing the yard again. As Mrs Matt's had no upstairs windows facing that side, she'd gone quietly down the stairs in the dark and crossed the kitchen. Although she moved quickly, by the time she got to the door and silently slid back the bar securing the shutters she always closed over its glass panes at night, she was in time to see only the shaft of light from a torch turning out of the yard and into the lane.

Upstairs again, she had shut the windows, drawn the curtains across them, turned on her lamp and tried to lose herself in her book, but found her thoughts frequently wandering to the woman who had written it, more specifically to the time she'd spent alone in that huge house, answering each dead-of-night hammering at the door herself, despite, as Dolores had put it, what had happened to her 'best of all brothers', whose body – unable to move it and just as unable to leave it lying on the cold tile floor of the hall – she had held across her lap all night.

Eve guessed it had been *because* of Francis's murder rather than despite it that she fearlessly answered those ominous knocks at the door. She didn't doubt for a moment the woman's courage, or her steadfast refusal to be frightened, but she knew it would have seemed a matter of indifference to Evelyn Hope-Ross, in that period of her deepest grief, whether she lived or not. She had felt that same indifference after her own 'best of all brothers' was cut down in such a sudden, brutal way. Not that she would ever have taken her own life, or could ever have done that to her daughters, she simply hadn't cared as much about living.

This was no longer true. She now cared very much. The night before, she'd been longing for the relative security of a telephone and couldn't believe how long it was taking to have the new line installed. Lily and Rose had long been urging her to buy another mobile, as hers didn't work here, but the Hope-Rosses told her it would be a waste of money. There was still no mast near enough for reception.

She had gained a good measure of peace attempting to portray eternity as an endless flow of time. Contemplation of the idea, itself so timeless, had had the usual effect of lengthening her perspective and reducing her own moment on the continuum to a mere speck, of no importance whatsoever, the way one alternative cancer therapy asks a patient to imagine the cancer as a black spot and to concentrate on visually shrinking it, until it has been reduced to a harmless dot; and then is gone.

At the same time, fully grasping the brevity as well as the precarious nature of her allotted time also had its usual effect and impressed her with the senselessness of wasting any of it, and increased her desire to leave something, if only a slightly deeper footprint, behind.

She had almost left it too late.

She was sitting facing west with the sun behind her, completely absorbed in her thoughts, when without warning the huge shadow of someone coming silently up behind her fell across her and threw itself over the cliff. She leapt to her feet and lost her balance. She would have fallen if a hand had not gripped her arm and yanked her roughly back.

'Lord! I didn't mean to frighten you.'

'Henry!'

'You *are* frightened,' he accused.

'I didn't hear you.'

'Sorry, I thought you must have done.' His long fingers

remained wrapped round her upper arm like a blood-pressure cuff; it was beginning to hurt. 'What on earth made you lunge forward like that? You might have been killed.'

'My foot fell asleep. I lost my balance.' When he did not loosen his grip, she said, 'You can let go, Henry. I'm not going to jump.'

To hide her extreme pleasure at seeing him again, she sat, resuming her former position, knees drawn up, chin resting on them. After a moment, he sat beside her, arranging his own longer legs only with great difficulty. They fell into an uneasy silence, charged with electricity and punctuated by the pounding of the incoming waves two hundred feet below. Eve, determined not to speak before Henry did, fixed her eyes on his lower legs and feet, on the damp hems of his wide-wale corduroys and the bits of wet grass adhering to the rough suede of his lace-up ankle boots, the string laces of which were untied, a detail that suggested to her that he might have seen her from his bedroom window and, without stopping to tie his shoes, come after her.

Why then wouldn't he speak?

After an interminable silence, she opened her mouth to ask when he had arrived. But he chose that same moment.

'Evelyn Hope-Ross, from this very rock, watched the *Titanic* sail off into the sunset, on its first and, ah, last voyage.' He kept his own eyes fixed straight ahead, far out to sea, so intently he might have been willing the ship into safe harbour in New York after all.

'Did she?' Disappointed at this impersonal beginning, Eve made an effort to keep her voice light. 'Did she know someone? Did she have friends on the *Titanic*?'

'Yes,' Henry said, and then added, almost apologetically, as if he regretted having to be so melodramatic, 'My, ah, ah, my grandfather. Among others.'

'Your grandfather?' Eve turned to face him. 'Charlotte's son?'

Henry looked at her with surprise. He seemed pleased that she had connected the dots so quickly. 'One of them. Her youngest. He was of course not among the survivors.'

'How awful!'

He smiled at her vehemence. 'Yes. Yes, it must have been.'

'Why do you say "of course"?'

'Women and children and all that. The elderly.'

'When was it? I forget the date.'

'1912, April 14. Or 15. As you know, it went down in the night.'

'Was your father – No, it would have been your mother. Was she alive then? Had she been born?' Eve tapped the knuckles of one hand against her forehead. 'She would have to have been born, wouldn't she?'

He smiled again. 'Actually, she wasn't. But my grandmother had already had, as Mrs Matt used to say, the promise of her. Which apparently was why at the last minute she stayed behind.' He left a thoughtful pause.

'My mother was born seven months later. In fact, she was born here. Well, there.' He tossed his long hair in the direction in which Duneske House had once stood.

Eve fell silent, thinking how hard it would be for him ever to have to say goodbye to this piece of earth, where each rock and tree and path had its story, and its part in his own story. She didn't want to have to say goodbye to it herself and knew that when that day came, despite all other losses, it would be one of the saddest of her life.

She had unconsciously kept her eyes on his face while she was thinking this, on his deep-socketed eyes, so dark they seemed black, on his long bony nose and wide mouth. Now he looked away from her, his eyes on a buff-coloured curlew that had alighted on a nearby ledge of rock, its own black eyes darting rapidly from side to side.

'You're thinking how ancient I must be,' he said. 'But I, ah, came relatively, ah, late. My mother was thirty-eight. I'm not quite fifty.'

Before Eve could respond to this revelation, he reached round behind her for the book lying on her other side. She thought at first that he meant to put an arm around her, and then that he might be angry with her for having taken a rare first edition from a locked library cabinet and set it on a rock at the edge of a cliff two hundred feet above the sea. But neither seemed to be the case. Instead, he gave a Dolores-sized snort.

'*An American Cousin*. Dreadful stuff, isn't it?'

'Is it?' she said, a little offended; she'd been enjoying it.

In answer, he carefully turned the brittling pages to the end of the book, and read aloud.

'*Why did you send me away?*' he whispered.

'*I never sent you away,*' she answered, bewildered.

'*It doesn't matter now,*' he said at last. '*Nothing else will ever matter again.*'

He looked at her, eyebrows raised. 'I *say*.'

'That's enough.' She took it from him. 'You're ruining the ending for me. I've never read it before.' She waited a moment before adding, 'But you must have read it often, to go straight to that passage.'

'I could have chosen any number of them. There are –'

'Simply dozens, my dear,' she finished for him, and was rewarded with a bark of laughter, after which they fell into an easy silence before he spoke again.

'Thank you for your note. I'm sorry I didn't –'

'It's all right,' she said quickly. 'It didn't require a response.' Except the one he had given by appearing.

'Must go,' he said, glancing at his watch. 'They'll be at breakfast.' He sprang to his feet with amazing ease considering his difficulty getting down.

'Wait.' Eve set the book down beside her and leaned over to tie first one of his shoes and then the other. 'You'll break your neck.'

He smiled down at her. 'I'm looking forward to seeing the photographs. I'll stop by later, if I may?' His voice slid effortlessly from statement to question, then went to pieces, 'I did, I did – I arrived rather late last evening – I tried – when they'd gone up to bed, I –' then, like a gymnast, landed firmly on its feet, 'Your light was out.'

She stayed on for some time, looking out to sea, savouring

her relief that it had been Henry and not someone else in the yard the night before, and savouring even more the fact that it had been Henry at all.

The sea had been steadily filling with bright sunlight until it had turned now to a very tropical-looking ultramarine. How rapidly everything changed. It made her dizzy. She stretched her cramped legs out in front of her, then lay on her back looking up into the blue-seeming depths of the sky. And then her eyes remembered what her memory had forgotten, one of her – and her twin's – favourite lazy summer-day pastimes when they were children. She looked into the sky, without blinking, until her eyes performed the magic trick, and the void became a solid surface, a canvas, a vast field of pure colour.

AUTHOR'S NOTE

This is a work of fiction. Contemporary characters and localities are a product of the author's imagination, and any resemblance to actual people or places is coincidental.

Evelyn Hope-Ross is broadly based on Edith OE. Somerville, as encountered in Gifford Lewis's *Somerville and Ross: The World of the Irish R.M.* (Hammondsworth, Middlesex: Viking, 1985), *The Selected Letters of Somerville and Ross*, ed. Gifford Lewis (London and Boston: Faber and Faber, 1989), and the early novels of Somerville and Ross, including *An Irish Cousin*, *French Leave* and *Naboth's Vineyard*. Sections of *Sea Light*, particularly the nineteenth-century sections, are therefore deliberately peppered with phrases from various writings of Edith Somerville.

Evelyn Hope-Ross, however, is a fictional character. Edith Somerville, as far as I know, never attended a Dublin season or a castle ball, never met Edgar Degas, Berthe Morisot, or Virginia Woolf, or, for that matter, anyone like Stephen Clarke. Nor did her brother support the Free State or meet with Michael Collins.

For images and details of the life of an upper-class young woman in nineteenth-century Ireland, I drew on many sources but am especially indebted to George Moore's *Drama in Muslin*, and George Meredith's *Diana of the Crossways*.

For biographical information about Berthe Morisot, I am particularly grateful for *Berthe Morisot, Impressionist* by Charles F. Stuckey and William P. Scott (New York: Hudson Hills Press, 1987). And to George Moore again for his impressions and opinions of Degas in *Impressions and Opinions* (New York: Scribners, 1891).

For details of the life of an art student in Paris in the 1880s, I drew on Cecilia Beaux, *Background with Figures: Autobiography of Cecilia Beaux* (Boston: Houghton Mifflin, 1930); John Shirley-Fox, *An Art Student's Reminiscences of Paris in the Eighties* (London: Mills & Boon, 1909); Edith OE. Somerville, 'An Atelier des Dames', *Magazine of Art* (1887); J. Sutherland, 'An Art Student's Year in Paris: Women's Classes at Julian's School', *Art Amateur*, 32 (1895).